WHAT
BECAME
of MAGIC

Also by Paige Crutcher

The Lost Witch
The Orphan Witch

WHAT
BECAME
of MAGIC

PAIGE CRUTCHER

ST. MARTIN'S GRIFFIN
NEW YORK

First published in the United States by St. Martin's Griffin, an imprint of St. Martin's Publishing Group

WHAT BECAME OF MAGIC. Copyright © 2023 by Paige Crutcher. All rights reserved. Printed in the United States of America. For information, address St. Martin's Publishing Group, 120 Broadway, New York, NY 10271.

www.stmartins.com

Designed by Gabriel Guma

The Library of Congress Cataloging-in-Publication Data is available upon request.

ISBN 978-1-250-90552-9 (trade paperback)
ISBN 978-1-250-90553-6 (ebook)

Our books may be purchased in bulk for promotional, educational, or business use. Please contact your local bookseller or the Macmillan Corporate and Premium Sales Department at 1-800-221-7945, extension 5442, or by email at MacmillanSpecialMarkets@macmillan.com.

First Edition: 2023

10 9 8 7 6 5 4 3 2 1

For Marcus, Rivers, and Isla Doll,
to whom all roads of magic lead

this is the wonder that's keeping the stars apart
i carry your heart (i carry it in my heart)

—e. e. cummings

One

✳

ALINE WEIR HAD NEVER BEEN NORMAL A DAY OF HER LIFE. At the clever age of thirty, she was quite happy with this knowledge, but that wasn't always the case. There had been several years when she had tried to fit in, to be like the other people in her town of Whistleblown. When she was in middle school, she joined clubs, ran the bake sale, and organized the end-of-the-year party. She'd memorized all the names of the other kids in her class, and the compliments that seemed to make them feel best about themselves. She had a notebook with all her curated praises stored in it. If Aline understood anything, it was the need for and power of good praise.

Aline knew at the age of thirteen she wasn't like the other kids in her class. She had discovered this for certain during a horrifying trip to the girls' bathroom at W. B. Middle where she went to relieve herself from having one too many chocolate milks, sat down, and saw a list on the wall directly to her right.

It was scrawled in aggressive, certain lines by an ultrafine Sharpie.

It read:

"THE I HATE ALINE WEIR CLUB"

Beneath it were the names of nearly every female student in her class and the other eighth-grade class. Jen S.; Ashley; Devon; Rachel; Angie R. and Angie P.; Sara, Sarah, and Sariah; and even Whitney, for whom she had bought a chocolate milk that very morning when Whitney forgot her lunch money. The two Angies had even dotted their "I"s with hearts, which added insult to crushing injury.

There was a single line beneath all their names. It confirmed what Aline already knew.

There was something seriously wrong with her.

The weekend before the list was etched to life, Aline had been invited to her first-ever slumber party. It was for Jen S.'s birthday, and every girl in the grade had been included. Aline didn't care about clothes and boys and makeup in the same way the other girls did. She preferred reading and getting lost in the woods. Losing hours on websites about druids of the forest and the history of trees and the forgotten magic trapped inside them. She assumed this was why she was often overlooked for parties, even with all her volunteering for school functions. The truth was, Aline wanted, above everything else, to belong.

Jen S.'s parents had purchased an older Queen Anne home on the edge of town and renovated it. It was three stories tall and looked like something from the pages of a storybook. The

Slugger family had painted the brick a very trendy deep olive green and stained the wood mahogany. The home was large, but it wasn't imposing. It was an updated modern dollhouse. The steep, gabled roof and highly decorative woodwork left Aline sighing in relief. Inside was just as ornate as the outside. A plethora of large rooms, quite a few with high ceilings, and a library filled with books of all sizes.

The night went well . . . at first. Pizza was ordered, and Aline had memorized a compliment and topic for each girl. She was able to ask Whitney about her crush on Michael G. and talk to Sara and Sarah about how pretty the streaks of pink in Sariah's hair were. Then a new girl sat down next to Aline, one she had never seen before.

"Do you like books?" the girl asked, peering into Aline's overnight bag on the floor where her copy of S. Campbell's *Tree Magic* sat tucked inside.

"I am a huge reader," Aline said, feeling bolstered by the pizza and success of the evening so far.

The girl grinned. Aline thought how the smile transformed her face, and then she realized the girl was wearing a most peculiar dress. It was beige with lace trim and much longer than any of the other dresses in the room. It was lovely, though, and Aline admired how confidently the new girl wore it.

"Have you read *Anne of Green Gables*?" the girl asked.

"Oh yes, I've read all of them."

"All of them?" the girl asked, her eyes wide. "But there are only two."

Aline stared at her in confusion. "No, there are—"

It was then that she heard the whispers. Aline turned from the girl to see every other person at the party staring at her.

"Who are you talking to?" Jen S. asked, her brows drawn together like an angry caterpillar.

"Oh, I didn't get her name," Aline said, and turned back, but the girl was gone.

"You were talking to yourself," Whitney murmured, biting her lip. "About books?"

"No"—Aline shook her head and looked around—"I wasn't. I was talking to . . ."

But the girl had drifted off like the end of a bad joke and everyone at the party was now staring at Aline like she had sprouted three heads and a tail.

The night did not improve from there. While no one whispered *about* Aline again, they also didn't speak *to* her. She sat on her rolled-out sleeping bag, watching the shadows climb the walls, wondering where the girl in the odd dress had gone and if she might come back.

Eventually she fell asleep, crying only a little and very quietly so no one could hear. In the morning, she woke and planned to roll up her bag and walk the two miles home. She did not think the others would miss her or care.

And then she saw it.

Someone had gone from girl to girl and drawn on their faces, arms, and legs. Giving them mustaches and eyeglasses, beards and spots. Words had been trailed down a few of their arms: "a human girl who stings like a bee, kindred spirits are scarce here, I'm glad I don't live in a world filled with petty girls." On and on the lines went.

Twists on *Anne of Green Gables*. Aline knew the words right away. She looked down at her arm and did not see any writing anywhere. The other girls were waking as she sat up, and when they looked from one another, the room erupted in shouts and shrieks and angry growls as they all turned to look at Aline.

"*You* did this," Jen S. said, her words dripping with venom, the drawn-on unibrow making her appear extra stern. "I told Mom I didn't want you to come but she made me include everyone. You're a freak, Aline Weir, and now everyone knows."

The accusations flew, and Aline ducked and tried to dodge them, but they struck her in her side, her heart, her head. She balled up her sleeping bag, shoved it in her duffle, and ran from the house—her pockets filled with their angry words.

She didn't try to stop the tears, and her nose ran as she hurried onto the sidewalk. She rubbed it clean with the back of her arm, pausing only long enough to adjust the bag that was tumbling from her hands in her haste to leave. She looked up, and there, in the third-floor window, she saw the girl from the night before. The girl smiled and wrote with her finger, against the glass, a single word.

"Dragon."

❧

ALINE SLUNK HOME, AN ELECTRICAL CURRENT DOGGING HER STEPS AS SHE DRAGGED HER BAG BEHIND HER. It was as though she were splintered into two people. One was trying to ignore the cramp in her stomach from humiliation, the way the other girls had looked at her like she was something disgusting the neighborhood dog had spat up. Aline wanted them to like her, and now—now that was going to be so much harder to achieve.

Her nose burned, and she rubbed it, unsurprised to realize

her face was wet from tears. She wiped them with the back of her hand and thought of the writing on the forearms of so many of the girls at the slumber party.

She thought of "Dragon."

Aline didn't know how to process the fact that she had been making friends with a ghost, so she simply set it aside. She wasn't scared. She couldn't be afraid of another girl—let alone a kind one, dead or not. She thought she might be excited, but that was squelched each time she remembered the sneer on Jen S.'s face.

She walked the last ten blocks home, silently crying, wishing she could redo the night before. Wishing at least one of the girls hadn't whispered about her or made fun of her—that one of them would have held her hand instead, and they would have left together. Gone back to that girl's house to make brownies and watch movies and eat too much popcorn and fall asleep laughing and consoling each other.

She played it out in her mind. The way it could have gone. How safe and okay and ordinary it might have been. A chapter in a book of a feel-good story.

Instead, Aline reached her house with its long drive and overgrown shrubs by herself. She lifted her bag and carried it to the large front door, pulling the key out from where she wore it on a chain around her neck, and went inside.

Silence greeted her, making the sounds of emptiness that only those who live in the shadows can hear. She made toast and poured a glass of milk, then sat at the empty table in the cold kitchen with its hard tile floor and concrete counters. The house never held warmth, and she shivered as she picked at the toast, listening to the ticking of the clock across the hallway, in the study.

As she sat, she shifted from here to there, getting lost in her imagination. She thought of her parents coming home, finding her upset. Making her hot cocoa with tiny marshmallows and gooey grilled cheeses. How they would put on a movie about adventures and maybe cats, wrap her in a blanket like a burrito and rub her hair until she fell asleep, safe and content.

The door to the garage lifted, a grinding of gears and mechanical whirs. Aline stiffened in her seat. She threw away the toast and rinsed the cup, setting it in the dishwasher. She never knew what to do with her hands when her parents were around, so she held them tightly in front of her.

Her mother entered first, carrying a bag of bagels. Her tones were clipped and rushed, the only tones she had. Her hair was pulled into a low ponytail, and she wore a cream-colored sweater. Aline thought her impossibly beautiful. Her father moved like there was a small dog chasing at his feet, hurried steps that had him shifting around her mother to place a take-out tray with two drinks on the counter before reaching into the cabinets and pulling down two plates. Her mother got out the napkins, and they both moved to the table. Neither seeing her, or if they did, neither acknowledging her.

Once they were seated and making their plates, Aline cleared her throat.

Her father looked up. "Ah, Aline."

He went back to his plate, and Aline swallowed the rejection, digesting it quickly. She was fairly used to it now.

"I'm home early," she said.

"Are you?" her mother asked. "How was it then?"

"Um," Aline ripped at her thumbnail, shredding a layer off. "Not great."

Her mother looked up, her brow furrowed. "Why? What did you do?"

That was a very good question. Unfortunately, it was followed by her father making a soft huff. "It's the way of it, isn't it?" he said to her mother. "Young girls are like wolves."

"You mean hyenas," her mother corrected. "Eating their own."

"Hyenas don't do that," her father said. "The bottlenose aardvark might."

"More like bottleneck," her mother said.

They both laughed and resumed their conversation about the wilds of the jungles in countries far away. Aline and her cloud of sadness ignored or forgotten. She was never sure if they didn't see her or didn't want to. She'd once heard her father compare their having her to a sociological experiment, to see which of their traits were passed down. Apparently, none of the good ones. For they did not care for her feelings or well-being.

Aline was certain they did not care for her at all.

She went to her room and read for the rest of the day, pretending she was a girl in a story, a better one than her own, surrounded by people who saw her and loved her and needed her.

⫷⫷⫷

THE NEXT DAY WAS SUNDAY, WHICH LED INTO MONDAY, WHICH BECAME THE WORST DAY OF ALINE'S EXISTENCE SO FAR.

She took the bus, sitting alone, and went to class, where she was ignored. She made it to lunch, but when she carried her homemade peanut-butter-and-honey sandwich into the cafeteria, eyes and snickers followed her. Within a few moments she judged the lunchroom unsafe and hurried to the bathroom nearest her next class to eat in peace.

She chose the wrong stall, as luck would have it, because once she sat on the toilet and unwrapped her sandwich, she looked over to find a list had been created that morning. A list of names signed in agreement that they, too, hated Aline Weir.

The words swam before her eyes, a truth written in venom that scratched its way to her core. Name after name after name. Her cheeks and chest flushed from humiliation, her stomach curled in on itself, and her heart thunked heavy against her rib cage. The callous way they each autographed their signatures, like they were signing up for boxes of Girl Scout cookies or the latest craze of Jen A.'s mom's "fresh and funky" hair-barrette pyramid scheme, brought tears to her eyes.

It was every girl she had in her notebook, and she had a momentary feeling of panic, as if she should pull it out and note that Whitney dotted her "I"s with hearts and Steph added curls to her "S"s, so she could compliment them about it later.

It was quickly replaced with shame, followed by rage. At herself for caring, at the girls for being so horrible. She threw the sandwich in the toilet and unlocked the door; she slammed it open so hard it swung back and banged into the other door. The noise filled the dark bubble boiling inside her, and she marched toward the sinks, slamming her bag on the ground.

Overhead, the lights flickered. Aline didn't look up. She stared into the mirror, into her own eyes and the pale freckled surface of her face. "I wouldn't like me either," she said, her voice hiccupping on a sob at the end of the sentence.

"No," she said, shaking her head. "I would not. Doesn't matter." She blinked the tears away. She ran her fingers over her face, tugged at her strands of red hair, and let out an angry laugh.

"But still." She wished they would. Wished someone did.

"Why doesn't anyone care?" She yelled the words at herself, raised her hands, and slammed her palms into the mirror, on either side of her head. She opened her mouth to scream, and a gasp slipped out instead . . .

As Aline fell through the mirror and tumbled to the other side of nowhere.

※

THE WORLD AS SHE KNEW IT WAS FULL OF COLOR. Harsh angles and bright lines, adornments and decorations. Overhead lighting that stunned Aline's eyes and cacophonous laughter of students that left her wishing she could hide in a linen closet for an hour or eight.

When Aline rolled to a stop, she found the world around her was nothing like what it should be.

There was a haze permeating the ground, a rainy mist that felt like kisses when her fingers brushed against it and made her forget why she was upset in the first place. It lasted a few minutes, the daze from the haze. She stood, shaking out her hands and feet, making sure she was still real, because falling through a mirror certainly couldn't be. But she was fine, a little tenderness at the back of her head and the base of her spine, but outside of that, not a scratch or bruise.

"I've lost my hopes," Aline said, thinking she'd also misplaced all sense as she knew it.

"A perfect graveyard of buried hopes," a familiar voice said. Dragon stepped through the mist, her curls bouncing. "That's what she said, our Anne of Green Gables. Though I think you might be right, too. Or wrong. Or so wrong you've become right."

"Are you real? Is this?" Aline asked, as Dragon drew nearer, her eyes bright and everything about her appearance screaming "authentic."

"Sure am," Dragon said, and she sat down next to Aline. She blew out a slow, exceptionally long breath, scattering the haze back toward the edges of the perimeter of the road. It was a dirt road, bordered by tall trees. It smelled of pine and cinnamon and spearmint. A mingling of scents that shouldn't have worked, but together were soothing. "Aren't you a bright penny, turning up and finding me."

"I wasn't looking for you."

"Are you sure about that?"

"I was mad, and I was asking . . ."

Dragon smiled. "Asking?"

"Why no one cared."

"But you see, I do care. I care very much."

"They hate me," Aline said, her eyes narrowing. "Because of what you did." In a smaller voice she added, "Because you aren't real."

Dragon snorted. "If I'm not real, how are you talking to me?"

"I may have lost more than my hope."

They stared at each other.

"You're not real," Aline said, which was ridiculous because the girl was standing *right there,* in the same beige-and-lace dress, her blond hair tangled and her stark blue eyes blinking.

"I'm as real as you," the girl said. Then she held out her hand. "My name is Dragon."

"Aline," Aline said, and shook her hand.

"I felt stuck," she said. "Until you came along."

Aline looked up at her. "Why did you write on the other girls? They hate me now. That wasn't right, either."

"They're mean," Dragon said. "One day they might grow out of it, but from what I've seen of those girls, they like their mean. When you like being mean, you don't grow out of it."

"Oh."

"You don't know what you are, do you?" Dragon asked, her eyes losing some of their luster as she studied Aline. Her mouth pinched into a shape like a small rosebud. "How do you not know?"

"I'm Aline Weir," Aline said. "I know who I am." She cleared her throat, let out a slightly hysterical laugh. "People hate me."

"No, they're just scared of their own shadows. You're a shadow witch. You can cross from the now to the in-between now and then. You can see ghosts, talk to creatures not of this world."

"Like you."

Dragon shrugged.

"How do I get back?"

"Same way you came."

Aline looked around. "I don't see a mirror."

"Don't need one. You only need a door."

There were no doors in this forest of mist and magic. Only trees. Aline took tentative steps toward the closest one. It was a thick old thing, some sort of ancient tree that she didn't have a name for. Too many limbs and roots, it reminded her of an angry octopus. To its left was a tall, thin pine tree. It reminded her of home. She closed the distance to it and realized it had a hole at its base. It reminded her of a dog door, and she squatted down.

"I need to get back to school," she said. She needed to make sure she wasn't hallucinating, something she had done before when fevering as a very small child. "Do I click my heels three times?"

"Not unless you're aiming for Oz, and no one likes a flying monkey."

Aline grinned over her shoulder. She liked Dragon. "How will I find you?"

"You want to?"

Aline's brow furrowed. "I . . . we're friends, aren't we? You stood up for me, with the others."

Dragon nodded. "I did." She smiled, and it transformed her face into such a blind radiance, Aline blinked against it. "Yes. Let's be friends."

Aline nodded, and then thought about slamming her hands into the mirror, screaming, and falling through. She screamed the name of her school at the top of her lungs and slammed her hands into the hole. She tumbled through the tree and onto the floor of the bathroom. A bell rang. Aline stood, dusted off her shirt and pants, and bent over to pick up her bag. The light shimmered across the floor, and she saw a sparkle at the edge of the sinks. She crawled to it, thinking of Dragon and shadows, and not sure how any of it could be real but desperately needing it to be.

A small charm winked in the sunlight. Aline picked it up, turning it from side to side. A little ballerina, standing in position with a small loop at the top of her hand. She pocketed it and scooped up her bag, hurrying from the bathroom, looking over her shoulder once, and finding the mirror was just a mirror.

It did not matter. Because Aline had a friend.

Two

THE REST OF THE WEEK AT SCHOOL WAS THE SAME. **More names** were added to the list; Aline ignored them as she ate in the bathroom. She thought about trying to go through the mirror, but she was a little afraid. She hated to be afraid, so she worked on strengthening her courage, and she placed the ballerina charm on her wrist and read in the last stall.

On Friday, she worked up enough nerve to approach the mirror. She thought about how Andrea called her cringe and Mary Beth stuck gum on her seat. She remembered her parents ignoring her tears at the dinner table, and as she stared into the mirror, a scream built. She silently let it out the way a kettle whistles, closed her eyes, and pressed her hands into the mirror. This time she didn't fall but was pulled through.

It was like traveling underwater: one moment she was in the

school and the next she was in a state of floating, and then she was standing in the forest in between here and there, holding Dragon's hands.

"You're having quite the week," Dragon said, smiling at Aline until her eyes drifted to the charm on her wrist. "Sideways but rightways, that."

"What?"

"The charm," Dragon nodded.

"It shimmered," Aline said, rubbing a finger over it. As she did, a glimmer grew at the edge of the trees, and she saw a pair of horn-rimmed glasses and bright-green eyes peering from behind a weathered sycamore.

"Who is that?" Aline whispered.

Dragon looked over her shoulder to where the girl stood off in the distance. "I'd say she's the spirit looking for the key you're wearing."

"Key?" Aline looked at the charm, and it grew brighter, then flashed from a ballerina to the shape of a key and back again. "Whoa."

"I told you, you're a witch who opens doors," Dragon said. "You find keys, too, and can return them."

"She's looking for this?"

Dragon nodded, a slow, thoughtful nod. Her eyes grew wider as she stared at the girl, and a vacant expression came over her face. It was like Dragon was there and gone and then she blinked and was back again. "She can't move on without it."

"But who is she?"

"Ask her," Dragon said, giving her a nudge.

Aline cleared her throat. She thought, I'm in a forest in a place that shouldn't exist, talking to one ghost who is my only friend and I'm about to try and help another. It should have sounded odd to her, but instead it rooted in her bones and felt precisely right.

"Oh," she said, the sensation of having a purpose settling over her like a warm blanket on a rainy night.

She walked to the edge of the trees and stopped a few feet back. She took the bracelet off and held it up. It grew brighter as she lifted it in the direction of the girl. "Hi," she called. "Is this yours?"

The girl's head poked out from behind the tree; she was small and had green eyes and olive skin and dark curly hair. She was younger than Aline and appeared scared of her own shadow.

"It's okay," Aline called. "I won't hurt you."

"I'm Tera," the girl whispered, her "T" coming out as a "Th." She was missing her two front teeth.

"Are you . . . stuck?" Aline asked, unsure how else to phrase it.

"I was staying after school, and then on my walk home I saw a cat running into the street. I chased it to help it, and the next thing I knew . . . I was here."

Aline bit her lip. She'd heard the story of the little girl named Tera who died in front of the school thirty years or so earlier. Everyone knew. It was almost urban legend how she haunted the pipes and the basement. No one Aline knew had ever actually seen her, and Aline couldn't imagine this shy, terrified person being the ghoul of the school.

"I'm sorry," Aline said, her voice soft. "Here, let me help you." She crossed to her and dropped the charm into Tera's small, curled palm.

Tera shimmered like the charm had done when Aline found it, and then she looked deep into Aline's eyes. "Ash on an old man's sleeve," she said, and walked into Aline and then was gone. Aline shivered as she felt Tera's spirit pass through her. She looked over at Dragon, who was sitting on the ground building a castle from dirt.

"She's moved on," Dragon said.

"Where?"

She lifted a single shoulder, dropped it. "Home, perhaps. To where the light gets in. I'm not sure, but she is where she was meant to be, and that's because of you, and who you are meant to be."

"I'm meant to give ghosts charm bracelets?"

"You're meant to guide them home, to return keys to where they need to be to unlock the doors that are stuck."

"That sounds a lot like homework."

Dragon threw back her head and laughed. "It's a calling and will become a craving." She flashed her white teeth. "You'll see."

Aline returned to school, and the whispers and eye rolls cast in her direction didn't bother her quite as much as before. She tried to return to a typical life. But an atypical girl is not meant for a typical life, and Aline began to find things others would not, *could not* see.

Shadows that walked and talked to one another, people moving inside mirrors and from one puddle of water to the other. Then she met another person like Tera, an older gentleman in a back alley behind Sam's Sandwich Shop in town. He had lost his way home and needed her to find a key so he could open the right door.

She told Dragon, who had begun sneaking into her room at night and pulling her through the bathroom mirror during the week. Dragon nodded and simply said, "There are but a few who can find the keys to unlock the doors for those seeking it to find peace."

Two weeks later, Aline was in Ballory Cemetery, cutting through to get home and avoid the main path where the kids from school walked. She saw a key glowing in a ditch behind the old church on Ballory Street, three miles from the local bookstore, and two miles from Aline's home. She picked it up and the key shifted into a watch.

Aline slept with the watch under her pillow, waiting for the owner to show up. She dreamed she woke up to find the man sitting on the chair in her room. Aline took the watch out from under her pillow, stood, and walked over to place the watch around his wrist.

The man smiled. He bowed his head and Aline thought of Tera. She whispered, "Ash on an old man's sleeve."

Aline woke up. The man was gone, and so was the watch.

The next month, she dreamed of keys that, when she touched them, became a headlamp, a dog tag, and a gold ring in the shape of a singing sparrow. Soon after, she found more and more objects that did not belong anywhere, and yet she could not leave them alone. She told Dragon they were a strange sort of treasure. They didn't belong in a vault in the Smithsonian and wouldn't buy a small tropical island off the coast of a faraway land.

No, her treasure did something else.

It whispered. It sang. It shimmered and called to her to be returned home. Finding lost items, as Dragon had told her, was her gift. It was her magic.

Sometimes ghosts showed up for the items; other times the objects disappeared on their own. Being found, they could then be claimed. She could talk to the objects. Ruminate on them in her mind. They heard her, answered, and would always end up in her hands. Aline's skills sharpened, her craft grew, and as she slipped further and further into a life in the shadows, she found out what she was made of and what she was meant to do.

She learned no club could touch her, and she had something better than fair-weather friends. She had power, she had Dragon, and she was no longer afraid.

TIME PASSED, IN THE INEVITABLE AND INERT WAY IT DOES. Aline graduated from middle school to high school without another slumber-party invitation. She hid in the library, finding solace and a new plethora of friends in the books on the shelves. She read everything she could get her hands on about the paranormal, as well as the entire middle-grade fantasy collection and fifty-seven nonfiction biographies. Dragon sometimes showed up, asking her to read passages out loud or peeking over her shoulder. Aline might not have had friends in her peers, but she had something better in her Dragon.

Many times, she'd look for Dragon's key, but when she'd tell her, Dragon shrugged it off. "We're friends," Aline would remind her. "Friends look out for each other."

"We are friends, and that's the biggest help of all," Dragon would say, before launching into a discussion on the vibrations of magic or the unusualness of a turtle's belly button. Dragon liked knowledge even more than Aline, although she also said things that didn't make sense, like how she'd gotten in an argument with a star about eating planets or how the snowflakes were incendiary agents for good. Aline didn't mind her peculiarity, considering Aline herself was so often accused of being odd.

High school proved a bit easier for Aline . . . at first. She skated through her freshman and sophomore years by keeping her head down. She did well in school, if not at the top of her class, and while she didn't seek extracurriculars like debate or cheer or sportsball, as Dragon called it, she had plenty to keep her occupied after hours.

Her parents took to traveling more and more. Aline told herself it was fine, since it gave her plenty of time to look for keys in and around her town in her after-school hours, yet she found the constant emptiness of her home, and the dark that permeated there, settled deep into her. It was an ache that pulsed beneath the surface of her skin. An itch that never went away.

Dragon wasn't always able to be there—perhaps she was off hoarding gold or treasure; Aline could never get a straight answer out of her. The constant loneliness would steal Aline's breath at times. It was so awful she'd double over in pain as her stomach clenched and sweat broke out along her brow. Lonesomeness was a horrible kind of sickness.

It was during her junior year that three things happened to alter everything once again. The first being that Aline's parents had a blowout fight in Greece and came home to stay. Where their indifference had reigned, now the house was filled with their anger, which turned into eggshells Aline had to tiptoe around.

Then came Noah Bones with his swoopy brown hair and rocker tees and scuffed Vans. With a crooked grin and eyes that saw everything, Noah noticed Aline.

She sat under a tree outside the school, between the football field and soccer field, trying to blend in with the foliage. It was her reading spot when the days were warm enough, and she found that grounding into the earth with her shoes off and feet dug into the soil recharged the ache she carried like a backpack she couldn't put down.

Noah crossed through the soccer field. The wind brushed his hair back from his face, showing off his spectacularly stunning blue eyes and straight nose. The kind of nose on the sculptures in the museums her parents liked to visit before their pedantic personalities finally made everything go tits up. Roman, she thought. Like a soldier. He smiled and her stomach tried to drop into the soil next to her toes.

No one had ever smiled like that at Aline, like she was someone to be excited about.

"Hey," he said, dropping next to her like he had a standing invitation and they weren't complete strangers.

Aline sat, holding a book called *The Conscious Ghost.* Noah glanced at the title and smiled. "Light reading?"

"Research," she said. Aline didn't know how to talk to people, aside from Dragon. She wasn't well versed in social conversation and had long ago given up her notebook with data about those around her. She preferred the shadows now, but here was a light, shining in her space.

"Cool." He pulled out a ham sandwich and proceeded to eat it, leaning against her tree, crossing one foot over the other ankle, and not saying another word. She could feel him watching her. As he did, her cheeks flushed and her heart sped up. She didn't know if she should get up and run or stay very, very still.

"I'm Noah," he said.

She nodded. She'd heard his name. New transfers were always a popular choice on the whisper network, and news of the senior soccer captain had reached even her averted ears.

"Okay."

He laughed, a deep rumbly sound that warmed its way down to her toes. "I don't suppose you want to tell me who you are?"

"Aline," she said.

"Aye-lean."

"Something like that."

"I like it. What's it mean?"

"A place in a line. Meant to be parallel or straight."

"Are you?"

She glanced up, found herself trapped in the bright blue of his eyes.

"Straight? Into boys, girls, both?"

She looked back down. "Haven't tested the hypothesis fully, but you aren't horrible to look at."

He laughed again, that sexy rumble, and she shivered. "You're funny," he said, crumpling his empty wrapper and putting it back in his bag. "You're also not bad to look at, *Aline*."

Then he was gone, and Aline found the earth between her bare feet had warmed to mud.

For the next two weeks, Noah showed up at Aline's tree spot. Some days, he was there before her. He arrived with books in hand, written by authors whom she thought of as part of the Dead Angst Society: Hemingway, Kerouac, Ginsberg, and Salinger. Aline didn't trust people who only read stories by dead people, but then she spoke mostly to dead people, so she decided to cut him some slack.

"Why do you only sit out here?" he asked. "There's a whole world of, I don't know, tables inside. Great places to rest elbows and plates and cups."

"Also a lot of endless chatter and laughter and clanging forks."

"Do forks clang?"

"Yes, and that you haven't noticed says so much about you."

"So you're paying attention to me then?"

"It's hard not to when you keep turning up."

"I'll be your bad penny," he said. Then he reached into his pocket and pulled out a rock painted to look like the moon. He slid it to her and returned to his book and turkey-and-Swiss sandwich—a variation on the only two sandwiches he ever ate.

Soon, Noah wasn't only eating lunch with Aline. He was also walking her home, five blocks from the north side of the school. When her parents weren't home, he was coming in to work on schoolwork after soccer practice and binge-watch cooking shows and documentaries about dead rock stars. His ennui for generations of dead artists was fascinating. They didn't have classes together, or cross paths during school outside of lunch, but he was always there, her first friend who was real.

"You have a lot of books on magic and ghosts," Noah said, one rainy afternoon when Aline's parents were out of town on separate trips. The house was quiet, but it wasn't dark. It had Noah's light and laughter and it felt like home.

"I have many varied interests," she said, lying on her bed on her stomach, drawing a picture of Dragon in one of her notebooks.

"You really do," he said. He sat the book down and crossed to the edge of the bed. "I like them all. I like you . . . all of you."

Then Noah shifted the notebook out from Aline's grasp; he lay down beside her and traced her jaw and the outline of her lips with his fingertips. "Is this okay?" he asked, his voice low, his eyes dilating.

Aline didn't only read books on the supernatural and non-fiction biographies; she was also well versed in romance novels.

She knew what he was asking, what it meant that his bright-blue eyes had darkened. Her stomach flipped as heat between her thighs built.

"Yes," she said, her voice breathless.

Noah leaned in and brushed his lips over hers. Soft, promising, gentle. He took his time, taking the kiss deeper, nudging her lower lip open, nibbling and running his tongue across the seam there. Heat built in Aline until she was trembling with need. Her hands came up and into his hair, and she sealed their mouths, took the kiss deeper, growling as she did. He groaned and she rolled him over, finding the perfect position seated on top of him.

"I . . ." She paused, trying to catch her breath. "Don't know what I'm doing."

"What do you want to do?" he asked, his hands clenching her thighs, the touch still gentle but the urgency a current flooding into her.

Aline licked her lips. "Everything." She wanted to do everything.

Their clothes were discarded with clumsy speed, then they were under the covers laughing and kissing, and when Noah pressed his thigh between Aline's legs and rolled into her, she thought she might explode.

Then he was sliding on a condom and positioning himself over her. They locked eyes, and his were tender and dark. She nodded and he was slow to enter her, and when the pain came, it was fleeting and sharp. Then they were moving together. Her breath and his breath, lips and tongues tangled, moans and groans building. Then, it was over. He shuddered and shook, and slid off her. Aline blinked at the ceiling, curious as to what she might have missed. This was a big deal; she almost knew why, but hadn't quite understood.

Noah pulled her to him, kissing her forehead and squeezing her tight. "Thank you," he said.

She kissed him back, unsure what to say, until his phone alarm went off. Three shrill beeps. "Shit," Noah said, rolling away and clamoring up. He grabbed his clothes, running to the bathroom. She heard the water run, then a toilet flush, then he was back out and dressed in two minutes flat, about the same amount of time the sex had taken.

"I have to get to practice," he said, running his hands through his hair. "I'll call you later, okay?"

Aline shrugged. "Sure."

He smiled, and his grin shot straight to the place between her legs that was still unsatisfied. Then he took off running, and Aline was left to sit in bed, feeling for all the world emptier than she had in a long time.

She showered and changed, preparing to walk through Ballory Cemetery and see if she could find someone. Someone, perhaps, who could help her. She could call on Dragon, but this felt like something she wasn't ready to share . . . just yet.

Aline laced up her favorite pair of scuffed black Converse high-tops and walked to grab her bag, then saw Noah's sitting on her floor.

"Oh no," she said. She tried to text him and let him know, but he didn't reply. Chances were good he was already to the field and perhaps on it. But missing his extra clothes. She could leave it, or she could try and drop it off. Maybe set it on the top of his car. She could be in and out and not have to see any of the students she needed to avoid.

It was a short drive, and Aline's heart sank at the crowd of cars. She couldn't tell which was his in a sea of so many gray and silver used and new SUVs. It was like trying to find a cobalt scarf on a rack of a hundred blue scarves in every shade.

"Shit shit shit," Aline said. She got out, grabbed his bag, and did what she always did at school. She shrunk in on herself, trying to appear more invisible. She hurried, skittering not unlike a crab, between cars and into the fields, behind the stands and around to where the players sat. Noah was on the bench, drinking water from his favorite Yeti container. The green one that had the tricky top. She should really get him a new one; was that something friends who were more than friends did?

The idea left her smiling, a warm burst of hope flooding through her.

Noah stood up and looked around. He could sense her? No, he wasn't looking at her, but behind her. Aline glanced over her shoulder. A girl with long brown hair and expressive eyes waved to him. She wore a jean jacket and pink lipstick and appeared happy and friendly, and everything about her made Aline want to scream.

Noah jogged to her, running past Aline—never seeing her standing there, holding his bag—and swept the girl up in his arms. He kissed her so thoroughly Aline's knees knocked together and she had to grab hold of the fence post nearest to her to keep from falling over.

"Gotta get back, babe," she heard him say in a low growl, one she knew too well.

Noah kissed the other girl once more and turned to hurry back to his starting line. That's when he saw Aline. His face lost all its happy candor, going pale with shock. Aline lifted the bag and tossed it at his feet.

She spun on her heel and walked as slowly as she could manage out of the stadium and back to her car. Angry tears coursed down her face; great gasping hiccups escaped where she was trying to force them down. She was almost to her car when her knees gave out. She stumbled and went down hard. The skies overhead darkened, and thunder rumbled in the far-off distance. The storm outside also started building inside her. Humiliation, her childhood companion, had returned, but it had brought a destruction she'd not yet met. Devastation, a new heartbreak. She could taste Noah on her lips, smell him in her hair and on her skin. If she closed her eyes, she could feel his hands roaming down her spine.

"Aline!"

She crawled her way up. She refused to let him see her on her knees. She kept moving forward, ignoring him completely.

"Wait, Aline."

She spun at the irritation in his voice. As though he had any right to be put out by this situation.

"Go away, Noah."

"I'm—"

"If you say the word 'sorry' to me after what you've done, I will destroy you."

He scrubbed at his jaw. "I got carried away. I like you, you're funny and weird, and entertaining, but it's not like that with us."

"You mean the part where you had sex with me? That's not like that?"

"I mean . . ." He looked down at his cleats like there was an answer he might pry from one of them. "Look. I don't know what I want. I just know I don't want you."

Then, as she reeled back, he turned and walked away. The rain coming down and soaking him and doing nothing to cleanse the pain that ate at her bones.

Every cell in her body was awake. On fire. Aline was dying. She had to be. Nothing had ever felt this bad, this layered with mortification, rejection, and truth. Because she was nothing. She'd known it all along. Her parents showed it to her by ignoring her and leaving her behind; the students in the school showed it by never seeing her; and Noah had shown it by tricking her into thinking he might be falling in love with her, only to discover he found her a forgettable joke. One barely worth using before he tossed her away.

The vibration beneath Aline's feet increased. The road shook, the pavement breaking into pebbles. Aline reached inside herself, pulling out all the pain and rage and hurt, and she threw her head back and screamed. Light flashed into the parking lot, wind blew fast and furious, and the earth cracked. The pebbles rose into the air like a hundred thousand glittering lights, before they blew past Aline, and straight into Noah.

Three

THE PERK OF BEING INVISIBLE IS THAT NO ONE SAW ALINE AT THE SOCCER FIELDS. The meteoric storm, a freak of nature, came out of nowhere. There was damage to the stands, but thankfully no one in the field or on the stands was hurt. The same could not be said for the new soccer star, Noah Bones.

Noah was crushed by concrete that fell on him when a sinkhole occurred. It took two crews to recover his body.

Aline wasn't simply a lonely witch anymore; she was a murderer. She did not go to the funeral. She stopped going to school entirely.

"I don't feel safe," she told her parents. A half-truth.

"You don't have to feel safe. You just have to graduate," her father said.

"Then you can leave and do whatever you like," her mother said.

Aline didn't want to leave. She still had Dragon and her ghosts, though she hadn't been back to the cemetery since Noah died. His spirit was not one she wanted to cross. She cried a lot and stopped reading and watching her documentaries. Everything reminded her of Noah, and of his words. "I don't know what I want, but I know it isn't you."

She was still a freak, and unlovable. And her anger had cost Noah his life. She might hate him, but she hadn't planned to kill him. She wished she felt worse about that. And yet, she didn't.

Aline tried to find Dragon, but she was nowhere to be found. It was then the third unexpected thing happened.

It was on the way home from getting a packet about completing her GED that Aline stopped into the bookstore tucked inside a historic building in the center of town. The kind librarian from middle school, Chlo Moirai, had opened it the week prior. Chlo's library had been the only place Aline felt safe, and she needed to see if she could find such a space again. If one could even exist.

When she went inside, Aline looked for Chlo but didn't see anyone. She wandered around until she reached the children's section, with its brightly colored books and thick rugs and beanbags for reading chairs. She crumpled to the ground and reached for the first book she could find. For the rest of the afternoon, she shifted from the harsh world of Whistleblown and the destruction she had wreaked into the soft world of the Baby-Sitters Club. She was too old for such a book, but it was like going home again, so she read until the three owners—Chlo and her sisters, Liset and Atti Moirai—waltzed into the room in a cloud of Chanel N°5, chattering and carrying a tray full of chocolate milk and warm Pop-Tarts.

"Aline, dearest. You finally came," Chlo said, her brown frizzy hair moving around her face like a cloud of cotton candy being blown in the wind. She took Aline's chin in her hand and stared for so long into Aline's eyes, Aline nearly forgot what it meant to blink. "It is temporary, dearest."

"Oh yes, absolutely," agreed Liset, adjusting her pearls and pressing a perfectly manicured hand down her skirt. "Nothing is permanent, after all."

"Not a single blessed thing. You are always welcome here," Atti added, her large green eyes blinking bright under her thick fringe of bangs. "This is a safe haven, and the books are happy for the company, as are we."

Aline found her salvation with the bookstore and the trio of women who ran it. In the bookstore, Aline lived a life where she could escape. She didn't have to pretend the indifference or whispers from other kids cut into her like the angry blade of a serrated knife, or keep the peace during one of her parents' many arguments. She could study for her GED, and lose herself in worlds where the villains were clear and the heroes indefatigable. Where she could pretend for hours at a time she had not killed the first boy she'd ever loved.

"A broken heart is a terrible thing to waste," Chlo said to her one day, setting a chocolate Pop-Tart in front of her. The sisters had the misguided belief that chocolate was its own food group. "You are clearly grieving, dear. Can it really be all that bad?"

"Worse," Aline said with a grimace.

A wonderful thing about Chlo, and the other two sisters,

was they never lingered. Once a period was at the end of a sentence, they were gone, back to their offices or a nook and cranny where they could gossip and knit. They never minded how Aline treated the shop more like her own personal library and less like a brick-and-mortar store, or that she left chocolate smudged on the corners of half the pages she turned.

"How come you let me stay?" Aline asked, after watching them hurry out a few teenagers with sneers from the store.

"You are our favorite kind of female: wild and free," Atti said. "The shadows under your eyes won't always be there, dearie. One day you will soar."

Aline thought they liked her because she was as odd as they were. For owners of a store, they spent most of their time knitting and keeping an eye on the door for customers they more often than not ran off. On rainy days, they whispered in tones too low for Aline to properly hear, and on sunny days, they read Aline's palm and compared it to those found in their anatomy books.

It was on one of the rainy days that Aline stopped being scared of what had happened with Noah and started thinking about what could happen in her future. She sat, turning the pages on the latest adventure of Nancy and Ned, when a book tumbled from the third shelf up. *Anne of Green Gables*.

Aline sighed in relief as she took in the cover. She looked up and saw Dragon, leaning against a shelf of science fiction and smiling.

"You've been busy," Dragon said.

"I've been . . ." Aline's eyes filled and overflowed.

"No, no," Dragon said, rushing forward. "No crying, please."

"You don't know what I've done."

"You mean burying the boy alive? That was impressive, to be sure."

Aline sobbed harder. Dragon gave a huff. "It wasn't your fault."

"Oh yeah?" Aline looked up. "And whose fault was it?"

"Okay, so maybe you pulled the trigger, but he was the gun."

"Why don't the things you say make proper sense?"

Dragon rolled her eyes. She was still the same as ever. Blond curls, blue eyes, lace dress, perpetually a child. It should have been unnerving, but it was soothing. That something comforting didn't change.

"I told you that you are special. Your powers are too big, too unruly. You should have been trained, but you don't have a line of witches to step up. I'm not able to do it."

"And now I'm a murderer." Aline's sobs started anew.

"Stop that," Dragon said, tugging at her curls. "You had an accident."

"I didn't spill milk."

"And you didn't spill blood. You spilled earth. Blame the elements." She pointed to the door leading back into the bookstore's greater sanctum.

"They can help."

"The librarian and her sisters?"

"The three witches who guard the books," Dragon said. "You never noticed how safe you felt with Chlo? How nothing bad reached you in that library? How safe you feel here now?"

Aline shook her head. "But . . ."

"You're meant to be here. They've already cleaned up your mess once; why not let them help you find out how to prevent having another one."

Then Dragon leaned down, brushed a cool set of lips across Aline's cheek, and was gone.

⚜

Aline didn't understand what Dragon meant about them cleaning up her mess. She put the book back and went in search of the three women. She found them sitting in a circle, in threadbare green club chairs, knitting bags at their feet, yarn in their hands, and fingers curled around their needles. There was a fire in their old stone fireplace, and the red rug in front of it was worn and inviting. As though it had stories woven into its fibers from all the conversations it had overheard in the years gone by. Behind them was a long counter with three brightly colored glass Tiffany lamps. The type that looked like reproductions, but, knowing Chlo, were anything but. Twinkly lights were strung over the counter, and beyond it was the section of rare books the three owners were forever perusing. As Aline approached, she found them clacking their needles. Instead of finding the noise grating, like the discordance of forks in a cafeteria, Aline wanted to twist inside this soothing sound. Tuck herself into the threads and coil away there.

"Hello, dearie," Liset said, looking up from where she was knitting the world's teeniest pair of pants. "Did the snow fall in your sunshine?"

"My . . . what?"

"You look like your beach got washed out by a blizzard," Chlo clarified.

"More Pop-Tarts?" Atti offered. "They're a wonder. They don't pop and they aren't tart, but they can make mouths smile."

"No, thanks," Aline said. She picked at the cuticle on her pinky and bit her bottom lip.

"Ah," Chlo said. She nodded to the others. "I think we might need a minute or four very long ones eight times over."

"We'll put the kettle on," the sisters said, and got up, pausing to pat Aline on the shoulder, brush a hand down the back of her head. They stroked her like parents soothed small children in so many of the stories she read, and tears clogged the back of her throat at such unfettered kindness.

Chlo tapped the seat of the chair Atti had vacated. "Sit, darling. I think perhaps it's time we have a talk."

Aline sat, her face falling into her hands. She rolled her head from side to side, trying to shake loose the weight of the world on her shoulders.

"What's wrong?"

"Nothing."

"Nothing is wrong and that is a problem?"

"No, I mean. Everything should be wrong. I should be hunted by the police, thrown in jail, on trial, preparing for a life of an orange jumpsuit and bartering prison candy that I'll never have enough of because I have a *terrible* sweet tooth."

"Hmm."

Aline looked up at her, eyes rimmed red, cheeks splotchy. "Hmm? That's your reassuring reply?"

Chlo sighed. "I'm hmming, because I have good news, but it is big news and I really wish we had a Pop-Tart."

"Oh my goddess."

"No one is coming, Aline," Chlo said. "You unlocked the wrong door, and the boy got caught in the crosshairs."

Aline stilled. "Were you all protecting me?"

"It's what we do. My sisters and I look out for witches, and I've been looking out for you ever since you showed up in my library five years ago."

"You knew then?" she asked. "That I'm a . . . shadow witch?"

"I've known for longer, but it seemed it was the time to meet."

"Why?"

"Because you were coming into your powers."

"You never said anything, though."

Chlo shifted in the chair and crossed one long leg over the other. "You've had enough on your plate, Aline. A sadness permeating, an inability to find your place."

"Wouldn't knowing why help?" she asked, a bite to her tone.

"Being a witch doesn't make you unlovable. Having parents who don't know how to love anyone other than themselves and being surrounded by children who are intimidated by you simply put you in a position of adversity. You crack or polish."

"So you left me to crack?"

"I'd say you rather shine."

"And Noah?" she asked, her voice breaking. "If you had warned me what I could do . . ."

"He might have lived, yes. He did not, and we should have taken better care with you. I admit it. You'd done so well the past few years, I didn't see this coming." She frowned, her gaze dropping to her knitting. "I was looking in the wrong direction and this was as much my fault as anyone's." She looked up and met Aline's penetrating gaze. "So we cleaned it up."

"You . . . how?"

"We pulled the right thread, dearie. It was an accident caused by a seismic shift in the weather pattern. A freak occurrence in nature, but nature is known for her reckonings."

"That doesn't seem right."

"You lost control," Chlo said. "But it wasn't your fault. You can't let your pain, anger, and hurt rule you. When a witch like you does, it creates a door. You help spirits, and you didn't have one to help. You created one."

Aline swallowed hard, feeling like she were trying to swallow glass. "I didn't help Noah."

"No, but your instinct took over. We helped Noah. He has moved on, and you must as well."

Aline shook her head. It was impossible, and surreal. Sitting in a library where the soft instrumental tones of Chopin played and a light rain fell outside the three arched windows at the far end of the store. Where lights twinkled, a fire crackled, and the two other sisters emerged carrying a pot of fragrant mint tea and a tea set with pine trees painted on the sides. She was in the coziest place on earth, and here in this cocoon of warmth her world had turned inside out.

"All is not lost," Chlo said, as she accepted a cup of tea and nodded for Aline to do the same.

"No, not at all," Liset said, smiling and pausing to rub the lipstick from her teeth.

Atti yawned and sat. "Lost is temporary, after all."

"You are meant for greatness, Aline Weir," Chlo said, "and more than that, you are meant for a great love."

"Quite possibly," Atti said.

"If possible is still true after all this time," Liset added.

Chlo waved them off while Aline was tempted to put her

hands to her head to stop the spinning of their words and the weight of all they had laid in her lap.

"You'll stay here," Chlo said. "Work for us this summer. The books will heal you, and one day, I promise, you will feel strong again."

"What if I accidentally unlock a door and send you all through it?"

They laughed, loud titters that shook the saucer. Liset leaned over and brushed the hair back from Aline's shoulder where it had cascaded forward. "If only you could, dearie."

Aline decided, after two cups of tea and another Pop-Tart, to accept their invitation. She needed a job, after all, and the thing of it was she didn't want to leave the bookstore. The sisters prattled on, speaking of magic and town gossip and the grooming habits of ruffian men and women. They asked Aline her thoughts from time to time, but also left her be.

They had protected her. They were clearly magical themselves. Aline didn't have a family, and she didn't trust herself, but she thought, perhaps, she could trust them. She hoped, in her heart of hearts, she might have finally found a family.

Four

There are laws of magic, much like there are decrees for life. The thing about magical law is, as Atti was fond of saying, "Laws are guidelines and guidelines are good to know. Once you know the rules, however, they are perfectly fun to break."

Thus began Aline's education on magic according to the sisters Moirai. As the months wore on, Aline studied with Liset and passed her GED. The sisters were accredited professors, among other things, and they enrolled her in an online college early. When Aline told her parents, her mother simply left the room, while her father told her, "I didn't think you were particularly book smart, but if those ladies can help you get out on your own, good for them."

Aline didn't understand it. She had tried her best with the

bad situation that was her family, and yet nothing ever measured up.

"They won't see themselves clearly," Chlo told her one day, "so they can't possibly see you."

It was a simple but effective explanation, and Aline took to spending more and more time in the store and less and less at home. She loved the routine of it. Stocking books when new shipments came in, listing them online (most of the sales were done over the "inter nettle," as Atti called it), and tidying the shelves. The sisters even let her organize the children's section, changing the system from alphabetical by author to colors of the rainbow. It was a rainbow of books, and being in the room left Aline sighing in happiness.

It was in the children's and young adult section that Dragon finally returned one early September morning.

"Told you they could help," Dragon said, causing Aline to drop the stack of books she was shelving. She spun around and threw her arms around her friend, surprised to find her solid.

Dragon hesitated, before raising her arms and squeezing Aline back. She barely came to Aline's ribs, and Aline dropped her chin to Dragon's head. "I missed you. Where have you been?"

"Where I always go when I'm not with you."

"Which is?"

"Keeping an eye on things."

Dragon looked around the shop, her eyes narrowing at the edge of the worn carpet. Musty, and the unfortunate color of a ripe avocado, the carpet waved up in the corner of the children's room where the padding had gone from aged to tatters.

"I know, I told them they should consider natural wood flooring in here."

Dragon didn't move, just huffed a bit at the corner of the room. Aline followed Dragon's gaze to where an odd brick stood out on the far wall. When Aline looked at it directly, it blended in, but seeing it from the corner of her eye, she realized the brick was the wrong shade of red. It was, in fact, much lighter than the rest of the wall. More faded persimmon than burnt sienna.

"That's not right," Dragon said, a note of worry creeping into her voice.

Aline didn't know what to say to that, but she couldn't help but reach out for the brick.

"I don't think you should touch it," Dragon said.

"Dragon."

"No, Aline. I'm not sure about that."

Aline hesitated. She trusted Dragon. Hated to go against her wishes. But . . . a small voice in the back of her mind whispered, what did a ghost, even *her* ghost, know? Aline rubbed a single finger along it. She climbed to her knees, and the brick *whispered*. The brick told her it was not where it belonged. It was in the wrong place, and it wanted her help. Aline knew what it was like to need help. And before she came here, she knew what it was like when no one did anything. Aline pushed hard against the brick and told the wall to *move*. The wall groaned, and creaked, and puffed an awful stinky puff of air . . . and it slid back three inches.

Aline jumped up, gaping at the wall. Her hands shook; her heart thudded like angry thunder in her chest.

"Aline," Dragon said, her voice a slight tremble.

Perhaps Aline should have been scared. Dragon certainly sounded it. But the simple truth was the things that scared Aline were far more complex than a wall with a secret. Aline feared the way her mother looked at her like she was a mistake her mother couldn't undo, and how her father looked through her as though she didn't exist. The hollow emptiness in her house, a place where love should live . . . that terrified her.

In the store where she had found safety and hope—nothing worried her here.

"It's going to be okay. I'm not afraid, Dragon," she said.

She found it surprisingly easy to slide the wall farther in once it was opened. She slipped inside. She left enough room between the movable wall and seam for Dragon to join her, though she didn't seem inclined to follow.

Behind the wall was a shelf of books and an old vintage desk. Lined up along the floor was a row of the most eclectic hats. Bucket hats, bowler hats, sombreros, deerstalkers, fascinators, dunce caps, ball caps, fedoras, fezzes, half hats, hard hats, top hats, whoopee caps, mushroom hats, party hats, pillbox hats, and Aline's personal favorite, the porkpie.

She studied the hats, and as she did, the ground vibrated beneath her feet. As the first bud of worry bloomed, Aline dug her heels into it, sniffed the air, and caught a whiff of a familiar, happy scent. The room smelled of lavender, like Chlo. She scooped the porkpie up, dropping the felt hat with the low, flat crown, narrow brim, and small bow on the back on her head. As soon as the hat hit her hair, a wave of heat rushed over her. Her cheeks warmed, her hands tingled, and her nose tickled. A little dizzy, Aline stumbled a step forward and dropped into the swivel chair in front of the old-timey desk. After a moment, the heat passed, and she looked up to see a book tucked along the corner of the desk.

Mischief, A Beginner's Guide.

"Don't touch that," Dragon said, standing outside the room,

looking in but not moving closer. "That's not a book. That's a story."

"Books are stories," Aline said. She scooped up the book, sat on the floor by the chair, and began to read.

Mischief told of a town called Matchstick where magic began. It was the story of a powerful witch who was lonely, and magic was lost, so she created a safe place for it. A place along the ley lines that would keep them both safe and protect them always. Soon the magic there drew other powerful witches, and those who lived in the shadows. Ghosts. Oddities. People like Aline. Like Dragon. Like the sisters in the bookstore. Magic was more than magic.

It was a story like nothing Aline had ever read, and she found herself in the pages, in the people who wanted to be seen but hid, who made mistakes and lost people. Witches who wished they belonged, but knew they lived in a world where they never could. She fell in love with the powerful being in the story, the one who was broken but desperately wished to be whole. Who was aloof but terrified, who had dark hair and brooding eyes, and Aline understood him in those pages as well as she'd ever understood herself.

Aline cried when the story was over. She put the porkpie hat back, kept the book, and crawled out from behind the secret wall. Dragon was nowhere to be found, and neither were the sisters.

Aline went home to a house where one parent yelled at her for walking too loudly and the other didn't hear her footsteps at all. That night was the first night Aline dreamed of a town that did not exist. Of night and day, of magic, and of a crack between the worlds. Of a young man with eyes like a vortex, who whispered her name and ran his fingers along her forearm, causing sparks to rain from the sky.

The next day Aline returned to the bookstore. In the children's section, she found the curious brick that did not match the other bricks alone on the floor. In its place was a newer, shinier brick. The wall was now a wall, the strange brick just a brick, and the way in sealed shut. Aline scooped up the brick and went in search of the wise women who owned the store. When she told them of her adventure, and Dragon, and the book she had taken home, they exchanged a look. When she apologized and tried to pay for the book, they laughed and offered her more chocolate.

"I'm sure I've never heard of a secret room in this store," Chlo said, smiling. "Let alone a story hidden inside that is more than a story."

"But how nice to find a floor filled with hats and be able to put on any one you choose and become whomever you'd like to be," Atti added.

"Or whomever you are meant to be," Liset said.

"Yes," Chlo said, pushing a tray of pastries toward her. "What wonders there might lie ahead for you if such a thing could exist." Then she winked at her, and the three went back to their knitting and debating the future of trees.

Aline returned to work at the bookstore every afternoon as before, but she never found a way back into the secret room. She kept her copy of *Mischief, A Beginner's Guide,* and the brick, and every night she dreamed of a man with dark eyes, a knowing smile, and when he would touch her, sparks would flutter from the ether, wrapping them in a snow globe of their own. Inside that orb, Aline had everything she'd ever wanted.

A few months into working for the sisters, they took her into the forest beyond the town.

"It's one thing to open a door," Chlo said. "It's another to open a soul. If what had happened with Noah had occurred with a witch, you would have kept a little of their essence."

"What does that mean?"

"A bit of madness, a spot of magic, a hint of their power. It shows up in different ways," Liset said, studying the fading sun as it set in the sky.

"It's why there are no more hedge witches left," Atti said, leading them to a row of privets. "It's one thing to help the spirits cross. It's another to make them."

"I don't want to kill anyone," Aline said, her eyes filling again as she pictured Noah's face before he was gone. "I don't know how to live with what I've done." She didn't, outside of the bookstore walls; she was beginning to hate herself as much as it seemed everyone else disliked her.

"We all make mistakes," Chlo said, her shoulders rolled back, eyes on Aline.

"How are you feeling really, though?"

"What do you mean?"

"Any . . . cravings. Need for more doors? Desire for something beyond this world?"

"I would like to go back inside and read a book and eat a Pop-Tart, while ignoring the way your eyebrows are pointing toward your widow's peak. Is that what you mean?"

Liset bit back a giggle, poorly, and Chlo smiled. "Some are bitter pills to swallow; others blow away with the lightest breeze. The key is to understand whether you want to do it again."

"I *don't* want to do that ever again."

The others nodded.

"How do you know?"

"I'm not a psychopath," Aline said, her voice rising. "I messed up."

"True," Atti said.

"You know how to cross over into the in-between," Chlo said. "Right?"

"Right," Aline said, her jaw aching from how tightly she held it.

"You must get more adept at going in and out, and doing so while there are obstacles in your way."

"Like a bunch of chairs and snowballs?"

"No," Atti said. "Like dead bodies."

"What?"

"Kidding," Atti said. "We rarely throw dismembered heads anymore."

Aline stumbled back as the sun set and the sweet, quiet forest beyond the store filled with ghosts.

"Cross," Chlo called, as she and the three women shifted back closer to the entrance of the shop. "Don't be afraid."

Aline blew out a slow breath as the ghosts drifted closer. A child no more than ten wearing a ball cap; a man in his thirties with a large headset over his ears; a pair of octogenarians holding hands; a woman holding a baby, tears tracking down her cheeks.

Aline walked toward the hedge that the ghosts were all circling. She told herself it was simple; she'd part the brush and call for Dragon. Dive through into the in-between.

The spirits moved closer, their fingers running along Aline's arms and down her back, the baby's cry reaching her and settling into her palms where she cupped it and tried to give it back. Their sounds and pain swooshed into her.

"I don't have your keys," she called, her temper rising, her eyes flashing as she swallowed fear. "I can't help. You have to get back."

The whispers started low, like wind blowing across individual blades of grass before rustling leaves. Keys, needs, all seeking her.

The sisters stood from the door, talking loudly. "She can't do it," Chlo said. "We were wrong. She hasn't got the power."

"She'll muck it up for sure, might even get caught in the hedgerow," Liset added.

"Half in and out, the poor spirits will forever be stuck." Atti sighed the words.

"I'm not sure what kind of a witch we need," Chlo said, her voice rising, "but it isn't her."

Aline's feet shifted. Her body tightened; her muscles screamed. Her ligaments were as taut as a spring on a bow and arrow. Aline Weir, the odd girl who had no place, whom no one wanted, whom everyone poked and prodded at like she was a pincushion meant to be stabbed by rejection. The sky overhead shifted from a pale, cloudless gray to charcoal. The wind whipped up twice before it faded completely. Not a weed stirred, not a bird called. Static filled the air, lifting the hairs off Aline's arms and neck. She let out the growl, incapable of holding it back.

She was never enough, and she was tired of being underestimated.

"That's it," Chlo said, and Aline realized she was right there. Standing at her side. "That's the trigger, and that power is seeking its way out. All of life, all of magic is made of light and dark. You choose which you embrace. Right now you believe the hate that is rained on you, but words are only as powerful as you allow them to be."

Liset stepped forward. "You can release your power, decimate the land, the person nearest you, take your revenge on those words that cut you to the quick."

Atti moved to her other side. "Or you can send it out through your hands, open them, let go. You can shift it from dark to light. Tell your power to open the door, Aline."

"You can do anything," Chlo said, her whisper brushing against the shell of her ear. "You only have to believe and choose."

Rage was a lit fuse, the words of rejection, the slashes of pain. They were rivers raging inside of Aline's very soul. She'd never been enough, never been made right.

Aline tasted grapefruit on her tongue. Bitter with a hint of honey. She stared at the hedge, cloaked in a haze, the way to the in-between visible. The spirits around her were quiet, but she could sense them. Could close her eyes and locate where each of them stood, waiting. Hoping.

Aline liked power. It was a secret truth she kept tucked in the bottom of her shoe. She liked the strength coursing through her, how she could decimate anything that got in her way, anything that tried to break her. The dark was seductive, honest.

But it wasn't her. It wasn't who she'd spent her life trying to be. It wasn't Dragon, with her quirky goodness, or the spirits who were as lost as she was. It wasn't the loving compassion of the three sisters who had taken her in.

It tasted delicious, though.

Aline hesitated. For five seconds, ten. Tempted, *so, so* tempted to give in.

She heard the baby cry, and she felt the nudge of that sound—even more broken than what she carried. They all had scars, things they carried. Wounds and broken bits. She and the spirits. She knew that. She held out her hands, releasing the dark and letting the light shine through. She couldn't be certain, but she thought she heard the collective exhale of the three sisters surrounding her in a semicircle.

The hedge parted, and Aline stepped into the beyond.

※

DRAGON SAT ON THE PATH, HER CHIN IN HER HANDS, HER BROWS HIGH ON HER SMOOTH FOREHEAD. "Golly, ducky, for a minute there I wasn't sure which way you would go."

"Neither was I."

They laughed, and Dragon helped Aline find the different spots along the in-between to cross through. In and out, over and under, through the hedgerow she went.

For the next few years, Aline lived in and out of the shadows. The sisters guided her in her education, making sure she studied hard. She passed her college entrance exams with flying colors, enrolled in a well-regarded state school's online program, one with a secret study of magic and the occult. Though she lived at home, she spent less and less time in the house that had never been hers. It was as though she was turning into one of the specters she guided. Her parents saw her less and less, no matter how solidly she stood before them.

"People can't always see around themselves," Dragon explained. "The key is not to become one of those people."

Dragon was a favorite of Aline's and soon the sisters'. They were cagey with her at first. It did seem a bit unnatural to spend time with a ghost who didn't wish to find their way home, but Chlo said, "That one has a path of her own to walk, and it's good she has you now to walk it with her."

One year turned into two, two into ten. Aline's degrees piled up. She held a Master of Business Administration, Master's of Library Science, and Mistress of the Dark Arts. As her knowledge of running the store grew, and her ability to cross back and forth into the in-between and help guide spirits and their keys to their proper space, the sisters began to travel more and more.

"You don't need us as you once did, dearie," Atti said.

"No, the world needs us more, and it's a far more complicated puzzle than even you," Liset offered, while pouring Aline a fresh cup of lavender tea.

"The winds are changing," Chlo would say. "We must change with them, or all is lost."

Aline never fully understood what they meant, but they had always spoken this way, in fragmented riddles. She found it comforting. Almost as comforting as the nonsense Dragon sometimes spoke.

The three sisters' trips away grew longer. "We've the wheel of fortune to attend," Chlo said, "and you're on the path solid now."

Aline missed them, but they sent back books and journals for Aline to fill. Chlo sent notes wrapped around rose crystal hearts, reminding her that her heart was still out there, love was waiting, and to stay the course and believe.

Aline tried, but mostly she believed in Dragon. In the books, and in the few townspeople who became her acquaintances as they shopped at the store. Until one week turned into two, and Dragon didn't show up. Aline searched in the in-between for her; she tried everything she could think of to summon her—setting out her favorite cookies, reading passages from *Anne of Green Gables,* playing her favorite recording of the violin. Nothing worked.

Aline couldn't sit still, waiting for the sisters and her dearest friend to return. She tried to reach the sisters, but the numbers they gave didn't work. Which wasn't a surprise. They hated technology and were forever losing their phones or "accidentally" misplacing them. Aline hired a local college student with a sweet disposition and experience in retail who had previously helped during the holidays to watch the store. Aline explained she had book festivals to attend, and the sisters wouldn't be back for a bit.

Then she went abroad to help spirits in Venice and Ireland. In Scotland and Iceland. It was on her return trip home that reports came in from around the world like a flood of group texts from befuddled leaders.

Aline returned to news that trees had stopped producing yellow leaves that fall, leaving only crimson and orange, and rivers in certain parts of the world had run completely dry. There were whispers of growing pandemonium across the world, and rising despair that rolled through towns like a common virus.

Aline tried not to worry. She focused on her work with spirits and the quiet of life in Whistleblown. She waited for the sisters to return, waited for Dragon, surrounded by books and memories, backed by a series of degrees.

She was thirty years old, tired and alone. She spent her days curled up in a silver-and-gold wingback chair pilling at the edges, staring at stacks of middle-grade novels that once felt like home, wishing—quite desperately—the sisters would return.

It was on a particularly gray afternoon, when the wind wouldn't seem to die down and the shutters on the windows banged against the stone every few minutes, causing Aline's eye to twitch, that a new door opened.

⫷⫸

THE CHIME TINKLED AND THE SIDE DOOR HARDLY ANYONE KNEW WAS THERE SLID OPEN. Aline sat up from where she was slouched. Business at the bookshop was slow, particularly on Tuesdays.

A tall woman wearing a long maroon dress that dipped dangerously in the front entered. She had hair the color of silver spun with cream and moved with the sort of grace Aline had only seen in old black-and-white films starring Katharine Hepburn or Grace Kelly. Aline couldn't take her eyes off her hair, the way it seemed to move of its own accord. The longer she stared at it, the more she felt herself losing focus—as though she were turning inside out.

The woman cleared her throat and Aline blinked, shaking herself from the reverie. She clearly needed to get more sleep. Aline's gaze shifted to the stranger's face. She was beautiful, with a striking jawline and brown eyes that were piercing and a little terrifying as she trained them on Aline.

"You're not Chlo," the woman said, her voice deep and gravelly as though she didn't use it often.

"No, I'm Aline," Aline said, slipping the book under the counter where she kept it when it wasn't in her bag. "The sisters are out."

The woman tilted her head, her swanlike neck elongating and showing off a sharp, square jawline. "Interesting." She turned and looked around the shop, then back to Aline. "I was afraid of this."

"Of what?"

"The winds are changing, and mischief is afoot."

The way she said "mischief" reminded Aline of her favorite book, the one that never failed to bring her dreams of the man with the dark eyes and gentle touch, who in her dreams was everything she was not. Everything she wanted love to be.

Aline pushed herself out of her chair and made her way closer to the woman. As she did, she found gravity arguing with her feet, trying to root her to the spot.

Aline paused. Power comes in many forms. Aline had come across witches and druids and so many Others over the past seventeen years. But none of them made gravity afraid.

"What is it you're looking for?" she asked, leaning on the long wooden counter, crossing one Converse-clad foot over the other ankle.

The woman looked down to Aline's feet and back up. She smiled in a way that had Aline wanting to duck. A knife thrown in the form of a flash of perfectly white teeth.

"Help."

Aline's eyes drifted to the key around her neck. It glowed bright.

"That's not yours," Aline said, her voice soft.

"What isn't?"

"The necklace."

The woman took a step closer to Aline.

"No?"

Aline's own movements were slow, as though she were moving underwater. The key whispered to her. It begged.

Help me, help me, help me.

She reached up and brushed her fingers across it and the key shifted into a shape.

Of a small, green dragon.

Dragon.

Aline met the woman's eyes. "That is most definitely not yours."

The woman laughed, a full and happy sound that filled the room and caused the books to shake on the stacks. They began to fall, one after the other, until the once organized books were scattered across the floor.

The woman reached out a hand and plucked an envelope from thin air. She dropped it on the counter as she walked past Aline.

"It's not yours, either. But perhaps you can help me find the one it belongs to."

"Dragon?" Aline said, and her heart fluttered in her chest. Mournful notes rose up, the sounds of Dragon, the lazy violin and cello, sounds she heard whenever her friend was near. But Dragon wasn't in the shop. She hadn't been for far too many months. "Stop that," Aline said to the witch, who was rubbing her two fingers together, back and forth, a tiny violin making a large sound meant to cut into Aline's soul.

"We have a friend in common," the woman said. "About yay high, unruly curls, and a mouth that runs too often."

"You have her necklace."

"Yes. She came to me, not for the first time. She needed our

House of Knowledge, and when I went to check on her this was left behind, and she was gone."

"What does that mean?"

"It means that Dragon tried to access very old, unpredictable scrolls. The kind that should never be opened. She's looking for a key, and I would assume, now that I see you, she's looking to help you."

"Why would she be trying to help me, and who are you?"

"I am a friend, and Dragon knows change is at hand. The sisters are gone, and they never leave; and you are here, and the world is shifting. The forests are unhappy, the leaves are revolting, the soil hardening. Soon the stars will take notice and the tides will run away from the shores."

"Dragon went looking for a key because Chlo, Liset, and Atti left the store?"

"No, she went looking for a way to help. It's clear the reason is you. You stand before me recognizing her necklace, because magic is fractured in the world. It started twelve years ago. Cracks in the foundation. A slow eruption, leading to a larger disruption over time."

Aline's stomach clenched. Twelve years ago, she had lost control and Noah had paid the price. The sisters had covered it up, and they had all pretended like everything had gone back to normal. Or as normal as it could be for a coven of witches.

"You think Dragon, what, stole the manuscript?"

"The manuscript is still in the House of Knowledge. I think someone stole Dragon."

Aline stared at the woman. "You haven't said. Who are you?"

"I'm a friend; that's all I can say now."

"How could anyone steal Dragon?"

"Magic has gone missing, Aline Weir. The world is crumbling. Your Dragon needs you; the sisters need you, and I need you."

She slid a card across the table to her. "I have said all I can reveal. It is up to you to decide."

The mysterious witch sauntered out of the room, not bothering to clean up the books she upended or look back.

Aline's mind raced. She flipped the card over and saw a line of trees shimmer across the surface with the name of a town printed across it. She grabbed the invitation and her book from under the counter and ran upstairs to the little apartment over the bookstore. She pulled a brick, heavy and pink, from under her bed. The invitation listed a name Aline dreamed of most nights when she was standing beneath the stars with a man who could not exist.

She flipped open the book she'd kept all these years, the one that was like an extension to her being. *Mischief, A Beginner's Guide*. She looked from the name of the town written in the book to the name inscribed on the brick, to the invitation. They were all the same.

Matchstick.

She blew out a slow breath. It didn't matter how powerful the woman who refused to give up her name had been. Or that being in her presence left Aline wishing to run and hide under the bed. It only mattered that Aline hadn't been able to contact Dragon in months, and the sisters were gone. It didn't make sense, but nothing about magic ever made sense; nothing about her powers ever ran off logic.

If there was even an iota of truth to what the woman told

her, if something had happened to Dragon and the sisters, there wasn't a choice. Aline was going to Matchstick. She was going to find them or bring the world down looking for them.

Magie's Rules for Keeping Mischief Out
(found crumpled in a yew tree in the forest of Matchstick)

Item One
DO NOT INVITE IN STRANGERS

Item Two
DO NOT ALLOW ANYONE TO SEE YOU

Item Three
DO NOT REVEAL THE ESSENCE OF MAGIC EVEN IN THE MOST DIRE OF SITUATIONS

Item Four
NEVER TRUST A PRETTY FACE

Item Five
STOP WRITING DOWN ITEMS

Five

THE TOWN OF MATCHSTICK, DURING THE DAY, WAS AS PICTUR-
ESQUE AS A NORMAN ROCKWELL PAINTING. If, that is, the painting
featured a cherubic human licking a caramel apple while ped-
dling down Main Street, USA. It was a slice of provincial life,
and Day liked the idyllic.

There was so much to see in a town like Matchstick, with its
unique layout of hamlets instead of neighborhoods, and witches
riding around on golf carts instead of brooms. Even the houses
were hopeful. Burnt-orange cottages, yellow federalist homes,
robin's-egg–blue farmhouses, and gray Craftsmans. Then, there
were the flowering crepe myrtles and pink and white dogwoods
standing proud in the manicured front yards, pear and apple
trees tucked in the back, and a large organic farm spanning the
length of three football fields along the far north hamlet.

Matchstick was the kind of place people would visit and never wish to leave . . . if people were allowed to visit at all.

Day spent quite a lot of time listening in on conversations in Matchstick. Learning about the latest brew at the Witchery or the newest shipment of books into Alchemist's Tales. Plus, the General Store always afforded a revolving door of witches to eavesdrop on as they went in for a sandwich and came out with a mouthful of gossip. The town wasn't so different from other towns Day had heard about, except, of course, for Magic. Magic was terrifying. It was also part of why Day was trapped.

There were so many things about Magic that confused Day. Rules that shifted and changed. Day wished Night were around more often, so Day could ask Night why change was so confusing, and why Day was stuck here. When the sun set, Day could almost remember why, but then the thought was gone, and Night was always quick to brush in and rush out so that even when he tried to stay, he ended up pulled away.

The sound of an unusual growling caught Day's attention. Day shifted focus to see a surprising sight coming into the perimeter of Matchstick, on the road that led in and out of the town.

Someone, a *new* someone, was coming. Day watched the vibration rumble across the air, a golden glittering light distending down across the perimeters of town, as a car cascaded down the road. The song of sunrise filled her, even though she was approaching Dusk. The power from the witch driving down the road was familiar, free, focused, and had a darkness Day had known once before.

Could it be? A new arrival? Driving erratically in an ancient truck that sputtered as it hurried up the road. The woman looked kind, with her clear, hazel eyes and the focused tilt of her heart-shaped face.

Day had an eerie worry settle over her. She hoped she and Night could find a way to keep her safe from Magic and the powers that be in Matchstick. Day feared not even Night would have the answers to this new development.

⟪⟪⟪

ALINE TOOK LESS THAN TWO MINUTES TO DECIDE TO FOLLOW THE STRANGE WITCH TO THE MYSTERIOUS TOWN OF MATCHSTICK. She wasn't impulsive by nature, or at least she thought she wasn't—though her past actions might have disagreed with her if actions were allowed to speak. But she loved Dragon, and she was worried for her and the sisters . . . and she was going to find a town she thought had only existed in her favorite fairy tale. So really, there was never a choice to begin with, though she was sure that if Chlo were there she would disagree.

"There is a choice every day to be who you are, and become who you want to be," Chlo was fond of saying.

Aline wanted to be the kind of person who didn't hesitate to help her family. So that was that. She hired Louise, the college graduate from down the street, to run the shop. Louise had previously stepped in when Aline had gone on trips abroad to return lost keys. The bookstore was mostly self-sufficient, in ways that didn't make sense, but the girl didn't know that electric bills never came, and mortgages were never late, regardless of payments not coming in or going out. The fridge was always stocked with chocolate milk, the pantry full of Pop-Tarts, and the books seemed to look after themselves just fine.

Whatever type of witches the sisters were, and Aline had

spent a decade trying to figure it out and never got further than *powerful*, they were an authority unlike any other. One that preferred to remain unknown. Though their power was not quite as seductive as the stranger who had come bearing bad news.

Once Aline had the shop covered, she packed her bag with enough clothes for one week, the strange brick from so many years ago, and a handful of magical objects stored in the emergency pocket of her handbag. She always traveled with a few charmed objects, usually those that became talismans and those that served as protectors. These were keys she'd never been able to return.

Aline shifted from fourth to third gear, her body jerking as she ground in the clutch. In Whistleblown, she never needed to drive anywhere. It was a walking town, consisting of a main street, second, third, fourth, and a few back alleys before you reached the outer edges that led to byways into other, bigger towns. Whistleblown was small and unassuming. Even with the minimal square footage, Aline barely knew her neighbors. People kept to themselves in Whistleblown . . . and away from Aline. She might know their preferences for the books they enjoyed, having shifted from keeping a notebook full of compliments to an Excel sheet full of purchases, but no one knew anything about her. They still liked it that way, and so did she.

The aging pale-yellow truck she was working hard to tame had sat in her garage for over a year. Chlo reminded her to "drive the damn beast and prevent the battery from corroding and falling out," which Aline wasn't entirely certain was a thing a battery could do, but she wouldn't put it past the vintage C10. The truck had been a graduation gift from Chlo, Liset, and Atti. She wondered what they would think of her driving it all these hours to a place that didn't exist on Google Maps as far as Aline could find, but decided they would love it and remind her that all magical mysteries are meant to be followed. She could hear them now.

"Let me tell you a story," Chlo would begin.

"A story is the evolution of something," Atti would add, before Liset leaned her pointed chin on her slender hand and said, in her crisp, cool tone, "A piece of the past."

A bluebird darted down toward the front of the truck as Aline took a sharp curve too fast, her hands gripping the wheel like she could crush it. She forced herself to blow out a breath as the bird flew off, unharmed.

Birds and the sisters and Dragon weren't the only ones good at leaving. People flew away without a backward glance. It's what her parents did when they moved abroad, what every single guy she had slept with had done since she lost her virginity to Noah. The recurring factor in everyone leaving was clear; it was the thing she whispered to herself in the middle of the night when she woke from the dream about the man who didn't exist.

It was her.

Each time she was left behind, she felt the loss like a tear in her soul. And at thirty, she had so many cracks she might as well be asphalt. The little dot that she took for herself on the charmed invitation was moving up the map, nearing a spot that had appeared only an hour before. It looked like an upside-down exclamation point, if the point sat on top of the line. It was a tiny matchstick, and it would have been charming if the wind weren't blowing so warm.

It was the beginning of October, and the outside world was a cool sixty degrees. Or so it had been, before Aline paused at the crossroads twelve miles back. Once she crossed the intersection, the earth rumbled beneath the tires and the air warmed to a balmier seventy degrees. The heat, she knew, was caused by how the trees vibrated. It rumbled beneath the car, shaking her hands as they gripped the steering wheel. Magic was energy manipulated. And this magic was manipulating the earth at such a level that Aline had to grit her teeth to keep from losing focus. She took another curve and the trees shifted from maples and oaks to a sea of firs. Tall, lean, and imposing. They leaned forward as she drove past, craning their tall necks.

A long enclosure ran alongside her to the left. It looked like a wall, impenetrable . . . and not quite right. Like pieces of a jigsaw puzzle forced together. Aline's scalp tingled painfully—a call of magic she knew too well. Magic didn't like being wrong, and if you gave it a misdirection, it was ready to do more than ignore it. The painful tug meant Aline was going the wrong way, and magic wasn't having it.

She stopped looking at the invitation and turned the car around. Aline understood tests. She'd been taking them all her life. People calling her names to see if they could bait her. Her parents forgetting to make her dinner to see if she would react or be able to fix her own. After the horrible slumber party in eighth grade, and with the guidance of Dragon, she rarely, if ever, failed.

She drove up the road and put the truck in Park. She grabbed her knapsack, where she kept her copy of *Mischief, A Beginner's Guide,* and exited the vehicle. The magic hit her like a hundred bees climbing through the strands of her thick auburn hair. It coated her, pushing and pulling, leaving her to clench her hands into fists. She walked on toward the wall of tall pines. She turned three-quarters of the way to the left and discovered a gap in the trees. A hidden section made of stone and brick, with one solitary gray stone in the center. The rest of the stones were faded. Aged or magicked . . . to the color of ripe persimmons.

Aline studied that gray stone, adrift like an unseeing eye in a storm, long and hard. It wasn't an easy task to do. Staring at the brick made her palms itch and her heart race. It made her throat dry and her eyes water. It was a mystery doused in magic, and one she solved without trying.

She stalked back to the truck, stumbling as she went. Tall yellow wildflowers and prickly weeds brushed against her calves, scratching across her skin. She reached the truck and yanked the door open. On the passenger seat sat her suitcase. Aline threw it open, digging through her pile of poorly folded clothes and meager belongings until her fingers closed over what she was seeking. She marched back to the wall, leaving both the suitcase and the door to her truck wide open. Squared off in front of the stones, she took a deep breath and crouched down until she was eye level with the odd brick. The one that was soft gray in color. The one that did not belong among its persimmon sisters.

Aline's scalp pulled tight as she studied it, and she heard the whisper. *Wind, wind, wind.* She leaned forward and blew on the stone in the wall. Ten letters floated to the surface in a row.

KCITSHCTAM

She held up the brick she had pulled from her suitcase and ran the tip of her pinky along the inscription she had studied for so many nights of her life.

MATCHSTICK

She turned the brick around and lined up the words, so they were facing the one in the wall. Then, with a sure hand, she pressed the two bricks together. The air cooled, the wall trembled, and the brick hovered off her palm. It slushed forward, like water being pooled back into ice, and merged with the gray stone sitting in the wall. As it did, the color shifted from reddish-orange into a sharper contrast.

Two became one. The rumbling of the wall grew, and the ground began to shake. Aline backed up, stumbling over her feet as she went. The trees cracked and groaned around her. She fell to the ground and crawled farther away.

The strange section of brick wall was sucked down into the earth. The ground sealed over where it had been, a fresh patch of green grass dotted with purple daisies popping up in its place.

Standing in the center of where the stone wall had been a moment before was the woman from the bookstore. She looked Aline up and down, and Aline felt the blush creep over her cheeks.

"Aren't you as fragile as a feeling?" the woman asked, her voice as quiet as the middle of the night.

Aline pushed herself to standing, dusting her pants as she went up. "*Excuse me?*"

"You've fight, good. You'll need it," the woman said, before pulling a timepiece with six hands instead of two from her pocket and checking it. "You're excused, and you may call me Florence; I'll have to apologize for not introducing myself in your shop. Names spoken outside of Matchstick have a tricky habit of falling into the wrong hands or getting swept into the gutters and lost below. Consider me the welcome committee."

Florence spun on her heel, stepping to the other side of the wall. Aline gaped at her. The tall woman with the imposing lip stain and gorgeous brown eyes looked over her shoulder at her.

"I'm short on time and I'm not one to repeat what has been spoken. Come along."

Aline looked back to where she'd come from. "What about my truck?"

The statuesque woman calling herself a welcome committee and exuding as much warmth as a doused fire snapped her fingers. Aline's sleeping truck revved its engine to life. It swung its open door closed, turned on its lights, and took off—undriven—down the road.

"Your transportation here has more sense than you," Florence said, cocking her head. "Get out of the street and onto the road to your future, Aline Weir, unless you prefer to be left behind."

Florence stalked off ahead, through a dense grouping of pines.

Aline didn't like being questioned and she hated being told what to do. But she wasn't going to stop now that she was so close to seeing Matchstick and finding Dragon and hopefully where the three sisters might have gone, so she shook out her shoulders and charged ahead.

THE OTHER SIDE OF THE WALL LOOKED EXACTLY LIKE THE VIEW FROM THE STREET. There was a dirt path worn before them, one that cut through the thick woods. To the left were tall pines showcasing needles that boasted little nuts and tiny pine cones that looked as though they belonged on a holiday wreath instead of in a forest. Aline looked up and nearly lost her balance. It was like looking into a maze. Thick branches snaking into the sky, surrounded by yellow and green leaves that bunched together blocking the sun so only slivers of light blue and gray could make it through. She dropped her gaze and glanced to the right where maples with golden leaves browning at the edges and beech trees with crimson leaves the color of an angry sunset bordered the wall. Between them were scrawny birches with peeling bark the color of ash.

Aline found its beauty picture-worthy, and yet couldn't dampen her disappointment at the ordinary view of the forest. She had expected something more from the mystical town she'd been reading about since she was eighteen. This was the place that would tempt her Dragon to leave her behind?

Then Florence turned to look at her and offered a smile the Cheshire cat would have envied. She took a step forward . . . and disappeared.

Aline's breath caught in her chest. She hurried ahead. One step. Two. A thin gauze, invisible to the eye and smelling of hibiscus and lime, brushed against her face like the strands of a spiderweb catching her cheeks. Aline pressed forward against the magical barrier, and the unsettling fabric moved over her.

She blinked her eyes to clear the haze of magic, and Aline faced an entirely different view. A picturesque village sat before her. It was surrounded on one side by a long curving stone wall. Streets lined with alabaster paths paved in stone ran to the left and right, with a roundabout directly ahead. On both sides of the street were houses differing in size, style, and craftsmanship. Each featured a well-kept lawn with sunflowers, zinnias, jasmine vines, and gardenias. A twisted iron street sign featuring Holliver Lane was posted at the end of the street to her right, as well as a handcrafted stop sign wrapped in ornate metalwork. The houses themselves featured an array of tin, darkly shingled, and thatched roofs. The houses' sidings were the color of an orange robin's chest, pale blue, soft cream. Then there were those with stone and brick exteriors that looked like something from a time lost long ago.

It was twilight in the village, and the lamps on the street and the porches glowed warm yellow. Daybed swings, oversized rockers, and sleek tables hand-carved from wood sat in yards and on verandas.

"This is—" Florence started, waving for Aline to keep up.

"*Matchstick,*" Aline interrupted, unable to keep the wonder from her voice. The view was entrancing, charming. But that wasn't why her breath caught in her throat. No, the racing of her pulse was entirely centered on the acute awareness that it was all true.

The story had been true. Matchstick was *real.* Which meant the man she'd been dreaming of, the love Chlo had prophesied, could be just as real, too.

"I'm here," Aline said to Florence. "Now tell me what you meant at the bookstore. Who took Dragon, where have the sisters gone, and why did you say magic is missing?"

Florence leveled her gaze. "First things always come first, and you're the first thing. We'll get to the second thing soon enough. Come along."

(MORE THAN A FEW FULL MOONS AGO . . .)

Night gets lonely. It seeks. It yearns. Night, for all its bravado and supposed fearlessness, waits impatiently for the moments it brushes up against Day. Nonmagical humans no longer remember this. They assume Night and Day are two separate entities, never thinking they might have been forced apart, forced to interlock. As if they didn't have a choice in the matter to be side by side for all eternity.

Night is also an impeccable watcher. And on this, the night

before the autumnal equinox, Night is paying close attention to the hidden town of Matchstick. The town responsible for Night's place in the sky.

East of the Sun and west of the Moon, tucked in the foothills of a state known for its southern roots and rolling range, Matchstick is forgettable. So forgettable, in fact, no one remembers it exists.

No one except those who call it home.

Esther Chatham does not live in Matchstick. No, she is a bit lost on this misty evening, maneuvering her car down the quiet back road of Hickory Bend. It has been a very long time since Esther has felt so free. As she drives, she is thinking about the words sung to her on the radio. About women, and glasses of beer. About waiting for summer, and pastures to change. "Change" is a sacred word, one she once believed a myth. She is not thinking about the town of Matchstick, or Night. She is not really watching where she is going . . . until it's too late to see.

An impenetrable wall of pine trees runs alongside Hickory Bend. No one is sure how the trees came to stand so close together, only that they have been there for as long as the locals living outside the wall can recall. It's a surprisingly solid grove of trees, with few cracks between them to peek through to the forest beyond.

It is unfortunate that Esther happens to drive by a very specific break in the wall. It is horrible timing that a deer runs across the road, right as Esther's headlights flash across the night-soaked street.

The deer knows the wall. It knows where the gaps are. The deer, unlike the humans, have not forgotten the secrets of Matchstick.

This deer, a doe, bounds across the road and into the path of Esther's aging Jeep Wrangler. Esther doesn't have time to do more than gasp as she yanks the wheel to the right and careens toward a ditch. She glances in her rearview while her car skids across the narrow road, checking if the deer is alive, and sees the wall of trees shimmer.

A woman with bright-silver hair materializes in the space of the missing wall, holding a broom and wearing a dour frown. Esther opens her mouth—to scream, to cry out, to curse the reckless deer—and the woman snaps her fingers and disappears.

The Jeep careens down a cliffside that did not exist three seconds before. Esther plummets to her demise as the singer on the radio calls good night to the moonlight ladies.

Night gives something akin to a shudder, cold wind blowing through the trees, as the woman on the other side of the wall bows her head. A cream mist rises from where the car has gone over into a ditch that should never have been a ditch to begin with. The woman lays her broom down across the gap in the stretching pine. The space, and the cream mist, disappears. The woman is gone. Esther Chatham is gone, and Night is left to bear one more secret about a town that barely exists.

Six

Florence walked ahead of Aline, her feet fast, her tone clipped, her shoulders rigid. She gave Aline a tour of the town, in the manner of a ready-to-retire guide forced to show tourists around one last time. "This is a street. This is a fountain. This is grass. There is the bush Jameson Beale once fell into while piss-drunk, and it took five nearly as sozzled people to fish him out." She had a few more pertinent facts to add, such as, "This is our main street. To the left and right you will find homes for our residents. We have three hamlets in Matchstick. They are Sun, Moon, and Dusk. We are in Dusk."

"Any reason for the names?"

Florence waved a hand. "Because it always stays dusk in this part of town."

"And sunny and moony in the others?"

Florence tapped her nose. "We have homes in every section, along with our live/work buildings—shops below and apartments above—and the businesses."

"How do you do business if no one knows your town exists?"

"The residents are not often in the wide world outside of Matchstick, but their business holdings are. We do quite well, and so the businesses prosper."

"How does that work?"

Florence paused in front of a lamppost. "There's a grand invention, the internet. Heard of it?"

Then she turned and kept walking, Aline struggling to keep up.

"In this hamlet, we have the bike shop, flower shop, and tea shop. In the others, you'll find restaurants, an apothecary, a spa, the garden and organic farm, and our yoga and meditation studios. There are also several metaphysical shops. Each one as lovely as the next."

"I'm sure."

"You'll be staying at the Inn. It's where the horse farm is, along with our recently updated farmhouse. It's quite charming and cozy."

"All that sounds fascinating, but where is the House of Knowledge? I'm only here to find Dragon." And snoop and wish on a star or two for love she didn't think she believed in any longer, regardless of what Chlo said.

"It's down the way, but it's locked up tight. Night closes it and won't open it again until Day arrives."

"Night. As in the hours when the sun goes down?"

"Yes."

"You say this like it should make sense."

"Life should never make sense, but this is the way it is." Florence shrugged. "You've one of the charming cottages we reserve for the rare visiting witch."

"How rare is it for a witch to visit?"

"You are the first in fifty years. Most who visit never leave. It's hard to walk away from Matchstick, or so I'm told."

"Unless you're Dragon."

"So it seems."

Aline looked around, fear pressing against her sternum. Claustrophobia and a sense of impending doom. Or change. Both felt the same to her.

"You can leave," Aline said. "You came to my shop."

"We're not bound here, but we prefer to be here. I have business and occasionally travel for it. Most don't, but that's their prerogative."

"I just want to find my friend." Aline swallowed. "I'm good at that, at least. I find lost objects and return them to those needing them to pass on."

"You find lost *magical* objects."

"Right." She studied Florence. "So what's the second thing? If I'm the first?"

"That's for tomorrow. I'll see you in precisely seven hours."

Florence flashed a grin so disarming, Aline's knees threatened to buckle. Power snapped out from the witch at every turn. Florence gave a quick nod and marched down the lane in the opposite direction, leaving Aline to stand on the path and stare off after her, wondering what the woman with the cream-and-silver hair was waiting to tell her, and what she might have really gotten herself into.

Aline stood there, her thoughts a swirling vortex of all that might come to pass, when a soft light drew her attention back to the present. The light shifted, brightening, and she turned her attention to the nearest streetlamp. It glowed yellow, a burst of color, before fading into an ombré of gold and white.

It took Aline a moment to realize that a person was standing beneath it, and he was watching her. She was certain he had not been there moments before.

Tall and lithe, he was almost willowy in form, and standing angled so his broad shoulders and wide chest were shifting away from her.

He turned, and every nerve ending in her body sparked into a flame. His features were stunning, dark arched brows, wide deep-set eyes, and a straight nose that offset the nearly perfect purse of full lips. The look he wore was knowing—the way the lips met and pressed, something in them matching the gleam of his eyes. Eyes, like a vortex. Dark, compelling, and Aline was certain, much later, that they held an entire conversation with hers.

It was impossible. A mistake. A joke.

Here stood the man she had been dreaming of for half her life, and he was devastatingly gorgeous, and *real*.

As he stood there, staring back at her without a care in the world, need started in the tip of her pinky finger and pressed itself firmly into the palm of her hand. She wanted to run a finger along the ridge of his perfect eyebrow, travel his wide and smirking lips. Aline had always been in control of her desire. Taking what she needed, giving what she could, and then moving on. She had never, ever, felt such a reaction as this—*pulled* from her—except in her dreams. But this was no dream: she was awake.

She took a shaky breath, and he smiled as though he heard it from the distance. A slow and delicious curve of his lips followed. It sent a shock down her spine, a hot speeding jolt of desire and greed that wrapped itself around her, and Aline took a step back.

Suddenly, he was right in front of her.

"You were lost," he said, his eyes locking her in place.

"Not even a little," she said, the magnetic pull to him growing.

Aline understood magic. She had spent years researching every magically inclined book, documentary, and tome she could get her hands on. She knew her power. She *did not* understand how her reaction to the witch who stood before her could be this forceful. It was not lust; it was not need; it was something else. A recognition that hit her like a fever. Because he was the man Chlo had prophesized, and suddenly faced with the thing she'd been too afraid to believe could exist, Aline was *terrified*.

Thunder rumbled across the sky, and the first drops of rain kissed Aline down her cheek.

"What is a hedge witch doing in Matchstick?" he asked, his voice a deep rumble that she felt down into her toes.

"I'm a solitary witch," she said, swallowing hard. She looked at him closer, studying the gold magic misting the air around him. "What is a chaos witch doing in Matchstick?"

He lifted a single brow. "You think me a chaos witch?"

"What else do you call the aggressive power you're throwing at me?"

"I'm not doing anything," he said, lifting his hands up.

Aline pointed to the sky and the lights flickered overhead. "You're throwing elements into the vibration around us."

He tossed his head back and let loose a laugh that rumbled its way into her belly. "You might be solitary, but you're a hedge witch, and I'm not what you think I am." His eyes drifted to her knapsack, and she felt the weight of *Mischief, A Beginner's Guide* tucked inside. Suddenly he flashed a grin and Aline's knees betrayed her when they threatened to buckle. "You'll figure it out soon enough, though."

The skies, still holding to dusk, rumbled. Rain broke through the thick purple and gray clouds overhead, falling fast onto Aline. She glanced up, to track the storm, and when she looked back again, he was gone.

She blinked, looked left and right, but did not see him anywhere. Aline stepped off the curb, feeling confused and . . . empty. She didn't understand it. He was more than what she remembered from the dreams, tangible and delicious, and she had craved to study him until the sun faded into the night and the night returned into day.

It was a kind of madness to feel this way.

Aline walked toward the streetlamp. She looked up the side streets leading off the roundabout, curious where he could have gone, but the street was empty. The beautiful, pristine houses sat quiet. Night was the only witness to her cursing her own reaction to losing the stranger she wanted to claim as her own.

A cool wind cut through the street, and Aline shivered. Keeping her shoulders back and gaze focused, she walked back to the path and up to where Florence had said her cottage waited.

But Aline couldn't help but look back, and when she did, she was certain she heard a male voice, deep and tender, whisper her name.

⊱

THE COTTAGE ALINE WAS TO STAY IN SAT TWENTY FEET BACK FROM THE INN. It was two stories tall and looked more like a carriage house with a converted garage than a home. As Aline studied the tidy house, she realized she hadn't seen a single car inside of Matchstick. Perhaps they had no need of garages.

She wanted to go hunting, find the shadows and follow them to the House of Knowledge; surely she could uncover her way. But as soon as she hefted her bag and walked to the navy front door, exhaustion poured into her. Her mind stayed on the man beneath the streetlamp with the penetrating eyes and their strange conversation, but Aline's limbs grew heavy and her steps slowed.

She thought of what he had called her. A hedge witch was an archaic term for witches with the ability to see beyond the natural plane and cross over into unknown dimensions. Aline didn't live in between the hedgerow, but she could travel back and forth through it. He had spoken with a funny cadence to his tone, and it wrapped itself around her as she recalled the way his smile had her gritting her teeth and wanting to lick his lips at the same time.

The door to the cottage opened with ease. Aline supposed no one needed locks in a town no one could find, and she moved inside, catching the scent of fresh mint. The small entryway into the home featured a row of Celtic knots that doubled as coat hooks and led into a living room–and–kitchen combo that boasted two light-gray sofas, a bright-red rug, and a dark oak coffee table. The walls were white, with paintings of ancient yew trees framed on them. There were thick gray floating shelves adorned with pristine books, tiny lanterns, and pretty glass bottles. The space could have doubled as an ad for a Restoration Hardware catalog.

The lamps on the matching modern side tables were pale blue and featured a set of driftwood coasters and a fresh journal with a ballpoint pen. If Aline could have reached into her dreams and plucked out her ideal retreat, it would have looked just like this. The art was abstract and soothing, swaths of blue and white, evocative paintings that reminded her of a feeling she'd had once, when she was lost in a forest during a school hiking trip and had accidentally wandered off while watching a blue jay. She'd gotten turned around, but instead of being scared, she'd been relieved. The woods were dark and deep. Quiet and welcoming. Being in them had felt not like being lost but being found.

Aline set her bag on the small white ottoman and summoned her last dregs of energy to explore the kitchen. A dense wooden table with bright-red, green, blue, and orange chairs offset the sparkling white granite countertops. The small island cabinets were a brilliant jade green, with the rest of the kitchen cabinets a lighter shade of the same color. It could have been chaotic. Instead, it was bright and happy. The perfect contrast to the sitting room.

Aline lovingly ran her hand over the countertops. She thought back to the small cluttered apartment she kept above the bookstore in Whistleblown. How age and wear and tear had left it looking like the before picture of a home-improvement project, while this house was better than any after shot. She peeked in the cabinets, gave a quick pet to the black matte silverware tucked away in the drawer closest to the oversized stainless-steel farmhouse sink. The refrigerator was stocked with three bottles of Matchstick Magic, a rosé-inspired wine that was wrapped in a label featuring the sun winking at the moon. The faucet in the sink featured a top-of-the-line water-filtering system, and the compact pantry held a fresh jar of almond butter, honey, and homemade sourdough bread—the three ingredients needed for Aline's favorite meal.

She got a glass of water and went back to the sofa, tugging the plush white chenille blanket off the back of the couch and tucking it around her shoulders. She was too tired to traverse upstairs and explore the area there.

Aline found her thoughts—which were usually busy things picking apart each minute of every hour, weighing words and expressions (hers and others), and judging each one of her character defects (of which she was sure she had many)—were as slow as a turtle taking a nap. She set her glass of tepid but refreshing water on the driftwood coaster and reached for the offered journal and pen on the table. She opened it and gave in to the urge to write her name at the top of the page, claiming it for her own. She tapped the pen against the sheet, three times, leaving three simple dots as her opening.

Aline did not have a clue what was to come, what ellipses of adventure she would step into tomorrow. She only knew she would find Dragon. She refused to let her friend down. She took out her copy of *Mischief* and curled around it like a child holding a beloved teddy bear. Her mind wandered as she let it return to the story world. The creature who spoke in riddles, the traveler who was out of time, and the man made of power and lies because the truth had been locked away from him. How she loved these people. She curled her hand under her chin, snuggling farther into the sofa. She thought of her magic man, leaned her head back, and let her last worry go.

It could have been a moment or hundred, but at some point, Aline came awake with the sense of someone watching her. She looked over and saw the man from her dream sitting on the floor, beside a small bookshelf in the corner. The bookshelf had not been there when Aline had drifted off.

"You snore when you sleep. Did you know that?" he asked, wrinkling his nose, holding a copy of *Anne of Green Gables*.

Aline rubbed her eyes. "Are you really here?" she asked, shifting so she was no longer slumped over the side of the exquisite sofa, her book open and lying across her lap. She slid to the floor to be closer to him.

"Of course, I'm here. You're talking to me. I'm responding. Hello, Aline."

Aline reached for him and found his form solid. She leaned in, noting he smelled faintly of the life and death of a book. Musky with a hint of vanilla and a waft of pipe smoke.

"You are an affectionate creature, aren't you?"

"I'm not convinced you're real."

"I'm not convinced you're safe," he said.

"What do you mean?"

"Matchstick is a secret place, hard to see into, impossible to understand. Savior or destructor, this is not the place for you."

"I don't understand what you're saying. You're speaking in fragments, and I hate puzzles. Especially word puzzles."

He lifted a brow. "Words are puzzles."

Aline studied the man before her, and curious want flamed into need so visceral she dug her nails into her palms to keep her hands to herself.

"There is darkness here. Old magic and ways and traps and cunning," she said. "Anyone who crosses your border feels it. I'm not afraid. I've been reading about Matchstick my whole life. I'm meant to be here. I know it. I have to find my friends. That's all that really matters." That and licking the side of his lip to see if he tasted as good as he looked.

"They will ask more than you can give. More than I can

give. But I won't let you down," he said, then he leaned in. His eyelashes were ridiculously long, and they cast shadows over his sharp cheekbones. He tilted his head, and Aline groaned at the way he studied her mouth. He dipped his chin, she lifted hers, and . . .

❄❄

ALINE JERKED UPRIGHT. She struggled to unwrap the blanket from where it had tangled around her waist and nearly fell off the couch unwinding it. She was dripping wet, sweat pooling under her neck, along her hairline, and beneath her bra.

Aline shook off the dream, physically shaking her arms and hands and knocking the book to the ground. She looked for him, but he was gone. When her body temperature had shifted from overheated to mildly uncomfortable, she moved to stand up. It would be cool outside, easier to think.

But Aline didn't cross to the door. The journal she had set down was no longer where she had left it on the table. It sat instead by her bag, on the ottoman. It was flipped to a new page, and a strange, looping handwriting had scrawled across it.

Follow the lights.

Don't trust the Night.

Beware the Watcher.

Find my key.

Seven

NIGHT DID NOT TRUST FALSE LIGHT. Lamps, headlights, flashlights, twinkling bulbs attached precariously to string, all the varieties of false light made Night irritable. Night preferred the stars. They knew their place, up in the sky. Knew to stay where they belonged, to fall in with the order of the Universe as the gods willed it.

Matchstick was a place of light, even in the dark. Axes in the world were like that. Scholars sometimes mistakenly referred to them as ley lines, but axes were the true portals and road maps for magic, and there were only six in all the world.

Three light, three dark.

Three beginnings and endings. Each one more than what they seemed.

Matchstick resided on a dark ley line, and yet the moon, the stars, even Day itself were drawn to it. Trapped by it. Because of it. The stranger was important. Night could feel her magic. It was familiar. She both felt like Matchstick and nothing like Matchstick. But how?

Night watched as the woman with bright-auburn hair and eyes like a cat on the prowl stepped out from the little cottage. She was soaking up the last of Night even if it looked to her like dusk, her hands clutching the blanket she had wrapped tightly around her form.

Night had been paying attention to her since her arrival and saw what happened under the false light the night before. Saw the ripple in the axis and who had taken notice of her. Danger was here, only Night wasn't sure where . . . yet.

The woman with red hair and false confidence glowed bright, almost as bright as Day. She could save them if she were careful with the other one. The one that would gobble her up like Night wished to gobble up Day.

Day would be here soon, and for once, Night was not sad to be going. Night would miss Day, but as Night studied the woman, and thought about what Night had seen and what it knew, Night decided it might be better for Day to be the recorder of the coming events.

Of what it meant now that Magic was meeting its match.

The truth was that some things were too dark even for Night.

ALINE BREATHED IN AS MUCH OF THE CRISP AIR AS SHE COULD, AND THEN WENT BACK INSIDE THE COTTAGE. She'd had the strangest sensation while she was standing beneath the fading light that someone was watching her. She thought of the words in the journal, of the man. Had he written them? Or was it someone else?

Since Florence said newcomers were rare, perhaps everyone was watching her. Aline didn't necessarily mind. People had ignored her in Whistleblown. It was a strange and disconcerting awareness and would take getting used to.

Florence showed up not a second later than she said she would. She knocked twice and Aline opened the door. "Time is wasting," Florence said, the train of her dress getting caught in the wind and kicking up. She stepped over a small bush blooming cheerful pink flowers and crossed onto the main road.

Aline followed and her head spun at the power pushing up against her feet. "Whoa. What is that?"

"You're on an axis. Power flows here much like water follows the current of a river."

"I'm on an axis? As in a ley line?"

"Yes. There are six axes of magic in the world. They are spread along the ley lines that run across the world. The axes are the source of all magic. Old and powerful, strong, and immortal. Matchstick resides on one."

"What does that have to do with Dragon?"

"The scrolls have to be housed under protection, and where else could we keep them safe but on a dark axis? One so powerful it grinds the bones of those unworthy to dust if they try and pass through its doors," Florence said, speeding up.

"I'm sorry, what?" Aline grabbed Florence's wrist, and the power shot into her hand, up her arm, sending a scorching burn along its path. She jerked back.

"Power here is not like power in the main world," Florence said. She glanced at the red streak marring Aline's skin. "You'll need a balm for that."

Aline rubbed at it. "You want me to enter a house that can kill me?"

"You're a hedge witch who carries the mark of Dragon. You'll be fine."

"What mark?"

She waved a hand as though batting an annoying gnat away. "All magical creatures have their own aura and essence. Dragon's is all over you. She's like your shadow."

Aline looked down. She saw nothing out of the ordinary, but she liked the idea that even when apart, Dragon was somehow with her.

They walked along the main road, cobblestones beneath their feet. In the distance were tall pines and fir trees, and beyond them Aline could see the darkness of night. She turned and looked in the other direction, and as she squinted, thought she was peering into sunrise, the horizon bathed in first light of pink and purple. She took a deep breath and smelled a hint of rain in the distance, wet pavement, and the lingering scent of lavender.

They came to a building shaped like a circle. It was the color of ripe cherries, with a curved thatch roof, a wide arching door, and stained glass windows dripping colors of cream and silver. It was free of shrubs and trees, and instead featured two lines of teak Adirondack chairs on the left and right of the lawn facing the street.

"Welcome to the House of Knowledge," Florence said, before sweeping her skirt into one hand and climbing the short steps up to the door.

The house pushed back against Aline. It was a presence, like an unwanted ghost, shoving at her—poking to see if it could get her to falter. Her skin buzzed, her eyes watered, and she thought of Dragon.

Aline walked, step by forced step, up to the landing. Her feet were like lead, her bones aching and popping with every inch she moved. She finally grasped the wrought iron handle and it turned blue, a frigid burn blasting against her palm. She gritted her teeth, said a prayer to the sisters—her only true family—and pushed the door open.

Silence fell around her, total and complete like the inside of a forgotten snow globe.

Florence faded from her view.

The House of Knowledge looked like a modest building from the outside, but inside was another story. There was a circle in the center, but it opened to a large, domed skylight. Surrounding it were sections of shelving stuffed full of manuscripts and texts. Beyond that were row after row of books leading down as far as the eye could see. To Aline it felt like the interior of a university library, vast and expansive. On the outside, it looked like a fraction of what it was.

"It's like the TARDIS," Aline said, studying the marbled floors and banisters, columns, and wide stone tables to the left of the shelving. "Bigger on the inside."

"It is the location of knowledge. All story has a place here, and all books a home. The House of Knowledge is protected and needs no one."

"And Dragon?"

"You have to ask." Florence nodded to a table in the center of the room. "It already knows what you need."

Aline kept her chin tilted, her eyes blank. Something in the way Florence stared without blinking at her made her feel she was missing an important piece of the conversation.

"What is it you think I need?"

"What do you know of magic, Aline Weir?" Florence leaned back, lifting her brows. Waiting. Aline could feel the words trying to tumble from her lips, the truth seeking a way out. She took a slow breath in and smelled primrose and bluebell. Aline reached into her bag and rooted around for the right jar. She pulled it out and sprinkled it on the table in front of her in the shape of a crescent moon. Protection.

Florence smiled.

"I know enough." Aline asked, wrinkling her nose, "You really tried to cast a truth spell on me?"

"The House of Knowledge is always casting for the truth. For knowledge."

"Yet you didn't warn me."

"I wanted to see what you would do. You surprised me," she said, nodding to the angelica sprinkled on the table.

"Why don't we lay our cards on the table?" Aline asked. "Unless you want me to walk away. I'm tired of tests, and I won't fail. I never do. How do I find Dragon?"

Florence pulled gloves from her pocket and instructed Aline to slip them on, then she nodded for her to pull a rolled-up parchment from the rows of text. A low whisper, urgent and unintelligible, called to her from the lowest level of the circular shelves. Aline pulled it out. The papyrus was faded to the color of a dusky sepia, and the writing barely visible.

She brought it back to the stone table, sat it down. "As it began, so it begins." The library, which should have been impervious to wind, whispered the words on a swift breeze. The air around them hummed with the vibration of magic.

The parchment unrolled itself onto the table, stretching out, the fabric imprinting into the stone. Words floated up onto the page before they elevated off it entirely. Aline bit back a gasp as they rose and drifted over, shifting across her skin, and slinking into it. She had a momentary flashback to waking up at the slumber party with Dragon having written across the skin on the girls' arms and legs.

This time the words didn't leave a stain; they went *into* Aline, and she found herself lost beneath them. It wasn't unlike picking up a book and slipping into the first page of it. Reading the words, following the pages until suddenly you're living alongside the characters and the story. It was similar to reading *Mischief* that very first time.

A tapping caught her attention. Aline let out a breath she didn't realize she'd been holding. At first, she thought she was still sitting in the House of Knowledge, staring at the stone table and the papyrus on it. But then she realized it wasn't the *same* parchment. This one was tan and crisp, and there was a person sitting with his back to her, his pen moving over the page. Aline crossed to him and read over his shoulder. As she did, he began to speak, his voice a gentle caress as he pulled each word from the pen and cast it onto the parchment.

"Once upon a time, there was a lonely and powerful Supreme Witch. She spent all her days tracing ley lines of magic and following them from town to town, country to country, continent to continent. As she traveled, she found more and more witches whose magic was waning. Magic was losing its strength, and she couldn't understand why . . . until the Supreme Witch ended up in the town of Alexandria and found a crack in the world. Not in the earth as she expected, but in the sky. She sought the Watcher's counsel, for the Watcher knew all, but he would only say that a barely decipherable rip was throwing off the vibration of magic and siphoning it out. The Supreme Witch searched high and low in the city, until she found a local witch reputed for his compassion and unparalleled skill at harnessing the elements. With his help, they sealed the crack and pooled the magic from it into the ley line that ran beneath them."

He paused, brought the pen to his lip, tapping the end of the bone quill there, before nodding to himself and continuing. "They did not know untethered magic needed a place to settle. That magic is as lonely as the rest of the world, and so the untethered magic took place within the Elemental Witch, shifting inside him and transforming him into Magic itself."

The man gave a single shudder, and the ground beneath them rumbled. He resumed writing, his hand digging into the paper harder now. "As the old power found a place to root, its imbalance tilted the earth off its axis. An earthquake shook the land, rivers rose, and the earth's vibration sent a blast of power across the seven seas and Europe fell into the Dark Ages. Drawn by the call of such a majestic power, witches, and beings of old (and new), and some who had been forgotten from time altogether, began their search for Magic. All felt the new power rise and desired to tap into the shifting and growing source.

"Soon the being Magic was hunted, and the Supreme Witch had no choice but to find a safe harbor for the one who had helped her. She took him back to America and they worked to right the tilted axis, setting a new point of origin. Together, they poured enough power into the ley lines surrounding their new axis to hide the town and being from those who sought to rule and destroy him . . . and snuff out the light of magic altogether. They knew they were playing with fire, and that it would likely only be a matter of time before the others found them. And so, they named their town Matchstick, and confided only in the Fates of its location."

The air around Aline thinned, her breath grew shallow, and the words inside her constricted. She tried to draw in a breath and failed. Her heart pounded in desperation in her chest. Her vision blurred. She was being suffocated by the story, attacked by the words. She clawed at her throat, a low keening erupting from her chest, and then, suddenly, the attack stopped. The man writing at the table lifted his head. He looked up, turned, and stared straight at Aline. Familiar dark hair and eyes, a cunning mouth and nimble fingers pressing hard into the stone table before him. He was here, the witch of her dreams, but how?

It was impossible. Because the papyrus he wrote on was new when it should be old. Hundreds, maybe thousands of years old.

"You don't belong here," he said, his voice a low whisper as he raked his eyes over hers.

They held each other's gaze in the way a child might hold that of another's if they were playing the staring game. Heat flickered through Aline, but she did not look away. He held up his left hand, and Aline lifted her right. She had not meant to do it but couldn't prevent the motion. He snapped his fingers, and she mimicked his. Her eyes tracked to his necklace, and the key he wore around it. A skeleton key, old and rusted.

"I don't belong anywhere," she said, unable to stop herself, her truth rising to mirror his own.

He cocked his head, his eyes narrowing, and then he reached for the key around his neck and gave it a yank. It broke free and he tossed it in the air. Aline broke eye contact as she caught it with one hand, and light exploded around her.

ALINE CAME BACK TO HERSELF IN THE MANNER OF WATER DRIPPING FROM A FAUCET. Breath by breath, drop by drop, filling back up. She saw the white marble floor first, the speckled black lines running through it, then the legs of the stone table and the chairs, and the parchment now rolled up into a scroll. Her eyes drifted from the scroll to Florence, who stood at the opposite end of the table.

"What did it show you?" Florence asked, shifting closer.

"You didn't read it, too?"

"The scrolls in the House of Knowledge don't reveal the same things to everyone, and they don't often reveal them the same way."

Aline hesitated. There was something about how Florence leaned forward as she asked, like she was trying to hold herself back. It reminded Aline of being a kid and waiting for an ice-cream cone to be scooped, ready to snatch the treat at the opportune moment. "I read a story in it, about a Supreme Witch and an uprising in magic."

Florence nodded. "Yes."

"That magic became more than magic."

"A being."

"Yes." Aline shifted her own weight, thinking of the dark eyes of the strange witch, doing the math of how old he would be to have been the one to write the scroll. "And that it came here, to Matchstick."

"Matchstick was created for Magic," Florence said, and Aline let out a little sigh of relief that Florence's recount matched what she saw. Perhaps Florence was impatient, but not because Aline knew something she did not. Because she really did need her.

"And Dragon?"

"Is looking for the rest of the untethered magic splintered along the ley lines."

"To help me?"

"Yes."

"Why?"

"Because the Fates cursed you, Aline Weir. Why do you think you can see ghosts?"

"I see ghosts because I can help them find the keys to moving on," she said. "There's no such thing as the Fates anyway."

"You are a finder of lost things. A witch with powers to move between worlds, to reach between them. A gift given to you by three very clever, very stupid Fates."

"I don't believe you."

"Which is why they left. I believe they came to love you and couldn't face you. Chlo, Liset, and Atti have always been so easily bewitched by their own weaving."

Aline's stomach dropped, her head spun, and she placed a hand on the table to steady herself.

"The sisters are not Fates."

Florence made a sound that from a less polished person would have been a scoff.

"They are many things, and there's so much you don't know." Florence sighed. "The axes, all of them, have become unsteady. If we don't ground them, you will die. That's your fate, and that's what Dragon came here for—a scroll with a plan to stop it from happening."

As Aline battled a wave of nausea, Florence looked back to the table, to the chair nearest to them. As though she had not upended everything in Aline's world, while threatening to crash it down.

"The axes and the ley lines running from them are unstable."

Aline tried to think, tried to stop the buzzing that was expanding in her ears. "What can I do?"

"What you're meant to. No more, no less," Florence said, her gaze drifting to Aline's hands. "All is not lost. Only a witch with the ability to disrupt Fortuna's Wheel could pull that from the scroll. Not even Dragon succeeded."

Aline became aware, quite suddenly, that she was gripping something tight in her hand. She opened it slowly and found a key, rusted and ancient, curled into her palm. As she stared at it, it shifted, reworking itself.

The rusted metal heated and sparked—and blew apart. Aline held her breath as the memory of her own power doing the exact same thing before blasting into Noah slammed into her. She bit the inside of her cheek until she tasted blood, refusing to let herself return to the past. Before her, the pieces floated into the air, metal becoming fragments, the pieces shifting into atoms, reworking their shape into a sphere resembling a globe.

Florence and Aline reached for it at the same moment, and the sphere sped into Aline's hand, where she cupped it, finding it vibrating, humming softly, before it quieted.

Florence stared at it, her hand still outstretched.

"Fortuna's Wheel?" Aline said. She hadn't meant to pull the

key, to snatch the globe it had rewoven itself into, but now that she had it, she refused to release it. She waited for Florence to ask for the key, but instead Florence sighed. A heavy, mournful sound. Then she led Aline down the hall, past rows and rows of books and scrolls to a door that led outside.

"Fortuna, the two-faced queen who leads the Fates."

Aline shook her head. There were no Fates. She was wrong about that. But Florence didn't see. She simply opened the door. The backside of the House of Knowledge led into what could only be described as an expansive and majestic garden. As soon as Aline stepped into it, she was overcome by the intoxicating scents of lavender, rose, hyacinth, pine, and several delicious scents too comingled to separate.

"It's like being inside a holiday candle," Aline said, breathing deep, and Florence let loose her light, airy laugh.

"This is one of my favorite places in all of Matchstick."

"I can see why." Aline said, watching Florence stare at the sphere curled in her hand. "Aren't you going to ask me for this?"

"I could perhaps trade you," Florence said, tapping the dragon around her neck, "but you see, that key came to you." Her mouth pursed in distaste. "It does not want me."

"And the one around your neck?"

"Has only *ever* wanted me. It's why she left it for me, after all."

Aline wanted to ask a dozen questions, but a breeze broke through the garden and the scent of spice, strong and bold, came with it. Distracting and pulling her attention. The man from her dreams, the same one from beneath the lamp, whom she had seen putting pen to the scroll, walked into the garden.

"Her?" he said to Florence, his eyes on Aline.

"So it appears."

"I'm not a fan of riddles," Aline said, studying the man.

"Then you've come to the wrong place," he said, the slight press of a smile carved into his nearly perfect mouth.

Aline forced herself to tear her gaze from him. She turned back to Florence. "Why is he here, and what does he have to do with Dragon and the sisters?"

"She's asking you to help save magic in all its forms and those whose lives depend upon it," the man said, stepping closer. "Which is saving your Dragon, and the three. But more than that, to save me."

"You?" Aline asked, looking between the two of them. "Why would I need to save you?"

"Aline Weir," Florence said, with a small, indecipherable smile, "meet the only being who can aid you in stabilizing the ley lines. Whose fate is in as much peril as yours." She nodded her head to the man. "Meet Magic."

Eight

Once upon a time the world was run by current. Byways and riverways that covered the land and seas. If you were to look at the world from space, you would see these currents as a labyrinth, spreading out across the world in a series of lines. These lines have been called many names: dream lines, dragon lines, spirit lines, and what most Westerners refer to them as: ley lines.

Magic knew something most did not. He knew the lines were more than lines. More than ways to follow the flow of the river or the lay of the land. They were coordinates, the logical progression of the vibration of the earth and the places where magic could freely flow. Animals knew this. They gathered at the points where the lines intersected. The spaces where they were safest, able to tap into the magic zigzagging across the earth's surface. Here was magic that allowed for the tides to rise, the sun to set, the moon to heal. Magic blessed into the soil by the gods. Forgotten magic that was allowed to flourish. Magic himself was here because of the lines, but there was something wrong. Wrong with the world. He knew this because he'd been having nightmares of the seas overflowing, of the tides running backward, and of a rip in the earth that opened to a darkness he could not run from.

He'd also been dreaming of the woman who stood before him. For so many years, the dreams had become a kind of safety blanket. Fall asleep, see her cinnamon eyes and slightly crooked smile, and find a way to release the tension that coiled inside him at all times.

"*Your* name is Magic?" the witch asked, her eyes widening as she looked him up and down. Her eyes were so close to red he wondered if the color of her hair had somehow seeped into her pigmentation. Everything about her glowed. Bright, red, fiery. Like the orb she grasped.

"I *am* Magic," he said, and crossed his arms so he wouldn't do something foolish like reach for her, run a hand through those gorgeous tendrils. Instead, he returned to the key clutched in her hand. He had held it once, long ago, but hadn't touched it in centuries. "You seem to have found something that does not belong to you."

She stared at him, then shifted her gaze, looking between Magic and Florence, as though making up her mind about something.

"He's not lost," she said to Florence. Her hands were shaking. He could see her trying to put the pieces together and being unable to make a puzzle out of clouds. "I find lost things, but if this is what was missing, now it's found."

Then she threw the orb to Magic.

His fingers closed around it, digging into the mouth and

throat of what had been the key. Power pulsed into his hands and suddenly he couldn't breathe. Magic saw a younger version of *her,* with hair the color of a sunset, sitting in a bathroom stall weeping, her eyes taking in a list of names. The scene diluted like tea with too much cream, and suddenly he was looking back through his memories. Through dreams of the two of them, and also of moments that didn't belong to him at all. Images of Aline lying on the floor of a bookstore, a book clutched like a promise in her hands. She was in a small room holding a story that was more than a story. She glowed like Day before Day tried to kiss goodbye to Night.

Magic blinked and there Aline was, sitting in the bookstore, older, shifting the elusive keys for spirits that few could ever touch, making plans to return them. Doing everything she could to help. Ghosts lingering behind her like a rustling wind after a storm, but she did not mind. Her sadness wasn't just a feeling, it was a being . . . and it was everywhere.

Magic finally drew in a breath, and when he did, he was in the garden, staring at Aline, with tears streaming down his face.

This was too much. This was the beginning of his end, and as much as he wanted to help, to touch her, to taste her, his self-preservation kicked in.

"*No,*" he said to Florence.

Then he threw the globe back to the hedge witch, snapped his fingers, and was gone.

ALINE'S HEART SPASMED AT THE LOSS OF THE BEFORE SIGHT OF MAGIC. Never mind that he was a being of power, and not a man as she'd spent half her life believing. He'd stared at her, been asked to work with her, and he had disappeared.

It was one more break in the cracks of her soul. One more piece of proof that she was not enough.

She thought of the House of Knowledge instead. It helped to focus on a different mystery. One that had yet to reject her. It was a strange house with more ancient scrolls than the Library of Alexandria. In fact, Aline wasn't sure she hadn't discovered the lost scrolls *from* the lost library. Aline didn't know what happened to Magic when she returned the key, but *she* had nearly crumbled as soon as he'd clutched it.

It had taken all her strength not to fold in on herself, as buried shames, the ones that used to keep her awake at night, flooded to the surface. Piece after piece of Aline shifted around inside her, remembering itself as her heart cracked around them. For a moment, she thought he might pull her apart simply by the way he stared at her. His black eyes flashing, his mouth pinched into a thin line, as though he not only saw into her but through her.

Tears had pooled at the edges of his eyes. They finally broke and Aline could breathe. She watched as they cascaded down his cheeks. Then he'd blinked. His eyes had turned cruel, harder than the clench of his perfect jaw. He'd looked at her like he wanted to obliterate her.

She knew this for certain, because it was the same way she'd felt when he'd pooled longing from her last night before disappearing. Poof. Leaving behind the smell of ash and pine. She'd wanted to destroy him then.

No one should drive such longing from another person. It was inhumane.

"That was interesting," Florence murmured, tilting her head back to look up at the sky, which had taken on a purple hue.

"Yeah, sure," Aline said. She turned to leave the garden.

"You're leaving?"

"Nope." She had no intention of leaving Matchstick. She might not trust the strange people here, but she would find the answers she sought.

"You'll help us then?"

"Not with whatever that was," Aline said, waving a hand at the air where Magic had been moments before. "I'm going to help myself."

"Magic is breaking."

"Get him a therapist."

"In the world, Aline. The foundation of it cannot hold anymore. All those souls you try to help, they will be lost. You will be lost."

"The only people I need to find are Dragon, Chlo, Liset, and Atti," she said, refusing to think of her parents, not daring to remember how Magic had completed her when he stood beside her in her dreams.

"It's reported everywhere. You know it is. The currents are reversing, trees are ignoring rain and drying up, the bees have begun attacking the flowers. There's a hundred different ways the world is failing."

"Isn't it always?" Aline turned to glare at Florence. "You act like this is the end-all, but we've been tearing each other down since the beginning of time. Ask any ghost. Why do you think they're stuck? Unfinished business because we never forgive, or we forgive too late. People killing, raping, hating. Taking. It's all about power and control and it's a tale as old as time, and if you ask me, time is a total asshole."

"You're not wrong. And yet, the ley lines need a guide," Florence said. "They need you, and they need Magic. It was prophesized long ago. Only a hedge witch blessed by the Fates and an elemental witch blessed by Magic can save us. To find Dragon and your Fates, this is the only way to gain what you seek."

"I'm no guide and I wouldn't know where to start."

Florence nodded to the globe still clutched in her hand. "Follow the lights."

The key around Florence's neck flashed—shifting forms in the blink of an eye. A little dragon staring back at Aline, its features twisted in horror and disgust.

A warning.

"The lights?"

"Yes."

"The only lights I want right now are my family. I want Chlo, Liset, and Atti. And you can't help me with that. This can't help with that."

Florence hesitated. "The Fates came home, Aline. A little ahead of schedule, but then they have never been what one would call predictable." She tilted her head, the dragon a key again, its golden body glinting in the fading light.

"Fortuna's line," Florence said. "They're bound to it all, too. Rather than being reborn, when the wheel of Fortuna spins again, the Fates, like us, will blink out of existence."

"I don't believe you."

"Well, then," Florence said, her grin turning into a sneer. "Follow the lights."

✻

ALINE LIFTED THE ORB INSTEAD AND WENT BACK INSIDE THE HOUSE
OF KNOWLEDGE... alone. Florence stood on the pavement outside in the garden watching, and Aline wondered if the witch
could have followed her even if she had wanted, or if the House
of Knowledge would prevent it. There was power and then
there was corruption, and she wasn't yet sure which side of that
line Florence leaned into.

Once inside the House of Knowledge, the quiet space erupted
into whispers. One after the other, tripping over each other as
the pages shook, the scrolls bucked, and ink floated into the air.
It might have been terrifying, if not for how the curved words
dripping from the ink reminded Aline of Dragon's handwriting
on the mean girls so long ago. The memory of that night once
brought only pain and shame, but now offered her a bit of comfort, and a reminder of her first real friend. Then the memory disappeared as a most peculiar and beautiful magic caught her eye.

As soon as the ink hit the orb, a light brightened inside it,
illuminating the tiny globe from within and casting a beam in
one direction.

Aline's hands warmed, her scalp tingled, and her feet moved.
She walked without thought, following the light out of the House
of Knowledge and into the garden, through its curving paths and
past its twisting trellises to a pond that was surrounded by statues.
Six, to be exact. Faceless beings in varied shapes and sizes bordered
the water, and in the center, two creatures folded into one another.
An embrace in the inky darkness of water that reminded her of
sludge or a spilled oil slick.

Beyond the pond a cozy-looking bungalow the color of clotted cream waited with its pretty baby-blue door and smart red flowers tucked in bright-green pots. The cottage had a black tin roof and a stone chimney with smoke billowing from it. The sight of it left Aline exhaling in relief. Hung over its light-blue door was a sign: STORIES & MAGIC.

Beneath it was a plaque of sorts. The letters appeared to move, backward and forward, reverse and straightaway.

"'Welcome to the rest stop for stories. We serve both books and magical necessities. The Fates created the first of us, as they created all stores and shops that spin tales. Here you will find the mother of necessities, though she is not mother to any, and if you speak wrong, she will have you begging for your own before the sun goes down.'

"Lovely," Aline said, after reading the sign out loud.

Aline thought of Dragon and the sisters. She wondered why so many houses here seemed to want to kill her, or house a creature who might. Deciding it didn't matter and that the only way out was through, she took a reassuring breath and went up to the door to the bookstore.

Her hand wrapped around the handle shaped like a curved key. Keys were everywhere here. Aline couldn't escape them. She let her hand close around the handle, the other grasping the orb with the bright light flashing as though to say she had made it to where it wanted her to go, and she found she didn't really want to escape.

Aline liked the taste of danger, the ambrosia and bitterness of it. It was like biting into a barely ripe plum. She grinned into the wind and pushed. A bell chimed, the air around Aline blew warm, and the scent of incense drifted out, swimming around her. She stepped inside.

The bookstore looked like a bookstore . . . if you didn't pay attention to the walls. Paintings—in all manner of styles and from various periods—adorned them. Only the prints were half-missing. It looked like someone had taken a butcher knife and hacked them in two, whacking straight down the middle. It was jarring to see, particularly among the organized shelves of books sorted by color, not genre or author. It was exactly what Aline had done in her bookstore, and seeing it reflected took her a moment to process. She decided the rainbow of story brightened the otherwise fractured room. To the left of the shelves was a charming counter created from an oversized suitcase. One that would have been modern in the 1940s.

Behind the counter sat a small girl, no older than ten, wearing a crown of blooming pink peonies atop her golden head, in a pair of jean overalls that had seen better days. She swung her slender ankles, flashing toenails painted in the shades of a rainbow. Her long hair cascaded down her back, and there was a curious glint to her emerald eyes. She smiled, flashing teeth as sharp as a razor's edge and thin as spindles, and held out a welcoming hand.

"You must be Chlo's girl," she said, her voice bright and soothing, and older than her ten years. She wore a thick gold nameplate with the words THE CRONE engraved into it like a name tag in a luxury hotel. She hopped off her stool and walked over to Aline.

Aline towered over her, and yet it felt as though they were eye-to-eye. "Yep. You're her. *A-line*. Start to finish, the one to restore the balance. Come on, then."

She took Aline's hand, capturing her nerves and words in her palm. A thousand needles stabbed at the place where their hands met, magic digging deep. The Crone smiled and Aline swayed where she stood.

"We can battle here, girl," the Crone said, flashing those spears for teeth, "or you can make a choice."

"What are the choices?" Aline asked, the words pained. Her head grew thick. Her legs trembled.

"You choose to trust me, or you choose to forfeit your life."

The world swam. Magic poured off the Crone, sifting into Aline and gathering her own power. It was a tricky spell. Aline opened her mouth to answer, and the Crone dropped her hand like she had been scorched. She shook it out, rubbed at her palm as the life poured and settled back into Aline. "I suppose I have to trust you."

The Crone stared at her for a long minute. "I don't really think you have a choice, do you?"

Without another word, she turned and headed for the back of the store. Aline looked over her shoulder to the entrance, prepared to run when the feeling fully returned to her feet.

"Won't do you any good," the Crone called as though she could read her thoughts—and maybe she could. "Plus you don't strike me as the type to give up so easy."

Aline debated. She wasn't the type to tuck and run, but she'd also never had a tiny sprite of a girl nearly suck her bones dry using powerful magic.

She thought of Dragon, of Chlo. There were answers here. She lifted her chin and walked to the back of the store where a collection of books, skulls, ventriloquist and Victorian dolls, an oversized tea set, and a large teddy bear sat.

"You know Chlo?" Aline asked, wiping her hand down her pants as she surveyed the creepy surroundings.

The Crone snorted and rolled her eyes. "Duh. Always hanging by a thread, that one." She flashed a grin. "Not quite ready to dye, she always has an end to tie, and when she's sewing, she inevitably needles a little space. Get it?"

Aline's eyes narrowed at the puns. "Where is Chlo? Where are the others?"

The girl only smiled, her needlelike teeth terrifying in her cherub's mouth.

Aline sighed. "Do you know or not?"

"They are where they always go when they run out of time. The Mother Tree. I suspect you're running out of time, too. We all are, but time never bothers me. Tricky fellow."

The Crone reached up and pulled a book from the closest stack, which featured an array of books colored from lead to obsidian. "And your Dragon? Is she with you or still missing? I know Magic's being tugged to you tighter than a current to the sea."

Aline took a breath. "You know Dragon? Have you seen her?"

The Crone smiled, her eyes widening as the swirls of time seemed to shift behind her pale violet irises. "I know more than I have ever wished to know. It's why I am who I am, and you know far less than you should."

"Let me guess, that's why I am who I am?"

"No. That's where you were failed, Aline. People are fallible. They will fault you, fail you, damn near break you. The Fates aren't much better, as they spin the yarn but do not dare to intercept it. Foolish lot of them." She said the last with great affection before tossing the book to Aline, who barely caught it by the edge of the cover. "You want to know a version of the truth? One closest to what will save you? Start here."

Then the Crone turned to leave.

"Hey, I have more questions," Aline called after her, irritated to be stuck with yet another story to read.

"The stories are more than just stories," the Crone called as she skipped out of the room, leaving Aline to gape after her.

"Wait, please," she said, before she looked down at the book, whose cover, she realized, nearly matched the one in her bag.

THE STORY OF THE FATES

Once upon a time the gods were not so greedy. They were merely curious. There was a watcher and his daughter, and a god born of lost time. These three lived in harmony in a single world. They created, they evolved, they played. Then, because they were so curious, they opened portals that might have been better remaining closed, and in doing so let magic and creatures into their playlands.

The world spiraled. The seas rose, chaos gods ran amuck, unicorns lost their horns, mermaids morphed into manatees, and the trees that knew every language under the sun grew silent, their roots sinking into the earth and spreading out across the plains of the land.

The trees were wise. They stopped speaking, but never forgot, and never lost their ability to understand. To wait, watch, and listen.

As magic began to break down the vibration of the world, the crack between worlds grew, and from it three beings emerged. These beings knew the trees. They knew this land as they knew all lands.

"I say," the first said, knitting a scarf that would fit a giant. "This won't end well."

"Never does," the other said, weaving a tiny intricate

hat with her pinky fingers. "Power is too seductive. It always causes them to forget to care for one another, for the forest and the beings that inhabit it."

"I have a theory," the last one said, studying the forest as she wrote on parchment, her eyes tracking the way the trees leaned, her left hand deft as it moved swiftly over the page. "That if we stop cleaning it up, they'll figure it out."

"That's some theory," the one knitting the scarf replied, wrapping it around her waist like a ballerina donning a tutu.

"It would leave a lot of them exposed, unprepared," the middle one said, curving her thumb and blowing across the tiny hat so it changed colors from red to green.

"Not," the scribe said, "if we stay."

"Stay?" the other two asked in unison.

"Yes." The scribe turned the parchment toward them. On it was a ticking, moving wheel that resembled a clock. "We lean into Fortuna. Give them one roll of her wheel and see what they can do."

"Is this a wager?" the knitter of the scarf that had become a skirt asked.

"No, of course not. It's better. An observation, an experiment."

"Do we leave and return?" the other asked, adding flaps for ears to the hat. "Seal the splinter they've set in the world?"

"No, the crack remains," the one rolling up the parchment into a scroll said. "We remain. In plain sight, but out of it. When the time comes, we do as we always do and record the chaos."

"Hmm," the woman with the tiny hat replied. She waited for a mouse to emerge from the base of the tree across from them. It scurried over, studying them, its small beady eyes wide, its pink nose wrinkling. The being crouched down and set the hat on its head, tugging tight. "Very well," she said, watching the mouse scurry off, before she reached into the pocket of her apron and pulled another small set of string from it. "I suppose if it goes too sideways, we can always kill them."

The other two nodded.

"Oh yes. Absolutely," said the one wearing the skirt, needles flying as it shifted into a dress. "But they'll do it for us if it comes to that."

"They always do," the last one said, before she turned, walking away from the tree and the forest.

Aline looked up from the book. "That's the worst bedtime story I've ever read." She looked around for the Crone, but she was nowhere to be found.

These Fates were supposed to be *her* Moirai sisters? They sounded more like bored homicidal gods than three loving bookworms who had made her life livable, who had loved her unconditionally.

Who then, were the three other players? The Watcher, his daughter, and the time creature? Aline stuffed the book in her bag and walked to the front. She found the Crone back behind her counter.

"Planning to pay for that or try your hand at the five-finger discount?" she asked, using a number-two pencil riddled with tiny teeth marks to point above her to a sign. It was a child's drawing of a dismembered hand, each finger cut from the bloody palm. Over it, scrawled in what looked far too realistically like blood, read: FIVE FINGERS DISCOUNTED.

Aline took the book out and set it on the counter, suppressing a shiver. The Crone might look like an ethereal ten-year-old, but she grinned like a psychopath on a prison break.

"Nope. I have questions."

The girl, who was definitely not a girl, leaned back in her antique leather swivel chair. "I'm no genie, so I'll answer two for you." She held up a single finger. "Not about Dragon."

"But—"

"You have the path in your pocket," the Crone said, barely suppressing a yawn. "The compass of the world, or rather her world, will guide you."

Aline thought of the key she carried that Magic had tossed to her. "How did you know that?"

"How does the sun know to rise or the moon to sleep? Some things are inevitable."

Aline bit her lip, thought of the story she'd read. "Where are the Fates?"

"Trapped."

Before Aline could open her mouth, the Crone lifted a single brow. "If you ask where, that will be your second question. Careful asking for things you might scry or spell for or even ask that compass about."

Aline wanted to ask her why the compass might help, then she wanted to ask why the Crone seemed to be helping her at all, then thought maybe that was her plan. To get her to waste a question—but then why answer any question at all? She rubbed at her temples as her thoughts tried to spiral out of containment.

"Why me?" she asked instead.

"Isn't that the question we all inevitably ask?" the Crone said, tugging her bottom lip. "You and Magic. You need each other, but ties usually need their binds. It's up to the two of you to help us all. Fair or no, it is what was set into motion, and you cannot change that any more than I can change being so very clever. Just remember . . . when unbound, the bind tends to die while the tie survives."

"That's not cryptic."

"Life is cryptic. That was a warning." The Crone set the story of the Fates back onto a small rolling rack to the left of her counter.

"I don't suppose I can pay for that book without losing my fingers?" Aline asked, turning the question over in her head and nodding to the story of the Fates.

The girl grinned again, flashing her sharp, menacing teeth. "Sure. I'll trade you for the one in your bag."

Aline sucked in a breath. Her hands protectively cradled the bag closer. "No, thanks."

"Smart girl," the Crone said. She leaned closer. "I'll give you a truth. Because you do not have a choice and I am sorry for that. Nothing in Matchstick is what you think it is, particularly the leader. Some things are movable, and others are fixed. Find the pieces you can shift, and you will change the board."

Then the girl yawned once more, climbed up on the desk, curled into a ball the most docile cat would envy, and fell asleep.

Nine

ALINE WAS NOT A FAN OF RIDDLES, BUT THE CRONE (LIKE FLORENCE) HAD SPOKEN CLEARLY ENOUGH. She was tied to Magic in more ways than she understood; the sisters were supposedly Fates, and they were trapped. Aline could no longer buy into the delusion that the Matchstick in her book was a lovely and giving world. It was Earth with claws, and she was going to have to do all she could not to get yanked under.

Aline knew reality was movable. She changed it for her ghosts all the time. Finder of the keys, she was able to send them from suffering to satisfaction. Or so she told herself. The truth was, she didn't know anything for sure.

Except she had to get a move on. She marched up Holliver Lane, holding the nearly translucent globe. It shimmered as she walked, splitting into three parts like a child's toy—the mantle, core, and outer layers of the earth—before it snapped back together. A soft light glowed, and she followed its path to a cemetery.

Some witches, much in the way of mortals, died. Not every witch was immortal; in fact very few had that gift—or curse, depending on how one's perspective embraced it. It was clear Matchstick honored its own. Aline had never been afraid of a graveyard. This was the land of her friends, the spirits she guided. A place of peace and calm. She was careful to mind where she stepped. Crossing up and down the rows, bowing her head in reverence for the lives once lived, the stories now silenced or forgotten.

She'd been walking for a good fifteen minutes when she saw a woman with dark-brown hair and light-brown skin sitting on a bench beneath a yew tree.

She was wearing bell-bottoms and a flannel shirt, her feet bare and her toenails a cheerful bright pink. Her smile tired, it was the kind that tugged down a little on one side but still managed to reach her eyes as she studied the gravestone in front of her.

The woman looked up to see Aline studying her, and tilted her head. "You must be the new witch everyone's talking about."

Aline gave a quick nod. "I've felt the stares. It's not the friendliest of places, which has been a little disappointing."

"Ah, there are a lot of those here. Stares and stars." The stranger looked up. They were in Dusk. There were fewer houses here, and a skyline that featured the first twinkling of stars Aline had seen. The two directly overhead gleamed bright, as though they were shiny eyes trying to blink down at them. "I'm sorry we've disappointed."

"I can't decide if people are unfriendly or busy," Aline said. "Florence said those who come to visit rarely leave, but I don't feel as though anyone is trying to influence me to stay."

"You're new, and everyone else is old. It's not a matter of dislike, but of uncertainty. Plus, the trees whisper about you. That makes those who don't speak to the trees but understand their talking nervous."

"What do the trees say about me?"

The woman looked off toward the pines at the edge of the perimeters. "Your name. Aline. The hedge witch who must find the ley lines and restore the balance."

"Such an easy and not at all vague task to be handed."

The woman grinned. "Do you know much of the way of the roots of Matchstick?"

Aline rubbed the chill from her forearms. "I read about the trees, in the bookstore."

"Then you met the Crone."

"I did."

The woman looked at her. "You survived, so that says you must be special."

"Not really." Aline sat down beside her. "I'm just Aline."

"Yes, and I'm Esther," the woman said, her warm smile flickering a little brighter.

"Do *you* speak to the trees?"

Esther yawned. "I used to speak for them. Before I ended up here. I came too early, or perhaps too late, but I haven't been inclined to leave, either."

"I'm supposed to help Magic," Aline said, studying the small white flowers dotted around the grave in front of them.

Esther snorted. "Magic should help himself."

"Maybe he doesn't know how," Aline said, thinking of the warmth of his eyes, of how his skin caressed hers in her dreams.

"Hmm," Esther said. "What do you want?"

Aline blinked at her, surprised at the care in the other woman's voice. She'd only heard that tone from Dragon and the Moirai sisters when Aline was having a tough day. "I . . . I suppose I'd like to save myself. And I would *really* like to find my friends."

Esther sighed. "I was afraid you might say that. Not that you shouldn't save yourself, but that you're going after them when they really should be left well enough alone." She stood up, nodded to Aline's globe. "Come along, then. It's better to go where you're bound to be headed with a little guidance."

⟨⟨⟨

Esther led Aline to the forest at the edge of the cemetery. Her hips swayed and she moved over the grass on her bare feet without stumbling over the rocks or sticks that littered the way. It smelled of October: burning leaves and crisp air. Aline could feel the veil between the world of Matchstick and the world outside it. Smell the occasional draft of citrus as it wafted through. The blades of grass beneath her feet shifted from vibrant and green to brittle and brown, crunching as she walked. The light in the orb bobbed as she followed it.

"A bit farther," Esther said, walking with measured steps.

They came to a clearing in the woods, where a trail widened. Aline followed Esther down to where the crunching of leaves underfoot softened to the pressing of rocks into a muddy embankment. Esther bounded over them, her bare feet not affecting her precision. Wind cut through the branches of the hanging limbs overhead, the wind chimes of the forest, rattling leaves and pine needles. The air grew colder, the chill settling into Aline's bones. She tucked one hand farther into her pocket, and the wind shifted in as its chill swirled around her.

The fog started low, barely visible as it brushed over the ground, driving the wind back. It grew to her ankles and stopped.

"Is this normally here?" she asked Esther, stepping away from the fog.

Esther sighed and looked contentedly up at the sky. "It's hard to tame memory mist," she said, with a careless shrug. "It can alter recall so that you forget you found it. It's not unlike thought itself in that way."

Aline swallowed panic. "You brought me here to erase my memory?"

"Oh no. I don't have that sort of power." She tilted her head. "Anymore. Besides, I don't like gaslights."

"Do you often rewrite your own thoughts?" Aline said, fighting the growing urge to cross to the closest tree and start climbing. She did not want anything tampering with her mind.

"No need. Time does it for me." Esther shuddered.

"Time sucks," Aline said, eyeing the fog that was now up to her shins and thinking of what the story of the Fates had said about the being out of time. "Noted."

Everywhere in Matchstick, it seemed, was trying to attack Aline. She looked down at the orb and found its exterior was covered in fog, the light hidden in the mist. Aline wasn't sure what to do without the guiding light. She swallowed and drew her bag closer to her. She slipped her hand inside and patted her emergency pocket. She sighed in relief. Surely something in there would help. It held powerful charmed objects she'd encountered over the years. Keys unclaimed, they stayed with her always—there was the empty Polaroid that showed you where you wanted to go, a tiny door that proved an exit when you needed one, and a clear marble that was the most powerful object Aline had encountered, and the most curious to use. It only ever whispered a single word, "seek," and it led the user to the safest location, which for Aline had often been where she might find tacos. She tended to bend the rules on safety when her stomach was growling.

The objects were talismans, but they were also incredibly powerful.

"The memory mist alters thought. It also reveals important knowledge hidden," Esther said. Her eyes were focused on the fog wrapping its way up Aline's leg like a red stripe circling a candy cane.

Aline did not want to lose her memories. She needed a way out of this predicament. She swung her bag around and unzipped the side compartment. She pulled from it a waterproof bag and reached inside, feeling around until her fingers closed over the marble. This marble she had been holding on to for years. She couldn't seem to let it go. Or maybe it refused to let go of her.

Aline held the marble in the palm of her hand. "Seek, seek, seek," it sang, as though happy to be in use.

She nodded at Esther. "Well, then, let's get on with it. We need to get to safety, on the count of three—"

Esther shook her head so hard her braid snapped against her shoulder. "You can't magic in Matchstick without respect."

The fog was up to Aline's thigh.

"I don't know what that means."

"We don't know we'll go the same way," Esther said, her

voice higher than normal. "You could go there, I could go here, and the fog could go everywhere."

Aline gritted her teeth together. "I don't understand."

"This is more than a look into what was, more than a story. It's a reveal."

A chill rolled over Aline's skin. *More than a story.* Like Dragon had said about the book of Matchstick so long ago, like the Crone had echoed.

Esther took a breath. "We have to do this right. Ready?"

"For?"

"Magic with respect."

Aline looked down at the marble in her hand. "Sure. Why the goddess not?"

Esther held up an open palm. "Repeat after me?"

Aline nodded and held up her marble.

"Two into one

"A blended hour

"To block what binds

"And unlock the veiled power."

THEY REPEATED THE WORDS TOGETHER THREE TIMES, AND AS THEY DID, ENERGY FIRED INSIDE ALINE. It started at her core and worked its way up her spine until it burst from the crown of her head. She savored the power in the sensation, and the marble in her palm heated and a flash burst from it. Aline looked down to her ankles. The mist was gone, and Esther was grinning.

"Nothing exploded," Aline said, glancing to Esther. Aline hadn't killed Esther; no rocks or boulders crushed her into dust.

Aline bit back a laugh, whispering thanks to the marble and putting it back into her bag.

"That should have been impossible," Esther said, spinning in a circle. "Improbable at the least, unmanageable at the most, and instead it's wholly done. The mist guarded what we needed, kept it secret and safe."

Aline noticed the way the crimson leaves on the trees looked more like velvet than crisp foliage and how the trunks of the trees, which had looked exceptionally ordinary, now had small arches inside them revealing little caves tucked in the trunks. She turned, though, at the mention of the mist having a purpose.

"What did the memory mist guard?"

The echo of a voice moved first from behind the largest tree that was directly in their path. It seemed to swim around to the front of the tree.

It said, simply, "Me."

(MEANWHILE, HIDDEN FROM PLAIN SIGHT . . .)

Dragon was tired. Or at least, she assumed tired was the feeling polluting her focus. It was hard to move about in the gaps of Matchstick and it tugged at her ability to remember. Names for feelings, places, even her purpose. Most places on and in the world were accessible to Dragon, though she could never stay long.

Only witches and certain nervous priests barred the doors to creatures of magic. Nuns were never afraid, which is why so many spirits sought refuge in nunneries. Women knew there were worse things on earth to fear than restless wanderers and guardians of the land. Matchstick, on the other hand, was a veritable fortress—and one Dragon had long avoided. It had taken all of Dragon's strength to follow Aline inside and enter from the in-between, and it had scattered her thoughts for almost an entire day. Which was unfortunate because Dragon was so much fonder of Day than she was of Night.

She'd lost track of Aline, only to find her again in the swamp with the broken creature. What was it with witches and water and broken things? And why the bloody hell had the Fates cursed her to be hidden like this?

It was frustrating and difficult, and Dragon was losing track of herself. She had gone down to the swampy lake to try and keep a closer eye on Aline, only to find the water did not welcome her. It spat and sputtered, gurgled and bubbled. It smelled of licorice and was the blended colors of a smudged rainbow. Like a trapped prism hovered beneath its surface. Beyond the water was a small cottage that was not a cottage. Dragon growled in irritation at the sight. Nothing in this spirit-forsaken place was what it was. Matchstick was a city of nesting dolls. One thing looked one way, until you got under the surface and then found it was actually something else. Similar but different. True but false.

It gave Dragon a headache. She was pretty sure that was what the ache was.

A body walked out of the house, clouded in mist. It seemed irritated, too. Swatting at the mist, stamping its feet. Dragon couldn't see the face, but she could hear its voice, cursing the mist and the lake. It sounded as though it was arguing with itself about a door.

Then, suddenly, the mist was gone.

Dragon saw the body and watched in wonder at its shifting form. From where Dragon stood on the edge of the embankment, she thought the body belonged to neither a man nor a woman. A being, perhaps, though Dragon had only heard rumors of other beings on the axis. She avoided the axis as a rule and had thought she was the only power so ancient that Time itself had forgotten how to find it.

Then this being—for as she studied it, she grew certain that was what it was—shifted. It seemed to sniff the air, to waver as though in a daze. Its features shifted from nondescript to clear. Thick dark hair, piercing eyes, a generous mouth, and a quizzical brow.

She heard him say, in astonishment, a single word.

"Her."

Then, like the mist, he was gone, too.

Leaving Dragon alone with the cottage that was not a home, and the feeling that everything was about to get much, much worse before it got better.

⫷⫸

ALINE TOOK A STEP FORWARD, AND ESTHER HISSED. A gust of wind blew up, swift and angry. Esther let out a yell, but it was swallowed by the squall. In the blink of an eye, she was wrenched away. Aline stared in surprise as the other witch was yanked off her feet.

Esther hovered in the air, like a suspended puppet, her hair framing her face, her arms reaching out. Aline's stomach gave a dangerous flip as fear spiked in her veins. Before she could get out a shout, a pine-tree branch splintered from the tree beside them and flew down to Esther's outstretched hand.

Esther caught it. She wrapped herself around the branch like a witch sitting on a broom right before the gust whipped her up into the air and tossed her over the trees. She flew away until she was a tiny dot on the horizon, and then nothing was there at all.

With Esther gone, the maelstrom stopped as quickly as it began. The forest went from raging to silent. The trees did not creak; the leaves refused to shift or sigh. Aline found the total embrace of silence far more terrifying than the storm. She was shaking, her hands raised in fists.

Magic walked out from behind the yew tree with the human-sized hole carved in its center. His steps were loud, crunching against the gravel of the path. His clothes were rumpled, and he reached up and tugged at the edge of one sleeve, unrolling it down his chiseled forearm. He looked a little worse for wear than he had earlier that morning, which considering he'd just summoned wind strong enough to toss a fully grown witch out of the forest, perhaps he should have looked like death.

Aline took a step back, trying to decide if she should break into a run or tiptoe backward a bit first.

"I'm not going to fight you," he said, his voice as rich as his unique eyes.

"Are we meant to battle?" Aline refused to meet those eyes, recalling too well what happened earlier that day. The zing from his touch, the desire unfurling in her belly like a flower seeking the sun—all from his gaze. Even now she struggled not to feel affected by the soothing cadence of his honey voice. Aline thought of the line from *Mischief*:

"*His world was made to bend to his will.*"

Everything about him made her want to reach out and crawl up him like a koala climbing a tree.

The air smelled of fresh pine and licorice. It was a strange and intoxicating blend. Magic sat down. On the grass. With zero warning or ceremony.

He just *plopped* down.

"She isn't hurt," he said, reaching out and plucking a strand of grass. "The one I sent out of the forest. Can't hurt that one any worse than what's been done. Not unless you splintered her soul, but I don't think you have it in you. I think you're better than that, better than the rest of us."

He held the blade of grass to his lips and blew. The sound that came from his mouth was not the soft whistle Aline expected. He blew out the deep sound of a trombone. One note, two, three. He tossed the blade, reached over, and picked up a new one, then blew anew. This time the lilting strings of a guitar played, the notes floating down and settling into her hair, brushing across her cheeks.

Aline dug her nails into her palms and shook off the effect.

"Stop it," she said, batting the notes from her hair.

He looked up. His eyes brightened. "What did you hear?"

"What do you think I heard? You playing instruments like a classically trained maestro from a single blade of grass. Quit trying to seduce me with your power."

He leaned back onto his wrists. "Is that what you think I'm doing?"

She couldn't stop the blush. *Wasn't* it what he was doing? Maybe it was unconscious. She felt utterly ridiculous at her emotions, and the realization it may all be one-sided. Cause and effect. He was Magic. He was hers. But did he know it? Remember her, even?

"What do you think you're doing?" she asked, her voice low.

"I'm not entirely sure." He looked at her, his eyes raking over the planes of her face, drifting down to her feet and back up again. "I suppose I'm trying to work out why you won't look at me."

It was her turn to take a deep breath and study him; she avoided meeting his gaze for too long and assessed his lean form as it was spread out on the grass. There were shadows under his eyes, and a growing stubble brushed across the square line of his jaw. She found his jaw more chiseled this afternoon than it had been this morning. Was that possible? His shoulders seemed broader, too, like there was suddenly more of him. She wanted to kiss the shadows away, find a way to take some of the weight he seemed to carry onto herself.

"Aline the hedge witch, with a bag full of tricks," he said, his tongue rolling over the words like they were notes in a song. The sweet melody of his cadence set her teeth on edge. Aline wanted to purr; the sound was so inviting.

"Cut it out," she said, her tone low.

He lifted his chin, and a dimple appeared in his left cheek. She wanted to press her finger against it and flick him in the nose. All at once.

"Aren't we past this?" he asked, sitting up, drawing his knees in.

She raised a brow. He was staring down at his hands, focused on the ridges in his knuckles. He looked . . . surprised and a little anxious.

"Do you . . . ," she said, struggling to spit it out, "remember?" When he didn't reply, she added, "Never mind."

"At first," he said, his voice low, velvet soft. "You were there.

Turning up when I closed my eyes. 'Like a starving, stray cat seeking milk from the farmer's door.'"

Aline thought of another line from *Mischief*. "'Like a curious cat tracking cheese to the mouse's lair.'"

"'The lair that is not a lair, from a mouse that is not a mouse.'"

"'When the cat is not a cat.'"

He laughed.

She smiled. Then frowned. How could this be real?

"I have known you, and not known you, and I don't understand." He leaned toward her. "But I want to know you."

She gulped. "I want to find my friends."

"Why do you want to find the Fates then, little hedge? For if you are in this part of the forest there is only one reason, aside from seeking me. Unless . . . were you seeking me?"

She might have done that, had she known she could.

Aline was great at finding lost things for other people, but she herself had felt lost for so long. If she was truly honest with herself, which she always tried to be, she wanted to find the lost thing she'd been searching for the longest. She wanted to find out why no one stayed. Aline needed to fix the broken parts of herself. She wanted to be enough. Dragon and the three sisters had been the one thing she had thought would stay. Fates or no.

"I need to know why they left, why everyone always goes."

He reached out, ran a finger across the back of her hand, tingles trailing where he touched. "I wonder if that would be enough."

He stood and held out a hand. She accepted and he slid his fingers into hers, as though they were always meant to be there. They started walking. Aline leaned into him, not questioning it.

He got under her skin like a tick or chigger or another creature that burrowed and refused to leave when it hadn't been invited. She had no choice but to follow him.

"Would it be enough for you?" she asked.

"What?"

"If I figure out what's wrong with magic and save you?"

He stopped, angled his body toward hers. "Wrong with me? I am free." He stared at her lips for so long they began to tingle. "I want, and can have, everything. Or I thought so, at least. Before you." His eyes dipped to her lips and then back up.

Aline smiled but released his hand. It was safer not to touch fire. The problem was Aline was very good at playing with matches.

He looked over his shoulder as though he had heard her thoughts and did a very human thing. He rolled his eyes. Then he held up a hand and flicked a wrist. The tree across the way, with a hole in its trunk the size of a small elephant, shifted from a view of bark to one of the doors into Aline's house. In Whistleblown.

Aline gaped at the sight and took a step forward.

With another flick of his wrist the barren hole in the tree was once more a vacant pit. He gave his shoulder a shrug. "As I said, I can have nearly everything."

"Except visitors?"

He raised his brows.

"You threw Esther into the wind. Literally raised the wind to toss her over the treetops and out of this forest."

"She didn't belong here."

"You didn't toss me."

"You belong with me."

Her jaw dropped. "What?"

Magic stopped walking. He turned on his heel and crossed back to her. His moves were swift and reminded her of a lion slinking up on a doe. Aline backed up until her back hit the thick trunk of the nearest tree. He leaned in, so close their noses were nearly touching.

"You are surprised," he said.

"No shit." She drew in a soft breath, careful not to make any quick moves. He was so close she could see the swirl of gold mixed with the obsidian of his eyes, but those eyes were calm.

"Because I said what you clearly know already?" He frowned into the words.

"Because it's a sexist thing to say." She pressed her palms into the bark. "Because you are in my face, violating my space."

He looked down, and back up. He seemed to realize he was close enough to stick out his tongue and lick the edge of her mouth. His gaze stayed on her lips for a moment longer as his cheeks flushed. He took a step back. "I apologize. I did not mean to be so forward."

What a strange way to say a thing. Aline brushed a hand through her hair, watching the tremble work its way up her arm. She wanted his hands back on her, in her hair, around her waist, and it was daunting how near impossible it was to stop the craving. "Yeah, well, you were."

"I don't talk to people, besides you, and I don't usually talk to you here in the waking world. People don't talk to me." He brushed a hand over his face. "I gave your friend a kindness, sending her on her way."

"I'd hate to see what you'd do when you are pissed," she said, mostly to her shoes. She looked up at him, and he was staring again, a look of amused confusion etched into his features.

"The waking world?" Aline asked.

"When we are not in between, when I am here and you are wherever you are."

"How can you find me? How could I find you?"

He shook his head. "I don't yet know, but there is little I can't figure out."

"That sounds presumptuous."

He grinned. "But true. Do you . . . like people?"

She blinked. "That's what you want to ask me right now?"

He crooked up the corner of his mouth.

She sighed. "I dunno. They don't like me much, either, aside from Dragon, Chlo, Liset, and Atti. But they're more than friends, they're my family."

"What about poetry?"

"I'm sorry?" More than sorry, Aline was severely confused.

"Do you know it? Like it?"

She bit back a grin, his expression was so earnest. "I do."

"Then I'll tell you a poem sometime, before this is done."

"What is *this*?"

Magic walked to the edge of the lake, to where decaying mud met the space between the land and water. They drew closer and Aline realized it wasn't mud but a shoreline—a beach of small and large pebbles of obsidian in varying shades of smoke.

"This is the start of now," he said. "This is where we try to save magic. This is the beginning of learning if we live or die."

Ten

ALINE STOOD VERY STILL. Magic faced her, his tawny black eyes searching hers, his hands relaxed against the fabric of his gray pants. He'd spoken so softly, for a moment she convinced herself she misheard him. Then the river behind him began to bubble. He took a step toward her, and then slowly circled her. She backed up to the edge of the rocky shoreline, tried to step out of it, and found she could not cross the line drawn there. She was stuck in his path.

Aline licked her lips and tugged her pack around, so it was more shield than bag. "I'd prefer we not die."

She could have sworn he bit back a grin.

"You can't really think we will."

"If we fail? Yes, I think we can and will," Magic said, his posture shifting, his eyes darkening.

Aline couldn't help but swallow hard as she watched him.

"I want to know why I feel this way." He looked at her, his gaze penetrating.

Aline forgot how to inhale. "What way?"

He let out a low hum, turning his gaze away.

"You know," he said, ignoring her question.

"I don't know." She slowly enunciated the next sentence. "It's always been this way, when I find you in my dreams, when you're near, I'm . . ."

"Found?"

"Perhaps."

"I am not lost. Which you know." He smiled or at least came close enough to one for her stomach to flip in a way that was more dangerous than his threat. The small stab of desire he brought out in her flickered to life as she stared at that smile. "But maybe I'm not whole?"

"Should we test it?" he asked, curling his fingers once more and summoning a bolt of light into his hand. It crackled, the energy zipping into Aline, causing the hair on her neck to lift. His power forced the leaves on the trees surrounding them to point upward like soldiers standing at attention.

"How are you doing that?"

He cocked his head. "I'm speaking to the elements."

"Yet nothing is blowing up," she said, squirming under the pressure of the energy flow as it came closer to her.

Magic turned his fist up and over, three times, and the bolt of light he cupped extinguished. Then he opened his hand.

Aline's marble, the object of her desire, sat in his palm.

"How did you—?"

Magic waved the hand, and the marble disappeared. Then

he emptied both of his pockets—pulling out her blank Polaroid and tiny door she kept tucked in her purse.

"Why would something blow up? It's transmutation, pulling from one place to the next, matter shifting and transforming. It's what we do."

She took in a shaky breath.

"You feel it all, don't you?" he asked, and took a step closer, reaching out and slipping the objects back into her bag.

Aline's heart kicked up another notch. "What?"

"This tether?" he asked, taking another tiny step. "From me to you, how it's more than magic."

Aline could not move. Excitement was working its way up her heel, like a curious lizard climbing along her calves, traipsing up her thigh, and clinging to her spine. Its slow march of want was sinking its way into her bones. But she held her ground. "I feel something."

"You don't want to feel it," he said, reading the barely masked fear on her face.

Magic hadn't pulled his gaze from hers, and the connection was as worrying as his words. She felt more danger from the need he pulled from her than from his threat of their impending death, and that was very stupid indeed.

"I feel . . . a crackling when you're near."

"That is *a* truth," he said, shifting even nearer.

They stood, face-to-face, the mist on the lake rising behind them like a wall. Aline tried to draw a breath, and instead pulled that deep, aching sense of longing from him deeper into herself. It *was* a rope, a binding of some kind, one she did not know how to break.

Magic drew his own shaky breath, his eyes widening. Then

his gaze dropped, for the second time, to her mouth. He looked back up, his pupils dilating.

A bind she was afraid she might not want to break.

"Matchstick isn't a safe place," he said. "But I'm not sure you're really looking for safe. The rule of the axis is simple, the price complex. I am no one's power, Aline Weir. I am my own, just as you are your own."

Aline blinked at the passion in his voice, the edge of anger curled there.

"We may not have a choice any longer, but if I can I will keep you safe."

She let loose a laugh, one she hadn't meant to free.

"You think that's funny?"

"No, I think only very few have ever cared to try and keep me safe from anything." She ignored the pang under her rib cage, reminding her how true that was. "Besides, maybe I'm meant to keep you safe."

"Perhaps." Magic's eyes narrowed, and his hand lifted. Aline went to step to the side, and his fingers grazed down her cheek. "But if only a few have tried to care for you, then you have been surrounded by fools."

Before she could reply, the light at the edge of her gaze wavered, shimmering. She turned and looked beyond him to a large yew tree. She had not seen it until he touched her, until his magic gave her the thing Esther had promised. Knowledge. Sight.

The tree was the size of a shed, wide and round, and ancient. In it, Aline could feel the magic of her three friends. Could smell the spices of their perfume, the sweetness of their comfort, the tang of their lack of goodbye. Chlo. Liset. Atti. The Crone and Florence had not lied: they were inside the tree, hidden away.

"They're trapped," she said, her voice cracking at the truth of it.

"Yes."

Magic ran his fingers through his hair. "The wheel of Fortuna spins, and time has shifted them into the place they must go. They are impenetrable in their cocoon."

"Nothing is impenetrable," she whispered, her thoughts rushing through possibilities. "The hardest of metals may be broken. Bent. Changed." Aline made up her mind as she studied the tree and heard the echoes of long ago. Of three women welcoming her in, providing support and safety and unconditional love.

"It's up to me to free them." She looked at him. "I won't be stopped."

"No, I doubt you could." His lips twitched. The tips of his elegant fingers still lingering against her skin.

"Would you like my assistance?" he asked, before his eyes dropped to her bag. Aline knew what he sought, though she did not stop to dwell on *how* she knew what he wanted. She reached in, pulled out the book, and pressed it into his hand.

"I'm going to that tree and I'm going to pry it open with my bare hands if I must. Do not interfere." At his narrowed gaze she held up a hand. "Please."

He reached for her again, pulling her close. Her side was electric where his hand not holding the book loosely cradled her hip. He was at least a head and a half taller than her, and he leaned down so his whisper slipped from his mouth into hers. "I will interfere with whatever I want."

His gaze darkened and a bubble of fear trapped there, his worry burst in her rib cage. His mouth was mesmerizing, his magic pushing at her. She opened her mouth to tell him to let her be, and his lips descended on hers.

Aline was so shocked, time seemed to stand still. Magic's lips were soft, gentle, and the kiss was barely a kiss. Until she groaned. Aline hadn't meant to do it, but as she'd finally taken in a breath, she'd taken in more than his lips: she'd opened herself to his power. To whatever was building between them. It was electric, sensual, and it sent every nerve ending in her body screaming for release.

Magic dropped the book, and both arms came around her. One hand cradling the back of her head, the other supporting her lower back. Aline slipped her arms up and around him and did something she had never done before. As she stood on tiptoes and took the kiss deeper, she yanked his hair. Tugged him down . . . and then his lips weren't gentle. His grasp wasn't guiding. He pressed his mouth to hers, his tongue sliding across the slit of her lips as he nudged her open. He moaned and she responded, their mouths fusing as their tongues tangled and Aline took the kiss deeper and deeper.

He scooped her into his arms, walking back to one of the large yews and pressing her into it. He pushed himself against her, and she pushed back, arching into the sensation as desire and a need for release built and built. Aline couldn't stop herself from grinding against him as she sought for release, and soon the sounds that were coming from both of their mouths were more animal than human.

Until.

"I say, Chlo, you were right about the sparks. I can practically see them through the wood." Liset's voice drifted out.

"Wood indeed," Chlo said.

"Didn't see this coming," Atti replied. "But then we never saw Aline until she was right in front of us."

"Oh gods, the puns," Aline said, pressing her forehead to Magic's heaving and extraordinarily broad chest as she unwound her legs from him. She pressed her fingers to her swollen lips and looked up into his eyes.

All the intense emotion, all the desire and drugged need had faded from them. His expression was as cold as the first snow in winter. Aline didn't have time to process what that meant, didn't want to untangle the twisted threads of what the shocking lack of feelings she saw there meant. She turned to face the tree.

"Atti? Liset? Chlo?"

"Hello, child," Chlo said, her voice muffled. "I hope this doesn't mean our store has burned down and the books have been forsaken."

"*My* store is fine. You're deflecting." Her voice broke and she looked over her shoulder to find Magic standing there, not moving or blinking. She turned back to the tree. "How could you leave me like that? What is going on?"

"We are sorry, dearest," she said, and Aline could hear the hurt in Chlo's voice. It was the same tone she heard when Aline had scraped her knees when Chlo was the librarian tending to her, or when she hurt herself in her attempts to control her magic and Chlo became something more. "Is the boy with you?"

"Magic, you mean?"

"That's the one."

"He's not a boy, but yes."

"When you are our age, dearie, everyone who is five millennia or younger is a child."

Aline looked at Magic. "How old *are you*?"

He did not reply.

She gulped and turned back to the yew.

"Can you come out now? I don't really like talking to a tree." She leaned closer, her voice dropping. "And I need you."

"You aren't alone," Atti said, snorting. "You have your guide."

Magic moved now, his eyes flashing. "You're playing with her."

"We're doing no such thing," Atti said. "Gods, he sounds angry. He won't explode, will he? Don't want him to hurt her."

"Well, it might be best if one of them kills the other," Liset said, her voice sounding sleepy and far-off. "It'll happen in the end."

"Not necessarily," Chlo said, her tone sharp. "And it won't happen to her. She's ours."

Magic took a step closer to Aline and she blinked rapidly up at him. He sighed, and shook his head, turned, and walked to where he'd dropped the book. He scooped it up and stood. Waiting.

"How can you say that? What do you mean, we'll kill each other?" she said, her voice quivering.

"Oh, ignore her," Chlo said, her voice soothing. "She's mad because she thought we had more time. We all did."

Aline didn't know what to think. Half of her wanted to run to Magic, finish what they'd started. Especially as the wind blew through his ruffled hair and his lips were nearly bruised from how she'd attacked him. He looked like sex. The other half imagined his eyes dead, if the sisters were speaking the truth, and everything inside her went cold.

"You're not making sense," Aline said to the tree.

"We are. You simply don't understand yet," Chlo said.

"You will," Atti added.

"Hopefully before it's too late," Liset mused.

Aline gently bonked her head into the tree. "What do I do?"

"It's as simple as complex," Chlo said, her voice fading. "You find the other axes along the ley lines before they are destroyed, and you protect yourself and him. We believe in you. We always have."

"It's more than a story," Liset called, her voice barely audible now, as mist shifted back into the forest. "Always remember that, and there are those who will help you, but you mustn't, above all else, trust the—"

Her words faded to nothing. Aline smacked the tree and tried to call them back, but the Fates had grown silent. She hit it harder, her hands curling to fists, punching and pushing, until she felt him there. Magic lifted his chin and held out a hand.

Aline tensed, pain flooding in at the reality of it all. The sisters, her family, were Fates. She was a pawn, and once again she had been rejected. Her knees shook. She nearly fell to the ground.

"I didn't get to ask about Dragon," she said, running her hands through her hair.

Magic said nothing. He simply waited for her to scream or cry or do both. When she took a shaky breath and went to straighten, he came to her and assisted her up. Then he slid her palm into his.

Together they shivered at the jolt of energy. She watched him experience the same reaction, and he swallowed.

"Fates are tricksters. It does not mean they do not love you," he said.

She shook her head, forcing the tears to stay banked.

"They speak of other axes," he said, his tone low.

"It doesn't track, though, not with what the scroll said. Not with what Florence said."

"Nothing tracks except when beyond the forest," he said. "It's why I come here. I dream here. I am more and things are clearer here. When I leave, they become less so. It's always been the way. With you here now, I don't think it has to be anymore."

"We have to do this. We have to find the other axes."

He nodded.

"And save magic?"

"Yes."

"And if we fail?"

He tilted his head from one side to the other. "Your Fates seem to think there's a chance I might end you."

"So we fail and you *kill* me?"

"Not today, I don't think." His gaze dropped to her lips, and she warmed all over. "Maybe tomorrow."

Then he tugged her forward, through the mist and toward his cottage.

Eleven

ALINE AND MAGIC CROSSED A SMALL WOODEN BRIDGE SHAPED LIKE A CAMEL'S HUMP TO GET TO HIS COTTAGE. The water beneath the bridge was calm and clear. Like ice melted in a glass. Rocks sat beneath it in shades of navy and purple. Magic opened the door and walked inside. Aline attempted to follow him and was repelled by what felt like a steel wall. It smacked her in the shoulder, and she fumbled back.

"What the—"

She tried to step forward again, more cautiously, and her foot connected with the barrier.

"Magic," she called to him, "I can't enter."

He paused in the doorway, and slowly turned around. "I've never had anyone over before."

"Maybe you have to invite me in? Like I'm a vampire?"

"Vampires don't need invitations; they only need a bit of the blood of the person they're preying upon to enter their domain."

"Okay, ew. I don't even want to know if you're telling the truth because I can't handle *vampires* right now." She looked down at her scuffed and well-worn Doc Martens Mary Janes and back up at him. "Why can't I come inside?"

"I don't know," he said. He walked back out and then in again. "I have no problems doing so."

Aline stood at the doorway, staring inside, wracking her brain. "You said things are murky when you aren't here?"

He nodded.

"How long have you been here?"

"I have always lived here, for as long as I've lived in Matchstick."

"Did you build this home yourself?"

He shook his head.

"Okay, did you magic it, Magic?"

"So clever, aren't you?" His lips twitched. "No, I did not. It was a gift."

"Ah."

"Why are your eyebrows doing that?"

"Doing what?"

"Trying to climb up your forehead like I've delivered a shock you already knew, and you're pretending it's still a revelation."

"I'm thinking. This is my thinking face."

He leaned against the doorjamb. "I think even if you could come in, I'd no longer allow it."

"You are exhausting."

"And we're out of our depths."

Aline shrugged. "I always am." She was also close to throwing herself at the door again, if only to smell him. She had to get out of the forest, and fast.

"Since I can't come inside, mind doing that tree trick and sending me back to my cottage?"

He considered. "I can still find you."

"You said not today, maybe tomorrow."

He laughed, and the sound was low, rich, and wonderful. "I meant we need to find the other ley lines, find out if this is true. I can't lose you."

He lifted a hand and flicked a wrist at the yew tree closest to his cottage. The air shimmered in front of the human-sized hole and then shifted to reveal the sitting room inside the cottage Aline was staying in. White couch, plush blanket, empty water glass.

"That's not creepy."

He simply smiled and nodded to the tree. "Run away, magic witch."

She rolled her eyes but found the way he watched her both charming and hard to walk away from. She forced herself to march toward the tree, and when she came within a few feet of it, there was a static filling the inside of her head. A popping sound like she was riding inside an airplane, being propelled up and down amidst turbulence that refused to break.

"Ouch," she said, her hands on her head. She tried to step forward and push past the pain . . . and the portal dropped. Aline swiveled to face him, the words she prepared to hurl at him drying on her lips at the shock on his face. He crossed to her, inspecting her, she assumed, for damage.

"Let me guess," she said. "That hasn't happened before?"

He swallowed, hard. "I don't know." His voice came out low, an exhale of a whisper. "I open doors, but . . ."

"But?"

This time, when his eyes met hers, there was something more than irritation and desire banked behind them. There was a ring of fear.

"I've never needed to cross through one before."

⟜⟜⟜

ALINE WALKED BACK TO TOWN. It took her a few exhausting minutes to convince Magic they needed to go separately and meet at the House of Knowledge.

She didn't trust Florence, but mostly she needed space to find herself. Being next to him, feeling his breath brush against her cheek, his hand graze her sleeve, it was like she was a slow fuse ready to ignite and he was the detonator.

As she sorted herself, she settled in for a long, annoying walk through a beautiful forest filled with large yew trees and knee-high grass. Tall pines that arched toward her as though following in her wake, and a dusty rose-colored night sky. Fireflies flickered, hovering but never coming close enough for her to touch them. Once, she was certain she saw a tiny face on one that looked more human than bug. She blinked and it flew away.

The trail was worn and wet, muddy in so many places the tops of her feet were flecked in mud-spattered freckles. It would be pleasant if she were in the right shoes, and if anything made sense. If her blood weren't still humming from the moments Magic leaned down to her as though he were going to inhale her, and if she weren't turning over everything the Fates said and didn't—and everything Florence implied.

Magic's power, to open doors, didn't work the way he thought, and that was problematic. He seemed splintered, as though something were missing or broken. He seemed bound to the forest and his home as well, for the most part, and if the Fates kept to that forest, Aline had to hope there was a chance they were protecting him.

Aline knew how to find and return lost objects. She wasn't sure how to put back together a lost person. Or what to do with all the scattered pieces of information.

She exited the trail, stepping into the dark of night, and feeling as though someone were watching her. She looked over her shoulder, expecting Esther, and found instead the Crone.

"I'm surprised you leave your store," Aline said.

"I'm surprised you survived the badlands," the Crone said, flashing those sharp teeth that were more needle than bone.

"Badlands?"

"The forest of fiction. Where memory fades and boundaries blur. Where the Fates wait."

"You know I don't know what you mean."

"You have an idea, though."

"There is something wrong with Matchstick and right with the forest?"

"There is something wrong with the world."

"Did the Fates build Magic that house?"

"They build many things. Stores, houses, protection spells."

Aline sighed and the Crone skipped to her. The Crone reached into her pocket and pulled out a pack of gum, unwrapping a piece and popping it in her mouth. "You found them?"

"The Fates?"

The Crone nodded.

"You might say that."

"You can't save them until you save yourself. You can't save yourself until you save him."

"Magic?"

The Crone grinned. "Yes. All of Magic."

"I don't suppose you're going to tell me where to start?"

"Duh." The Crone rolled her eyes. "You're already heading there. You want answers, go to the answer store."

The House of Knowledge.

"Is that where you're going?"

"Oh, I never go there. The house is more than a house and it reads people like *you* read story. I like my secrets kept in my own pockets."

"He saw me," Aline said. "In the scroll. Magic."

"Did he see you," the Crone asked, "or did he see the mirror reflecting back?"

Then she winked and skipped off, not bothering to look back or answer Aline when she called after her.

Aline sighed, returned to her cottage, and changed out of her muddy shoes and splattered pants. She took a quick shower, sighing in relief at the perfection of the temperature and pressure the shower afforded. She was exhausted when she got out, the events catching up to her, the shock shifting into a deep fatigue. She needed to find Magic, to process everything that was happening and to do what the Fates said.

She slipped into her most comfortable yoga pants and oversized tee and went into the bedroom. It was a gorgeous sight, with a king-size bed covered in the fluffiest light-blue comforter, matching pillows and a navy-blue chenille throw in the corner. There were two modern tables and lamps, and a dresser, along with a bookshelf filled with books on a variety of magical lore and spells.

Aline yawned, walked to the bed, and face-planted into it. It was, she thought, like dropping into a cloud. She would give herself a moment, two, and then get up and get on with it. Four deep breaths later, and she was sound asleep.

ALINE OPENED HER EYES TO FIND MAGIC LYING BESIDE HER. He was curled into her, his arm across her waist, the big spoon to her little spoon.

"Am I dreaming?"

"Not so much," he said, shifting on his side. "Or rather, you are and aren't."

"How do you mean?"

"There is something old here and it is waking. Blurring what can and cannot be done. You're sleeping but you're also waking. It's this place, I think."

"And you and me?"

"Always you and me," he said, smiling and reaching for Aline's hand, a voltage of pure desire fluttering into places she wasn't ready for it to go. "We have to be more careful."

"Of who?"

"Everyone."

"But not you?"

"Never me."

Aline nodded. She believed in Magic, in this connation that had existed for so many years. She trusted what he said.

It was a bone-deep certainty, that Magic wouldn't—or perhaps couldn't—lie to her.

"Florence. Tell me about her?"

"She is a collector. She is . . ." His face scrunched up, his straight nose wrinkling, full lips pursed. "Helpful until she is not."

His eyes drifted closed. "I am sleepy. I always rest better when you are with me. May I stay with you for a while? Here?"

"Of course."

He scooted closer, curling into Aline, his heat infusing her. "We have to be careful. 'Tomorrow is a new day with no mistakes in it . . . yet.'"

"*Anne of Green Gables,*" Aline murmured, her eyes flicking closed again. She held tight to him, and soon they were both asleep—and not asleep—together.

꧁

WHEN ALINE WOKE AGAIN, MAGIC WAS GONE. The scent of him remained in the air, sweet pine and a hint of smoke. She rolled off the bed, the feel of his fingers an echo of a caress against her palm. He'd quoted *Anne of Green Gables,* Dragon's favorite story pouring from his lips. She needed to find out why.

Aline didn't trust this town. She knew better than to trust the Crone, no matter how charming the Machiavellian almost-child was. She didn't trust Florence or Esther or even the Fates, as much as she loved them. They had hidden too much from her. She trusted herself, though. Aline knew her powers. She'd honed them, but there was the strange tether with Magic, and how he stirred everything awake in her.

First things first, she'd go to the House of Knowledge, regardless of the Crone's warning, and look for Magic.

She threw her hair into a high knot on top of her head and headed out. Night greeted her, steadfast in its darkness and rotating constellations. The sky had to have been bewitched, with how the three hamlets rotated skylines. It was reassuring and terrifying.

"Hello, Night," she said, and her breath caught as the stars seemed to glow brighter in response.

Aline studied the sky, the feeling that there was something in it she was missing. She pocketed the thought and hurried down the path in the direction of the House of Knowledge. As she went, she encountered several witches. Male and female, young and old. Few smiled, most appeared skeptical of her in the town. Furrowed brows, pursed lips, lingering stares that left cold shivers skittering along her spine.

As she crossed from Night into Dusk, it changed. The feeling of being watched increased, but it was like there was a current in the land, the vibrations of Matchstick, perhaps. While in Night, the townspeople had acted repelled by Aline, and now that she was in Dusk, they weren't smiling so much as drifting closer. If Aline were the sun, they were flowers seeking her warmth. As they moved near, she waved, and they waved back.

"You're the witch Florence told us about," a gruff man with a thick red beard, wearing a blue-and-green flannel shirt, said. "The one who talks to ghosts?"

"Oh." Aline paused, wiped her fast-to-dampen palms on her black jeans. "That's me, yeah. Hi."

Another woman in a pale-yellow dress with olive skin and

beautiful green eyes stepped closer. "A hedge witch? We haven't had a hedge in Matchstick in years. Do you hold séances? Are you any good at gardening? I'm Shell, by the way."

Aline's head swam at the line of questioning. "I wouldn't know where to begin with a séance and I accidentally killed every plant I've ever brought into the bookstore."

"You run a bookstore?" Shell said, her green eyes flashing with excitement. "The Crone mentioned you to me. You can trust her because the books do."

"Rubbish," the man with the beard said. "Books can't judge character. They're holders of characters."

"What do you know of character, Timpleton?" a woman with graying curly hair, wearing a bright-pink apron, asked. "You regularly skimp on tips at my café."

"Your gluten-free muffins are dry as a dehydrated cracker, Margaret," the man replied.

"And you like to talk seven inches lower than my face when we gather," Shell said to Timpleton, waving a hand in the direction of her chest.

"You wear a seeing eye on your forehead," he exclaimed, shielding his own eyes from it. "I don't trust you won't put a pox on me like you did Nuria years ago."

"Hogwash," Shell replied. "She spelled herself after drinking too much of the Matchstick punch and fell into the mirror. It's not my fault she got distracted by the other dimensions."

Aline bit back a chuckle as they kept on. It was like nothing she'd ever seen. Then Shell raised a hand and crooked a finger at Timpleton. He shrieked and rubbed his backside.

"How dare you?"

"How dare I?" Shell said. "Now you know what being ogled feels like, you twit!"

The air blew cold, and Aline shivered. The sun dimmed, and everyone quieted. Florence rode down the pavement on an electronic bike, her long silver-and-cream hair waving in the wind behind her.

As she pulled up beside the group and climbed off her bike, Aline had a strong sense of *wrong* nudging her. It was in the way Florence's hair waved and shimmered. How the sun seemed to dim when she drew near. Aline needed to get to the House of Knowledge, and she wanted to get away from Florence.

"I see you all met our Aline," Florence said, flashing a smile that left Aline's blood running cold. "Out getting to know the locals?"

"I was looking for Magic," she said, giving her a partial truth. "I was also getting answers to questions, like which businesses I need to frequent. I definitely want to check out the café Margaret runs."

"You want to get to know the town, then?" Florence said, the chill in her smile dimming another ten degrees. "I can help with that." She raised a hand, and more people drew near. Witches who had been watching from the porch, drinking tea and laying tarot cards or charming their flowers.

Aline was immediately inundated with hellos and pleasantries, and she broke out into a sweat at the proximity of the crowd. She smiled through her teeth, perspiring moisture down her back. She answered questions as best as she could about how she helped spirits and promised to try the café, clothing shop, and flower shop.

After what felt like a small forever, when another argument about the quality of flour in the café's scones broke out, Aline managed to slip away. She hurried on to the House of Knowledge, cutting through a series of backyards overflowing with hydrangeas, tomatoes, squash, and an assortment of herbs.

She did not know if Florence believed her enough when she gave her a half-truth. The sisters . . . Fates always said it was best to never lie directly to another witch, but they hadn't said anything about bending the truth. Aline only knew that she never wanted to be in the position of having the spotlight of twenty witches or more on her again.

The door to the House of Knowledge was open when Aline arrived, and she hesitated. It had allowed her in before, but what if it had changed its mind? She stepped up, held her hands in surrender, and walked inside. She went in on a hushed whisper, the wind at her back, and crossed through the stacks—up and down them until she came to the circular center of the room. The door might be open, but the building was empty.

She was thinking of Magic and what the Fates had said—how there was more than one axis in the world—and that's when she heard it. A rustling from one of the shelves filled with a section of yellowing scrolls.

She crossed to it, her fingers hovering over the scroll. It was at the bottom of the pile, and she hesitated. It had been an uncomfortable experience when the scroll had gone into her before—or she into it. She wasn't particularly looking forward to repeating it. Taking a deep breath, she reached and, gingerly, like she was attempting to pick up a ladybug, she scooped the scroll and tugged it out. Unrolling it with as much precision and care as possible, she read the words written down the page.

Rules of Magies

Item One:

DO NOT LET THE MAGICS CROSS PATHS WITH ONE ANOTHER

Item Two:

DO NOT LET THEM SEPARATE FROM THEIR SELVES OR BOND WITH
ANOTHER

Item Three:

DO NOT LET THE WATCHER OUT

Aline read the rules, finding herself more and more confused.
A rustling came from the door, so she quickly rolled the scroll
back up and slid it into the stacks. She smelled the perfume—
lilac and jasmine—and turned to find Florence walking beyond
the open windows in the garden.

"I do not think Magic would come here," she said. "He prefers the shadows to the light."

"I must have misunderstood him, then," Aline said, flashing her best the-customer-is-always-right smile. "I thought he
wanted to meet at the house. Maybe . . . maybe he meant his
house?"

She was thinking on her feet—or attempting, seeing as Florence had sent her heart racing and her skin flushing. Like a child
sneaking into the pantry for a cookie before supper, but she was
not a child and Florence was not her guardian.

"His house is in the shadows," Florence said, flashing her serene smile that made the skin crawl at the back of Aline's neck.

"Ah, well then."

Florence studied her. "There is something here that might help you, though."

Aline raised her brows. "Oh?"

"Your power, the scrolls are always willing to help when offered a price. I could help you give a little to take a little."

"Thanks, but I think I'll pass," Aline said, the idea of giving Florence any of her power leaving her skin flushing.

"Perhaps for now, but the time may come." Then she turned with the swishing of her long navy skirt and sauntered into the garden beyond.

Aline looked down at the nearest roll of scrolls, snorting. The woman had secrets sewn into the edges of her smile. As if Aline would ever take her advice.

"She's not wrong."

Aline jumped at the sound of the now-familiar voice, savoring how it sent her pulse scrambling. Magic shifted from the shadow beyond her and crossed to where she stood.

"How can anyone use this House of Knowledge if it's never empty?"

"I don't count," Magic said, laughing. "I'm in the pages."

She thought back to seeing him in the first one and wondered how true that was. "How can you be there and here?"

"I am a little fragmented, I suppose. Parts of me left behind in different spaces."

Aline flushed, thinking of how damaged she had always felt. "Yet you are here now."

"Of course. I said I would be."

He reached for her hand, and as soon as he was holding hers, everything in her settled.

"So, what, do you want to pick a scroll, lay it on the floor, hold hands, wink, double blink, and jump?"

He stared at her like she had grown a second head. "Is that how you think my magic works?"

"No, it's how the wonderful world of Mary Poppins works."

Magic let out a sound that could have been a growl or a grumble; either way it reverberated down her spine and into her bones, where she laughed around it.

"We do something easier."

"Oh yeah?"

"Yeah."

He crossed to her, standing directly in front of her, so close she could feel his breath fan across her cheeks. "Give me your hands and close your eyes."

"So it *is* like Mary Poppins," Aline said, her voice coming out breathless.

"Close your eyes," he said, an edge of amusement and something deeper, a current of need, beneath the words.

She did as he suggested, taking his hands and fighting the rush of energy that flooded in. She wanted to open her eyes and make sure her feet were still on the ground, so heady was the feeling.

"Now," he said, his voice soft, "call the scroll we need."

"How do I know which one—"

"The Fates gave you a key, a word but still a key."

Aline didn't think, she simply sighed his name. "Magic."

There was a rustling, a strong wind, and a rumble calling through the library. She heard Florence's voice cry out from the garden, thought she heard the Crone laughing, and then the doors to the House of Knowledge slammed shut one by one. Aline's eyes flew open, and Magic's own were staring back at her, focused on her lips, his own parted in surprise. The scrolls, at least fifteen of them, had flown from their spaces in the shelves and were hovering in the air. They were shifting and changing, pulling elements and distorting them. It was exactly like what Aline's power could do when she couldn't rein it in.

She didn't want to try to rein this in.

Words shot off the pages, swirling around them like a tempest. They didn't have to step inside; the words embraced them. It was like being a computer, downloading too many files at once, and it rocked her off her heels as the words settled and took root. Magic's hands tightened in hers, keeping her grounded.

"*It's more than a story,*" Aline said to him.

She could feel the vibrations of magic as they pulsed from Magic into her, could see the ley lines as they ran beneath them like roots from an ancient tree seeking their way home. Magic himself glowed, a faint blue aura wrapped around him like a snake, before a heavy line shot from him out into the earth. A fainter line pulsed from Aline into the earth, and then lines streaked from him to her. All of Magic was connected to Aline. All of Matchstick was alive with magic.

She thought of the book *Mischief, A Beginner's Guide.* Of how she read it and magic coursed into her. How inside the scrolls magic was waiting.

"It's not just me," he said, his voice shaking. "There are many of us."

Aline could feel it—the gravitational pull to something else. It hit her in the same potent way that she was called to Magic.

A single scroll shot up from a compartment in the floor. It wove around them.

The words sang off the page. A whisper from a scroll that did not belong here. It shifted into a floating face carved from paper: a large nose, blinking eyes, and pursed mouth. It cried out in a chant of many voices, *"One by one they were born, from the magic brought by another land. Then she came along and tried to take it, but the magic was too powerful. She needed a vessel to dilute it and so she stole the most powerful witches in the land surrounding the axes and filled them with the stolen magic. They held it, waiting until the day she was ready to take the power back and claim her dominion over the land. Six axes and six Magics, beings kept hidden from the world to feed her and a promise of her rise to power."*

The face gave a silent scream and the mouth elongated before it devoured itself, chewing the paper and spitting out the fragments. They floated down around Aline and Magic.

She swallowed her shock and turned to him. The axes, they were more than other points of Magic. They were other beings like Magic.

"Oh gods," he said, his face ashen.

The truth of what the scroll revealed clung to them, and fear flooded through her. Aline couldn't see what Magic saw, but she could feel as the rage built in him. It built in her, too, a tether between them. The scrolls tumbled one by one from their places on the shelves. All the stories, all of history upending as he let out a guttural bellow.

Magic's power was bursting forth, and it was tearing apart the house.

The stone in the walls fissured around them, cracks shooting from the top corner of the building down the marble walls, fissuring into the floors. Ripples fanning out as the earth shook like it was a ball in a snow globe shaken by an unruly child.

Aline stumbled, her hand ripping from Magic's as she fell to the ground. He cursed, helped her up, keeping his arm securely wrapped around her waist, and threw up his left hand, his fingers splaying out wide like a fan. A door appeared between the stacks. Beyond it sat his cottage.

"I lost control and endangered you," he said. "We have to go," and he pushed forward—but was shielded back.

"Magic," Aline whispered. The words swirling in her. Whispers from the scrolls running through her mind, mingling with the words stamped across her mind and in her heart.

She looked between them, the tether of his blue aura comingling with her golden one. It flowed evenly from him to her, from her to him, even as the rest of the power in the room sparkled along the ley lines in this part of the world in shades of gold.

She lifted her hand, mimicking his pose, and light shifted out from the door. Her legs crumpled beneath her.

He looked down at her, his eyes darkening in fear and pain. He scooped her up, whispering her name over and over, and carried her over and through the portal, right before it shuttered behind them.

Twelve

Night sighed, looking out at Dusk, wishing for Day. Dusk was unhelpful, and a little vengeful with all the red sunsets that never seemed to shift to softer purples or grays. Dusk had always been that way, and as Night studied the ripples in the air where the worlds had splintered, he gave a shiver.

"Won't be long now."

The words were not spoken, but he heard them. Dusk, whispering them on the wind out of the earth and up to where Night held the moon.

The rip in the sky was translucent, no bigger than a feather. It was many things. A warning, change, and least, or perhaps most of all: hope.

Who would have thought hope possible?

Day would. Night thought Day would have seen something beautiful, while Night lost every bit of beauty when he lost Day.

Dusk grumbled, the sky shifting into a fiery indigo. Beneath Night, Florence paced the perimeters of the forest, searching for a way in, unable to break the barrier set by the Fates. Now those three, that was a magic Night wouldn't have minded having. Though he didn't think the rebirth they went through every millennium would have been quite as enjoyable. But still. They were free. They weren't stuck, the man in the moon to bear witness to the world, neighbor to an angry twilight.

The ripple shimmered and Night peered into Dusk, where Magic held tight to their salvation before stepping beyond the hedgerow, and once more Night wondered what price this bit of hope would eventually cost them all.

※

MAGIC AND ALINE STEPPED THROUGH THE PORTAL AND OUT OF A YEW TREE. They were not by the cottage, as Aline had intended when she shoved them through the in-between, but on the other end of the forest by the river. It took her a moment—it was distracting going from inside a room filled with scrolls that appeared to be throwing a temper tantrum to the tranquility of a forest coated in green grass, tall pines, and fat, dark-brown yew trees. The sky was clear, and the sun was out. It was Day here, and the river was rushing.

At first, Aline thought it was the wind. In Whistleblown, when a storm would build, the wind would howl softly before the leaves trembled and the branches shook. It created a rushing that never failed to fill her with a sense of calm. She loved when the skies went from blue to black, when Mother Nature got tired of sunny days and gleaming springs and decided to take a bow. Aline hated sunny days. She was able to relax in the darkness, to breathe in the rain. She might not have gills, but she had a yearning for the pain that she carried under the surface of her skin to be ripped out and washed away.

But this was not a storm. This was the river that ran at the edge of Matchstick. The one she knew from the story. It was said it carried with it a protection spell to help keep the town hidden. Aline thought that perhaps everything in the book was real but not what she had thought, and that was a terrifying idea. Magic lowered her down and she turned to ask him, and found him drooping forward, bent over at the waist, his long fingers splayed against his firm thighs—had they filled out somehow in the past few hours?

His chest was heaving. Aline opened her mouth to ask if he was all right, and a high, desolate keening rolled from him. It was animalistic, terrifying, and had Aline stepping back until she hit the side of the yew tree.

He stood, jerking upright, and yanked at the hair on his head, yelling into the current of the river.

Aline waited for what felt like a tiny eternity but could have been moments; she couldn't tell over the shaking of her legs and the pounding of her heart. Then she cleared her throat.

He turned to her, his eyes flashing. "There are others like me? How could she have lied to me for so long? And my magic doesn't even work. I couldn't open the portal. I'm trapped here."

"You aren't trapped," Aline said.

"No?" He waved a portal open in every door in the forest that surrounded them. A rooftop in New York, an overgrown forest in a country Aline couldn't name, a patio in Paris, a boat in Vienna, a restaurant in Japan. He didn't wait. He charged forward, dove to the closest entrance, and was knocked back fifteen feet onto his back.

Blood poured from the cut across his brow. He brushed it aside, and the cut healed in a matter of seconds.

"Good to know gods bleed," she said, her voice shaky as she tried for a joke.

"I'm no god," Magic told Aline. "I'm . . ." He dropped his head into his hands. "I'm not sure what I am."

The mist rose from the river, shifting closer to them. Voices whispered with it, echoes of spells and words long forgotten.

"She lied to you," Aline said, crossing to him, placing her palms on either side of his face. He raised his head and met her eyes. "I think Florence is kind of an asshole, Magic. There's no surprise there."

"But you . . ." He rubbed a hand across his sternum. "You have an idea of what we should do next."

Aline's eyes narrowed. "What makes you think that?"

He pushed up, taller now somehow, which seemed impossible. He took her hands in his. "Because I can feel it. Hear it whispering in my head, the words too fast to understand." He leaned in. "Why can I feel you, Aline Weir?"

"I don't know," she said, lifting her chin.

He exhaled and his breath fanned across her cheeks. Her knees threatened to buckle.

"We know what I can do. I find lost things. Just now, when we crossed over, it was easier for me than it's ever been. We're meant to do this together."

"I'm broken."

"You're separated."

"From the other axes?"

"From the other Magics." Aline looked down to her palm and ran it across his. "Nothing is just a story."

"We are stronger together."

She nodded.

"Where do we go, Aline Weir?" Magic asked, trust in his eyes.

"To the next axis, closest on the ley lines," she said.

He opened the portal, and she waved it free. Then Aline took one step and another, pulling Magic in after her. She didn't look back. They entered the realm between worlds with all the conviction two broken, healing souls can have.

They never saw two others follow in behind them.

Thirteen

THE FOREST MAGIC AND ALINE STEPPED INTO WAS AN OVERGROWN EXPANSE OF LAND. Humid, warm, with evergreen trees wrapping around them like a thick blanket. It was quiet, calm, serene, and terrifying. Not a sound echoed out aside from their breath, and even then it was subdued, as though caught in a vacuum and hushed away.

"Where is everyone?" Magic asked, as he looked around.

Aline shook her head, and he wrapped an arm around her. Beyond them the trees swayed, the wind whipped through the leaves . . . but it never reached them.

"Where are we?" he asked, looking down at her.

"In between."

"Beyond the hedgerow?"

She nodded.

"Ah. I told you that you were a hedge witch."

She looked up at him, her mouth twisting in a laugh. Her eyes narrowing. He was grateful to see a look other than fear or confusion on her face.

"I don't need you telling me what I am or am not," she said. "You're incredibly bossy, do you know that? I am the one who pulled us through and you're trying to talk down to me? I don't think so."

He burst out laughing; he couldn't help it. No one had made him laugh in years, and no one had ever made him want to kiss them and run away from them at the same time. The feelings were too big, too uncharted. He'd wanted others before, witches with long legs and dizzying power. He'd never, though, not once that he could recall, desired. Not like this. He wanted to ask Aline a thousand questions, to find out what she was thinking, why when she looked at him, he found his stomach trying to turn inside out even as every part of him hardened with need.

The tether to her, the incessant need to touch her: it was all-consuming. He was obsessed with her hair, how individual threads shifted when there was a breeze. Then he was jealous of the wind for touching it.

There was no logic in how he craved her, only instinct and something deeper.

"My apologies," he said. "It's only, the in-between. I don't know anyone else who can travel there. I certainly cannot. It's an intoxicating power. I assume you're pleased."

"Pleased we're stuck?" She trembled beneath his arm, and he tugged her closer, happy when she leaned into him rather than pulled away. "I don't see Dragon, and I don't see any of the spirits."

"Hmm," he said, leaning down to smell her hair. Coconut

and mint. "Magic is breaking apart. Perhaps it affects here as well?"

She looked up at him, and he swallowed as heat flooded through his veins. His eyes fell to her full, Cupid's bow mouth. He wanted to kiss the bow, and then press a finger to her full bottom lip. To lay her down on the hard earth beneath their feet and lick a trail from her collarbone to the inside of her thigh.

"You can't look at me like that," she said, her voice shaking.

He nodded. She was right. They shouldn't linger here; they had much to do and if he let himself, he would never be able to stop touching her. He tore his gaze from hers and looked up, to the path before them.

"What do we do, then?"

"We keep walking," she said.

He nodded and together they continued forward, one step at a time, as the tension between them rose and the land ahead seemed endless.

＊＊＊

Dragon was worried. She'd been following Aline and Magic for some time, and they still didn't seem to realize how to exit the land of ghosts. It wasn't safe for Dragon to be following them. She wasn't meant to be on the ley lines, or anywhere near the axes. It was like placing a hammer close to a bell that wanted to ring. She'd shown Aline enough over the years, as had the Fates, that she should have found her way out. But Aline seemed . . . distracted.

Men.

No matter. Dragon would help Aline cross over, so they didn't accidentally *cross on*. The in-between was not a place to linger, and while they didn't seem to realize it, Magic and Aline had been inside it for days. So much longer than Aline had ever been inside it before. Dragon worried Magic's power was affecting her friend. Spirit time did not move in a linear line, and they were losing minutes of their lives by the second.

If she could only make them see her, it would all go so much easier, but the Fates' curses were like candles in the wind. You knew there was a light, but it wouldn't stay lit.

Dragon stood in the forest, careful not to touch the trees and find herself stuck to the sap or let the leaves fall onto her scalp and burn off her hair. This forest was as disrupted as the natural world. It was reshaping, made from memories of the countless ghosts that had passed through. It held all their emotions and pain and suffering.

"They're going to stay on this path until the end of Time," Dragon muttered, as she blew out an irritated breath. She looked at the rocks beneath her feet and thought of how they could rip into the fabric of the in-between when thrown. A thing Dragon studiously avoided.

Until now. She might not be able to guide her friend per usual, but she could show her the way.

Grinning, Dragon curtseyed to herself, squatted down, and picked up the biggest stone—one that was the size of her fist. Then she reached her thin arm high over her head and brought it down, releasing the rock as she did, watching as it soared through the skies and smacked into the earth just ahead of Magic and Aline.

⸎

ALINE AND MAGIC CLUNG TO EACH OTHER AS THEY FELL OUT OF THE SKY AND DROPPED INTO THE MULTILAYERED LEAVES INSIDE

A HUMID, VAST FOREST. Magic climbed his way up first, dusting himself off and pulling up Aline. After he checked her over, they both looked around, then let out a surprised laugh and hugged. And hugged. *And hugged.* Yet, oddly, they weren't aware of how attached they were. At least not from Esther's perspective. The two were as drawn to one another as any pair of magnets could be, and they fought it because they didn't yet understand. Esther understood, much as she knew this land, though she was not nearly as fond of it as she was the female witch who had *finally* exited the in-between.

That could be because she wasn't overly fond of the being who ruled over the rain forest Aline had brought them to—or the ley lines the creature lived on.

As Aline and Magic held hands and moved deeper into the forest, using their power to slice back overgrown banana leaves and vines and branches, they began to sag. Their shoulders drooping, hands flexing in pain, bodies wearing out. It wouldn't be long before they were depleted, not realizing what this sanctuary was or that they had spent two weeks in the in-between and had utterly exhausted their bones.

"You're going about this the wrong way," Esther finally said, speaking up from behind a wide evergreen, in case Magic should try and pitch her into the air again.

"Esther?" Aline asked, her jaw dropping. She moved to reach for her, and Magic tugged her back to him.

"She can't be here," he said. "She's not real."

"I'm realer than you," she said, rolling her eyes. He was *so* dramatic. "And I am most certainly here. I followed you in from the portal. You were foolish leaving it open like that."

"I didn't leave it open."

"Did so."

"Did not."

Aline snorted, and Esther smiled. "Don't worry, it's closed. Now. But still."

"What do you mean, we're going about this the wrong way?" Aline asked, shooting Magic a look that had him growling, but quietly. "And how is it closed now?"

"It timed out, and, well, you don't feel it?" Esther held out a hand, and a light drizzle hit her fingertips. "That's more than water from the sky."

Magic let out a hiss, comprehension causing his lip to curl. "Pocketing potion."

Esther nodded.

"What's a pocketing potion?" Aline asked, looking up at the sky, a few drops falling across the freckles on her nose.

"It pockets your power," Esther said. "A potion made for protecting the source here."

"Source?" Aline asked, looking at Magic. "As in a magical one?"

"As in an axis."

"How come it's not affecting you?" Magic asked Esther, his gaze narrowing.

"Who said it wasn't?" she replied, studying a thick vine in front of her. "I'm not the one, however, using my power like currency ready to be snatched. The two of you are worse than tourists who put all their coin in their backpacks with wide zippers and then pitch a fit when they discover they've had their pockets picked."

A slithering came from overhead, and Esther looked up to see a seven-foot-long lizard inching along a branch. She booked it over to Aline. "We need to get to the bridge. Now."

"Bridge?"

A single cry of high-pitched squealing sounded, and Aline jumped. It was followed by another, then a squeak, and finally a series of barking calls that had the hair on her forearms rising at attention.

"What *is* that?" Aline whispered, turning wide eyes to Esther.

A movement pierced the air, a tiny body flying across one branch to another, skittering like a spider on speed. The creature came to a halt, letting out a high screech. A tiny face with hair like one of the Beatles, mop-top and shaggy, and black ears that should have belonged on a bat peered down at all three of them.

"Toque macaques," Magic said, his brows lifting. He raised a hand. "Cute little—"

"Don't," Esther said, with such conviction that he dropped his hand. The monkey turned toward Esther, slow and methodical in its movements. It threw back its head and laughed before snapping its blackened teeth at them.

"Run," Esther said, not taking her eyes off the monkey as she gave lead to the chase, taking off in a sprint.

A rain forest is not a paved path. It is a lush, wet, beautiful bog of a land, fenced in by foliage. For every inch of movement they made, they were pushed back three more by broad, scaly, and needle-ridden leaves. Biomass roped around them like thick constricting vines, and still the monkeys overhead howled in their high-pitched and barking tones, pursuing and taunting them.

"This is ridiculous," Aline muttered as she shoved away a slick, flat, wide leaf with square edging where it cut into her face. "We survived the never-ending road in the in-between only to become dinner for those tiny little devils."

"Not devils, harvesters," Esther said, pausing to look over

her shoulder at Magic tending to the scrape on Aline's cheek before she ducked beneath the biomass vines. "There."

Up ahead, about twenty feet, was a bridge. Esther squinted at it, relieved to see it was the same as it ever was. A rope bridge, with sturdy wooden planks bound together, leading to one tree, where it formed a platform, before leading onto another, and another, until, she knew, ending at a tree house that was more tree than house and hid a cave of power far beneath it.

The tree house did not like being noticed. The roots beneath the home widened and grew, and the portion of tree on top of the house, sporting a rather large and solid Ipe tree covered in the most luscious rose-shaded flowers Aline had ever seen, moaned as it swayed.

Tucked between the two halves of the tree was a square house that could almost be labeled ranch-style, if not for the moss covering it or the way it moved with the tree as though part of an extension of it and not a building built into it.

Suddenly, as they stared, the tree house split into four versions of itself, two on top and two on the sides. The monkeys' calls grew and the path before them became overgrown with leaves and branches, closing in on them.

Esther sighed in irritation; of course the house was using duplication and elemental magic to confuse them. Juvenile of it, really.

She reached her arms up and sought the wind that was being held back on the other side of the rain forest, as though a wall forced it away. She yanked and, in a long, steady swoop, drew it to her. As she did, she realized her mistake. This was no ordinary wind. It was a spirit, and it would mark Aline like a homing beacon.

"*Go,*" she said, as the wind crushed into the forest. It broke up the leaves barring the path, and Aline took off running, with Magic behind her, casting surreptitious glances over his shoulder as he tried to block anything that might reach Aline.

"Bloody fool," Esther said with a shake of her head. Then she was racing behind them, navigating the bridge, noting the smell of pungent incense that soothed something deep inside her soul, and keeping her eyes out for the one who already knew they were there. Who would be waiting. Possibly panting in anticipation. Esther let out a huff and sought the skies with her eyes as the spirit wind closed in.

The restless dead swarmed overhead like a storm preparing to break wide open.

"I don't know how to get in there," Aline cried, as the tree house shifted form again, new walls and doors shooting up.

"Don't trust your eyes," Esther said. "Keep moving, and whatever you do, don't stop."

The group circled two tree-stump platforms that rose from the ground as the diminutive monkeys raced overhead, darting down to tug at their hair, bark and cackle in their ears. Aline shrieked back at them and batted at her face. Magic glowered as though his surly manner could scare half-dead monkeys away. Creatures that lived neither in this realm nor the other. Who only had one job and focus and could not be tempted away from it by anyone other than their guardian.

Finally, they reached the edge of the house, right as the storm broke.

Rain, spirit, and snow mingled and dove for them. Aline let out a terrified scream as the creatures seeking relief swarmed her and Magic tried to shield her.

Esther studied the house, found the green battered door unable to hide behind the thick layer of moss and subterfuge and sent her intention ahead. Her power shoved the door open, and she threw up both hands, pulling the purest part of the wind forward and tossing Magic and Aline safely inside.

She stood outside, the wind howling at her back, the spirits and elements raining on her, monkeys closing in.

"Esther?" Aline asked, brushing bits of twig and leaf and wet from her hair, scrubbing the scratches on her face. She was shaking like she'd been in the eye of a hurricane. "What are you doing? *Get in here.*" Her friend reached out, her hand nearing the entryway.

"Oh, sweet Aline," Esther said, flashing a wistful smile. "This can no longer be my fight."

A loud thumping came from inside the house that was more hut than home. A being—not quite either female or male—with eyes as deep as the seas and cold as an iceberg clamored forward. They leaned heavily on their cane, tracking the two strangers attempting to invade the home.

Finally, their eyes shifted to Esther, who stood outside the house, ignoring the monkeys and the unruly elements that swooped up and down behind her, closing in as though they had all the time in the world to topple their prey.

"Ah," the being said, the voice deep and ancient. Something that could have been called sadness or disappointment flashed across their smooth face. "So she got to you like I warned."

Esther sniffed, brushing at her pants and rolling out her neck. Oh, how she hated being wrong. "Now is not the time to gloat, or to ask for amends, though perhaps I have a few to be made." She glanced from Aline to Magic and back to the being. "They need your help. Not quite like us, they are special, with their bond . . . and, well, perhaps stranger things have saved worlds before."

The creature stared back at Esther, and a thousand memories attempted to flood in, to overtake her will, but they danced just out of distance behind their eyes. Finally, the creature released her gaze and turned to the two standing inside the home.

"I am Magic the Third. You must be Magic the First and this must be your witch. Come in, come in. If we are very lucky, the Supreme Witch won't strike us all dead before my monkeys fail to devour our dear Esther."

Then the door to the hut, one made of wood and twine and magic and blood and bone, was slamming shut, and Esther was on the outside. Where she belonged. Now.

She threw her head back and let loose an uproarious laugh, then spread her arms wide and leaned back, falling fast and far down from the bridge, away from the monkeys, into the river deep that waited below.

Fourteen

ALINE STOOD INSIDE THE HUT THAT LOOKED NOTHING LIKE IT DID ON THE OUTSIDE. It was filled with lace doilies and curtains and rocking chairs, an axe and a wall of sharp knives, mechanical clocks, and piles and piles of books. She was frozen for half a second, her heart pounding in her chest, ticking off the moments, before she rushed for the door. The floor slick beneath her feet, the air sweet and thick with humidity, it coated her but didn't stop her. Aline leapt toward the door as though diving though a marshy water, her hands gripping the sides of the doorframe as she landed in front of it.

"Esther!" she called to her friend, and threw the door open. The woman was gone, as were the terrifying monkeys. Aline swirled to face the creature that called itself Magic the Third.

"Where is she, you sniveling toad?" she said, lacing venom through her words.

Magic the Third choked for a moment before letting out a harsh laugh. "You are impressive, but your insults could use some work. You can call me Three, and that's an impressive spell trying to poison me with your own voice. I've not had that one before." He held his hand out, and Aline heard the echo of her words as he pulled them from his throat into his palm, shook them onto a piece of parchment, and rolled them up into a scroll.

"I . . ." She hadn't realized what she'd done. She looked back to Magic, whose brows were raised.

Three looked between the two of them. "Yes, you're a clever one, and your one is a two. Esther is fine. Or as fine as she can be now that she's a shade. Should have listened to me, but she's too much of a rebel. Unlike that one," Three said, pointing at Magic. "He's too much of an obey-and-go-along, or was until you came and changed the landscape. As for me? I'm the ultimate observer." He sat down in the smallest rocker, picking up a basket of lace and magically sewing the pieces together, melting the ends with his fingertips and suturing them into one. "What a lot we are."

"I don't understand," Aline said, crossing to the other side of the hut and looking down into the land beneath them. Her teeth were chattering, and she had to wrap her arms around herself to keep from falling apart.

"Esther is a ghost," Magic said, leaning against the side of the tree hut, his beautiful face devoid of expression.

Aline gave a bark of laughter. "Sure."

When neither Three nor Magic responded, Aline turned to face them. "Wait. She is?"

Three scoffed, grabbing a new sliver of lace from the wicker basket by his feet. "No, she is not."

"Oh, good," Aline said, with a small sigh of relief.

"She's more than a ghost."

"More?" Aline said.

"She is the reason the stars shifted, and the trees lost their leaves?" Magic asked.

"That wasn't Esther's fault," Three said, glancing over to Aline.

"Absolutely not," Esther said, from outside the window. Aline hurried over and found the ghost of the witch hovering in the air.

"Can . . . can you fly?" Aline asked, her voice rising on the last note.

"Witches cannot," Magic said.

"No, but Magics can do all manner of things," Esther said, with a gentle smile. "But what you're seeing is something you already know. You just would rather not."

"Magics?" Aline stared deep into Esther's deep-brown eyes with the bits of silver. She thought of how her friend had never touched her. How she wasn't affected by the rain or the monkeys. How she had met Aline in a cemetery. Aline bit back a sob. She didn't want it to be true. She didn't want her only friends to be impossible.

"You're a ghost of a Magic," she said, and Esther gave a small, sad smile.

"I'm a witch who became a Magic who became a spirit," Esther said, and gave a bow while floating in the air. "According to the laws of aviation, I should be in a grave and not capable of flight or haunting. But I, as I'm sure you've discovered, lovely Aline, do not care what others deem impossible."

"How is a Magic a ghost?" Aline said, and then she frowned. "Do *you* know where Dragon is?"

Esther shook her head. "I wish I did."

"Who or what is guarding your axis?" Magic asked, his arms still crossed.

"You might as well come in," Three said to Esther, waving the lace like a white flag.

"Or you could come out."

Three shot Esther an impatient glare.

"*I'm* not going anywhere."

"Scaredy-cat."

"Smart being."

"Fine," Esther said. "I'll pull up some air, but I'm staying out here. I'm free, and even if it's in noncorporeal form, I prefer the fresh breeze."

"Can you even taste the breeze?" Magic asked, his tone dry, his eyes sharp. "Or do the other spirits taint it?" He had moved closer to Aline as Three and Esther were talking. Aline hadn't realized he'd done it, but now he flanked her, as though everything else but him were the threat.

"I can remember it best, when I'm in it," Esther said, as the wind kicked up, swirling around her, a low moan filling the land around them.

"You know I hate that noise," Three said, shaking his head.

"How long has it been since you were in it?" Magic asked. "In this reality, not between them?"

Esther licked her lips. "A while."

Aline stared at the bell-bottoms and the fringe top. She'd thought Esther a bohemian witch at first, but now . . .

"Nineteen sixty-four?" Aline guessed.

"Sixty-eight," Esther replied. "I still made it to Woodstock, but it wasn't the same as it could have been."

"You're a hippie?"

"I am."

"Where were you?"

"On my axis, of course."

"Which was?"

Esther gave a little wave at her outfit. "The real rock that is magicked into pretending to be Alcatraz, outside of San Francisco."

"*Alcatraz* isn't real?"

"It is, and it isn't."

"I don't understand."

"It's real, but not really where people think it is."

"Which is why no one ever escaped," Three said. "Those who came close found themselves climbing down a volcano in the middle of a remote island uninhabited by humans. Bad luck for all."

"There are many places in the world that aren't where humans think they belong," Esther explained.

"I think I need to sit," Aline said, lowering herself to the floor. Magic waved a cushion over before Aline hit the ground. She put her head between her knees.

"You know magic is real," Magic said to her, crouching beside her, his voice gruff. "I'm real."

"Sure, but this is more than helping ghosts move on. It's one thing to try and find Dragon, to be told we have to stop the disrupting magic. It's something else to realize nothing is what I thought."

"Everything is topsy-turvy," Esther said, nodding.

"And the world is falling apart and you have to save it,"

Three said, and Aline rolled her cheek to her knee to face Magic as he turned sharply in Three's direction.

"Not helpful?" he hissed the words at Three.

"Way to go, Three," Esther said.

Aline lifted her face. "We can't save the world. This is madness. How can we realign the axis when I can't even find Dragon?" Her eyes filled, and she wrapped her arms tighter around herself. Magic sat in front of her, his arms cocooning her.

"You are not alone."

Aline pressed her fingers to the bridge of her nose and pinched. "It's all so insane."

"That's Magic," Three said. "Insane and true: the world is both of those things. Or it was. It's falling apart and soon it will be threads of time and nothing else. Not even those monkeys will remain."

"I think you're unhinged," Magic said, lifting a brow.

"I'm not," Three said, leaning away, their face contorting into insult. "I may be a little eccentric, but I'm fully hinged." They sighed and leaned into the desk behind them. "Let me tell you a story that is more than a story. One I think will help you with where to go next, if not how to do the impossible."

THE TALE OF THE WITCH & THE WATCHER

Family is a funny sort of magic. It's elemental because people are *made up* of the elements. Six, in fact. Around 99 percent of the human body is made up of six simple but complex elements: carbon, calcium, hydrogen, nitrogen, oxygen, and phosphorus. Those elements work together...like a family.

Yet family is often chaotic and unruly, but when one is lucky, it can go very, very right. Love, support, acceptance, all unconditional and completing. So often, however, one is unlucky in magic and in family. Such was the case for a young witch who crossed through the veil after the Fates with her father holding her hand, and her dreams guiding her footsteps.

Her name was Supreme and she was the most powerful witch to enter the world, second only to her father, who was more an observer than an action-oriented witch. They had left their realm in search of a stronger foothold, of new and clean magic. Of a place they could claim as their own.

The land they found was lush and untapped. They were able to build a settlement of huts and homes, and soon other witches crossed over through the rip in the world where they entered. These people came too late, for they could not absorb as much power as the Supreme Witch and her Watcher father, who had tried to gobble up all they could.

They decided to host the others because no one needed a ruler. No one wanted a ruler.

"We can provide you with safety and crops," her father, the Watcher, would explain. He was a tall man, built like a mug of ale, round and sturdy...and filled with a potent power. "Think of it as a community. We are all in this together. No one's voice is stronger or more important than another."

Their settlement was primitive at first, but it grew, and the people who came to stay flourished. They did not see how the words he spoke were poisoned with lies.

The Supreme Witch did. But she was his daughter, and so even knowing how and who he was, she tried to gain his favor. For she wanted nothing more in the world than to be seen by him and recognized for the talent she was. The equal she was.

As the skies filled with rain, she stood beneath a willow tree and called to him. "Father, I have grown the east side of the forest so the trees drop bushels of apples that can allow you to control your opponent's thoughts." Her father merely grunted and went back to training a group of men on how to control the rain.

One week after her father complained of the animals being too slow, she rode atop a blue mustang and waved to him. "Father, I have raised horses that can run as fast as a rushing cloud before a rainstorm." She took off with the speed of the forgotten gods, but when she looked back, he had returned to helping a different group of men plant in the shrunken garden on the east side.

A month later, she came to him, carrying a basket overflowing with ripened fruit. "Look, Father, I have created a fig tree that will never die, that will provide us fruit all year round. I can heal all the gardens and charm them to do this."

Her father barely batted an eye before he turned his attention to one of the most recent arrivals, a young man no older than Supreme whom he was training for battle. She watched as he took the boy under his tutelage, teaching him all there was of the world that he knew, and rather than give up, Supreme doubled her efforts. She spent six months working methodically from morning to night, nearly losing her sight in the process, only to find victory in the end.

Elated, she brought him the best news she could think to carry.

"Father, I have spent many cycles of the moon harvesting the tide. I now can control the water. Should anyone try to attack us, I will wash them to sea. I have called to the sun and can control when it goes to sleep and when it rises and can burn our enemies' eyes out."

Her father did not reply. Nothing she did was ever worthwhile to him. Until one evening when her father brought his apprentice to her.

"Daughter," he said, "you will join this witch in hand-fasting, and you will give him your magic so he may help me conquer lands beyond this one. This is how you will earn your keep."

At his words, the sea beyond them rustled and rushed, and tears flooded the Supreme Witch's eyes and tracked down her face, but her father did not see. He, the one who they called the Watcher, had never seen her, his daughter. He'd never tried.

The Supreme Witch left the village that night. She took off for the farthest end of the world, following the lines of magic as she went. When she reached Alexandria, she found a pocket of magic, one too potent for her to tap into without it destroying part of her. Elemental magic in this land was different from where they came from. It carried a cost when taken in. It could grant long life and power, but for a witch from their realm, it overwhelmed and would cause immediate decay.

The Supreme Witch had grown strong in her skills, trying as she might to turn her father's attention and win his praise. To affirm her worth. She did not, however, know how to harvest such a magic as the one in this part of the land without paying a heavy price.

She did what she had learned to do best. She took to studying in the library in the small Egyptian town, reading all she could on magic and the world that was forming beyond them. She soaked in the words, bathed in the knowledge, and when she was close to giving up, found one scroll written...by a creature even Time itself had forgotten.

"To harness Magic, one must beget Magic. Any container will not do, for the rarest of jewels desire the rarest of storage. A witch can hold magic, and with enough story Magic, Magic may hold the witch."

This creature, who was worse than the Fates when it came to forever meddling with all the worlds and all the realms, left instructions. A recipe for disaster.

To hold Magic, pour it in the proper living vessel. It will spread out from that vessel and connect to whatever ties are bound to it. Land, other people, places. Over time it will dilute so that it may be used by others to help make the world better, fuller of love and peace and prosperity.

The Supreme Witch stole the scroll. She slipped it under her robe and went in search of a witch who might serve as the perfect vessel. She did not want peace or love for the people of the world. No. She wanted power.

Ironic, since she did not consider that what she sought to do was the very thing her father had asked of her.

The mirror into her own soul was covered by her need for revenge and acceptance and, perhaps most of all, his love.

She would harness this new magic, let it dilute enough so she could take it for herself, and then she would show her father who she really was.

Three finished reading the story and climbed into their hammock, a large swinging bed that spanned the corner of the room. They swayed back and forth, their face troubled, eyes cloudy. Aline looked over at Magic, and how cold his face had grown.

"There are six axes and six Magics," Magic said.

Three nodded.

"The Supreme Witch used us to store it," Magic said, and his hand reached for the back of Aline's arm, brushing the skin there.

Three nodded. "She has another name, doesn't she? The witch with the gold-and-silver hair."

Aline groaned. "Florence. Of course. How could it be anyone else?"

"She has been waiting for a long time for the sign the magic was ready," Three said.

"The sign?" Aline asked, Magic's hand gripping hers so tightly she couldn't wiggle even her pinky finger.

"The Fates had to return to the Mother Tree. This cycle of life needed to come to an end."

"She killed Esther," Magic said, as though she weren't hovering nearby.

"Because Esther went looking for the Supreme Witch,"

Three said, looking over their shoulder at where she hovered in the night. "Isn't that right, dear?"

"I had to," she said. "I was tired of sitting on that godforsaken rock."

"How did you leave it?" Magic asked. "How did you break free?"

Esther smiled. "We aren't stuck. She lied to us all. We could always leave."

"I tried," Magic said. "I was locked to my forest and the town until Aline arrived and helped me."

"Cat of a different breed," Three said, before they steepled their fingers under their chiseled jaw. "What did it cost you to do it?"

Esther glared at them. "It didn't cost me anything."

Their smile grew an edge. "What did it cost those prisoners?"

Esther looked up at the sky before dropping her gaze. "I'm sorry, the rapists? It only cost them a little blood. A small sacrifice for my circle, considering their misdeeds."

"Vigilante," Three said, their voice infused with warmth.

"It was the least I could do, considering their actions."

Three shrugged a shoulder. "You had to know it wasn't going to go the way you wanted."

Esther scoffed, the wind whipping up behind her. "If we do nothing, and we know we could do something, we're nearly as bad as the problem. It is always worth it to try, Three."

"I'm still not killing my monkeys to escape," Three said, and shifted their skirt as they stood.

"Oh, the monkeys," Aline said, shivering. She stared at the full skirt and then back up at their face. "Are you . . ." Aline grimaced. "I'm sorry, that was rude."

"What was?"

"What I was going to ask."

Three grinned. "Don't let that stop you. If we're to help one another, which I hope we are, we might as well speak freely."

"Even if I'll sound like a jerk?"

"Oh, especially then. Honesty isn't often dressed in pretty clothes." Three swished their skirt.

Esther let out a snort of a laugh from where she floated on the other side of the window.

"Are you . . . that is, Esther is female, and Magic is male. I mean, I assume Magic is."

Magic nodded.

"But you." Aline cleared her throat. "Do you have pronouns?"

"You want to know what to call me?" Three said. "We're Magic. We are everything."

Aline cocked her head. "I still don't understand. Are you all gendered? If you're magic, do you need to be?"

"I chose to be female once I took the magic in," Esther said. "I found it gave me a better way to serve as a conduit for my power, and to help other women—which throughout the eras has been beneficial. No one suspected a long-haired hippie or a prairie farmer capable of striking a killing blow to the men who tried to overpower women, and any gender they didn't understand."

"Oh," Aline said, digesting the information, finding she was running out of space to process things. Esther likely had killed many people in the name of justice. Then not long ago, Florence killed Esther.

"And Florence is the Supreme Witch, and she wants to kill you all." She turned and looked at Magic. Her Magic. "But not you?"

"I was what Florence wanted," Magic said, his eyes tracking Aline. He reached out and shifted her, so she was standing upright. She hadn't realized she was listing to the side, about to topple over. "You're worn thin, Aline."

"You are different," Esther said, rubbing her nose, studying Magic. "You've been changing. Growing."

Magic's eyes stayed on Aline, and she found herself blushing at the intensity there.

"We choose," Three said. "I have never had another being to choose for. The monkeys don't care, and I certainly don't want to join their brethren. So, I'm simply me. Three."

"Okay." Aline nodded. "Magic the First, Third, and Esther."

"Magic the Fourth," she said, a faint smile not reaching her eyes. "There are three still out there."

Three reached over for a sliver of bark and plucked it from their hut. They used it to tap a soothing tune against the desk. "Aye. Three to save before the Supreme one finds them and does to them what she did to Esther."

"How did she even manage to kill a Magic?" Aline asked.

"She is the Supreme Witch," Three said, "and she can kill that which she made."

"She is Florence the deceiver," Esther said, her eyes flitting to Magic and the way his face contorted with anger.

"Florence," Aline whispered, as Magic stood up and threw the door open and disappeared outside. "She asked me to come."

The room sank back into silence.

"Should I go after him?" Aline asked, her gaze seeking into the setting sun.

"Not unless you want to get obliterated," Three said. "It's a lot to process, and he's not even dead. Yet."

"He won't hurt Aline," Esther said, tilting her head. "She means more to him than the worlds ever will. But I do think even Magic needs time to make sense of the discovery that everything he believed is suddenly untrue."

Fifteen

✳

FLORENCE WAS PISSED. In the blink of an eye her beloved House of Knowledge had been turned upside down—literally, the whole building was flipped on its ass—and her Magic and his . . . ugh, witch, were gone. Worse, it was all her fault. Florence shouldn't have brought Aline Weir here. The Fates had blessed the child, something they had not done in a millennium, and because of it, Aline was a true hedge. She could travel beyond the hedgerow, she could walk with ghosts, and she drew them to her and to Matchstick like a desert seeks the rain. Aline should have led Florence to Dragon, and the way to reclaim the magic; instead, Aline had thwarted her efforts.

To make aggravating matters worse, Florence couldn't access the forest at the edge of Matchstick where the Fates were tucked away. She had been trying to breach the perimeter for days. She knew down to the fibers in her hair that it was pointless. Magic and Aline had come to it only to go beyond, to leave Matchstick in search of the other Magics.

Florence knew Dragon was the only one who could locate them. And yet. Magic and Aline had found another way.

Florence thought she had the answer, a way to restore things and give her what should have been hers. She did not like being thwarted.

She walked to the water and looked in, seeing her reflection stare back. The price of a power such as hers was that Florence no longer knew who she was until she looked in the water. Then she saw the girl she had been. However, time was eating at her, and being alone in her truth for so long had her doubting herself. Her skin was sallow and her eyes far too sunken. Her frown was pronounced, tugging permanently at the edges of the once-smooth skin around her mouth.

She failed to hold all the magic of the axes the first time she tried. Like water into wine, the power was diluted enough now for her to take it in. And yet.

She ran a hand through her hair and walked from the forest into the lanes that led to the center of Matchstick. She would have to leave if she was going to stop them, and she'd have to leave tonight. The race was on, and Florence couldn't let any of the Magics go. They were *all* hers, and it was time they returned to where they belonged. No matter the cost.

"You won't know what hits you when it comes," she said, projecting her voice toward the lines only she could see in the sky that delineated Sun, Moon, and Dusk. Then she smiled, slow and serene, and let down her hair, lifting her hands and tugging the threads of silver and gold from it—a shifting form rising into the air as her hair shifted from spun color to a deep brown.

She whispered to the freed strands as they wavered on their own, a bit of magic shimmering beneath the night, before she looked back up at the stars.

"Let's see which one of them dies first."

⫸

MAGIC PRESSED AGAINST THE ROPED RAILING ON THE WALKING BRIDGE IN THE MIDDLE OF A RAIN FOREST. He was in the center of what he knew to be Bali, trying not to burn the fibers down with the heat emanating off him. He knew where he was, could feel the location like there was a beacon inside of him pointing him in the right direction. The direction of a magic, not unlike the magic that flowed in his veins. But he wasn't controlling his abilities as he usually could, which was terrifying. A fire had lit inside him when Aline started shaking, as the reality of what lay ahead of them settled in, and when Three had said what Magic had been trying like hell to forget—that Florence was responsible, that Magic himself had been her pawn—the blaze erupted.

Magic was made of sparks. Of stars and pieces of matter. Atoms and air. He was losing his grasp on each of them.

"You are going to have to get a handle on that, or you'll burn the whole place to the ground," Esther said, as she slipped over the railing to stand just downwind from him. "You, Three, and I can survive it, but with the state of our hedge witch, she'd pop through the veil, and we'd never see her again."

"I should have thrown you out of the stratosphere," he growled, not bothering to look over at her.

"You didn't." Esther studied him. "You also didn't tell her I was more spirit than witch."

"You were never a witch."

"Of course I was. Much like you."

Magic squinted out into the rain forest, sweat dripping from his brow.

"I couldn't remember either, until after. Then everything was clear . . . and lonely. Three knows too much, but that's because Florence made a poor choice in filling a clairvoyant with her power. Three is made of senses and emotions. I was an easier target."

"What were you?" Magic asked, his voice puffing out from between his clenched jaw.

"I was a solitary witch. Easy to get alone and prey on."

"And Aline?"

"You really don't know?"

"If she's not a hedge?" He shook his head. "If I don't understand, I can't protect her."

"If you don't get your chakras together you can't help anyone. Your erratic energy will implode her. Or she'll implode you."

"What does that mean?"

"I mean *pull it together,* First."

He cast her the briefest of glances. "I'm trying."

"Bah. You're grieving. You loved that devil called Flo." She stretched her neck from side to side. "The Supreme Witch always did favor you."

Sparks ignited from beneath his knuckles, and Esther stepped closer. "You're doing it again." She studied him, as though she were making up her mind. Finally, she said, "Inhale a long, slow breath. Imagine Aline's kind and vulnerable face, her sweet Cupid's bow of a mouth, the untamed freckles along her nose, her trusting eyes. Exhale that rage you're bubbling over with, send it down into the river deep, where it can harm none and where it will keep."

Magic hated being told what to do . . . but as he considered how his power could erupt and that there might even be a sliver of possibility it could harm Aline, he forgot how to breathe entirely.

Desperate, he listened to the ghost, and as he forced an exhale, the fire inside shifted him from furnace to blaze, and down to a flickering flame. He turned to look at Esther, allowed himself to see beyond the dated clothes to the power she had been. He should have realized it before. What she truly was.

Her hair never quite settled, floating around her head like a halo. Her eyes were too bright for a spirit, too knowing. She moved like she was trapped underwater, but she was still able to make her way through the world like a manifested being. She was no simple spirit. Esther was a true magic and sage.

"What is Aline, Esther?"

"You can't unknow if I tell you."

"I don't care."

Esther smiled. "You will, in the end. Too much. Both of you."

She slipped over the ledge and floated above the river that rushed beneath them. "She is both hedge and hereditary," she said, tapping off her fingers. "Adopted daughter of the Fates. Beloved friend of an impossible being. She is loved, but she does not know it, and her powers are theirs and not theirs. Hers and not hers."

"You're purposefully being vague."

Esther smiled, and he did not like the joy in it. "I thought you would have figured it out by now. All-knowing Magic."

"Spit it out, witch."

"Aline Weir is a daughter of Fortuna's Wheel."

He blinked, and his eyes narrowed.

"You understand what this means."

His jaw had turned to granite. "She is the daughter of two unhappy humans."

"She was born one way, and now has evolved into another. Blessed by the Fates. She carries the magic of their line, of her own, and . . . more."

"What's the more?"

Esther leaned in, but there was a shout from inside the hut. A high-pitched shriek that preceded the tree house shaking and shifting to reform itself again in protection.

She and Magic took off running at the same time. He passed through her and shook off her surprised shiver as he reached the door to the hut and blasted it off the handles. Darkness cloaked the inside of the home and extended out beyond it. Lightning cracked in the distance. Three held their arms over Aline, encasing them both in a protective glow of light.

"Seems like you've got a piggyback," Three said, as the contents of the hut—small bed, makeshift lamps, books and books and books, table, chair, plate, and lace and cups—flew around the room like a cyclone thrown off-kilter. Magic stepped into the room and ducked to avoid being smacked in the face by a hunk of hard cheese.

"Made that on my own," Three said, watching it fly out the window. "Damn good, and a terrible thing to waste."

"Florence?" Aline asked, from beneath the arms of Three.

"Not in the flesh, though likely of her influence," Three said. "*She* would have announced herself by now."

"What is it, then?" Magic asked, looking around.

"Madness," Esther said, slipping into the room.

"Madness?" Aline asked, looking around for a person or being.

"It's what remains when a Magic is broken. The cost. When you harm someone, when you wear them down to nothing, you fracture them. We are already splintered, so when she breaks us, the broken bits form into a true Madness. One she controls."

"How?" Magic asked.

"She spins it into her hair."

"The silver and cream," Aline said. "I thought it undulated, when she was in the bookstore for a moment. I was certain her hair was breathing, but then thought myself a bit . . ."

"Mad?" Esther supplied.

Aline nodded. "I felt upended and cold. As though everything was wrong and there was no right."

"What do we do?" Magic asked, studying the flying objects and sliding a hand into Aline's.

Esther looked at Three. "You fight or flee."

"You know I cannot flee," Three said, an enigmatic expression crossing their lovely face.

"You can." She slid her gaze from Three to Magic, to Aline, and back again. "You just have to give something up."

"I'm not giving up anything. It's a rule, and I cannot break any of the few I made before the time is naught. My word is my bond, after all."

"I'd say we're pretty damn naught, Three," Esther said.

"Not yet," they said, with a wink.

Esther let loose a low snarl. "Then you can stay and see how long you hold out before the madness takes over and breaks you. Then you're hers, anyway."

"I have surrounded myself well, little ghost, and you know I will not leave my cave."

"She'll take it regardless."

"Perhaps I will be the one to take her," Three said, and a terrifying light shifted into their eyes.

"I do not like this."

"And I did not like you doing what you did, but we can't control one another. Control is an illusion and my power is my choice."

Esther bit her lip, but nodded.

Magic tugged Aline closer to him, their hands tethering them together, their eyes on each other. The darkness wove around them but did not manage to slip between them. Three didn't bother to look Magic's way.

"She doesn't need your protection," Three said to him, the maniacal light still in their eyes. "Though by the end of it, you'll likely need hers."

"What's in the cave?" Aline asked, her hands shaking as she brushed one over her cheeks.

"None of your concern, dear hedge." Three cocked their head. "There is a door at the back of my desk. It leads to the center of this tree. If you're as powerful as I think, you'll be able to cast it open and take your Magic and your haunts and leave this behind."

Three shifted the light around themself, tucking it in like a child snuggling deeper into a blanket. Then they marched to the center of the room, shifted a small table with a stack of books on top. They waved the table aside, threw back the corner of a rug, revealing a hole cut in the center of the floor.

Three met Esther's gaze. "I hear the stones of the isle are particularly enchanting this time of year, and far easier to navigate than the lonely mountain or nowhere land."

Three nodded to Aline, narrowed their eyes at Magic . . . before they dropped through the floor.

As soon as Three disappeared, the darkness splintered, shifting down through the hole and swirling around the three remaining witches in the room.

"Where did they go?" Aline asked, her voice rough, tinged with fear.

"To buy us time," Esther said.

"What's in the cave?" Aline whispered, her eyes on the desk Three had said to move to access a door that could lead them out. "And why wouldn't they leave with us?"

"Power," Esther said, looking down into the hole. "Because Supreme hasn't taken their madness, and they are fool enough to think they stand a chance in defeating her."

"They think they can claim the magic for themself," Magic said. "You could smell the greed on them."

"Three dark and three light ley lines," Aline said.

"Observer, my ass," Esther said, "but Three *is* light. They are just caught up in a war. There is only gray here."

Aline shifted closer to the desk, her eyes tracking the edge of the room. Inside the tree house, the wind was blowing stiff air that banged across the room. The floors creaked, and the doors bucked against their hinges. "Is it just me, or is the swirling darkness growing louder?"

"It's hungry," Esther said. "And the spirits are desperate."

"Right," Aline said, and crossed the two steps to the desk and shoved it out of the way. Behind it was a large sliver of bark that didn't feel like any tree she'd ever touched.

"What do you feed madness?" she asked.

"Sanity?" Esther offered, studying the undulating swirls of cream and silver. The silver ones drifted closer to her.

"Is . . . is the madness trying to sniff you?" Magic asked, watching the silver close in on Esther.

"You can't sniff a ghost."

"You smell of ashes and rain," Aline said.

"What?" Magic and Esther turned to her.

"It's true. Most ghosts only smell of the earth. You smell of the rain right after a storm in the summer."

"San Francisco," Esther whispered, staring at the silver swirl as it expanded out. "That's what it always smells like. Even with the chill in the air."

"There's an axis there," Magic said. "It was yours?"

Esther nodded. She held out a hand toward the madness, her fingers dancing as though she wanted to curl them inside of it. "I can almost taste it. Isn't that odd? Like saltwater taffy. Caramel, perhaps."

"Yeah, Florence didn't unleash that so you could pet it and make nicey-nice," Aline said, and Magic reached out and pulsed a beam of light into the room. The madness slunk back against the walls, splaying out across them like swirling wallpaper before it regathered into itself and shifted closer again.

"We need to cloak ourselves," Aline said, tracking all the objects in the room, looking for something to help. "What if it's not hungry in the traditional sense but is drawn to energy? Ghosts have a serious amount of kinetic energy because they're not really here and not really there. They're looking for help. Maybe it is, too."

"Do you want me to go beyond the veil?" Esther asked. "You could send me to distract it."

"No." Aline shook her head. Her stomach cramped at the idea of sending Esther beyond this world only to lose the ability to pull her back. If magic was disrupting, which it clearly was, it was now also incredibly unpredictable.

"We stay together." She wouldn't lose anyone else and couldn't risk something happening to Esther in the in-between. Not until she assessed how that space was holding up.

She turned to Magic. "Your elemental magic, can you use it to pull a small whirlwind around us so that we can sneak over to that wall right there? The bark beyond the writing desk, I think it's made of the same wood from the trees in the forest. If I'm right, it's made with it on purpose. We can use it to cross over to the in-between."

He surveyed the room, the slinking madness that looked more like a hovering storm cloud disrupted by colors not found in nature. He turned back to Aline. "You're sure?"

"Dragon isn't here. Three's gone, and whatever *that* is, I think it might be trying to eat us. It's our only chance."

He nodded and closed his eyes, lifted his hand, and beckoned to the wind. A strong breeze barreled into the hut, rattling the wooden walls, flying through the windows and open door, banging up against the madness. The madness rushed back to one corner, hovering there. Magic pulled the wind around them in a protective cyclone, and they began to move, three as one, toward the wall where Three's writing desk had been and the odd bark waited.

When they reached it, Aline ran her hands along its sides, and found the edge where the desk and the tree met. She tugged and the bark pulled away. She dropped the panel on the floor where it broke away into brittle pieces. In front of the desk stood a gaping hole. Aline looked over her shoulder at Magic.

"The tree house can't be made from a yew tree. They don't grow here, and the top half is Ipe."

"It appears you're wrong about that," he said, his voice slightly out of breath. "Magics are masters of disguise, and Three worked hard to conceal this."

Aline nodded and looked at Esther. "What did Three mean? About the henge of stones and the lonely mountain and the nowhere land?"

"It's where we can go next," Esther said, her eyes on the madness in the corner, longing shifting across her face.

"That is not a sexy storm cloud," Aline said.

"No? It . . . calls to me."

"Great," Aline said. "Then come here."

Esther looked at her in surprise. "Me?"

Aline nodded, and Esther hesitated but stepped closer. Aline waved for her to move in front of her. Aline wasn't about to let Esther get lost inside the cloud of madness. She would use her instead to guide them. The Fates said it was about Magic and Aline, but what if it was about all of them? Working together.

"I need you to be my eyes. See the place Three mentioned, the one you think is safest for us. A place a driven spirit hoping to

help, my Dragon, might go." It was a trust of immense propor-
tion. Aline was talented at moving between worlds, but Esther
could lead them entirely off course.

She hesitated for a moment and looked over her shoulder.
Esther was still eyeing the madness like she wanted to crawl
inside it. And . . . were the silver strands sliding toward Esther
even with Magic pushing them back? She didn't know if a ghost
could be consumed by madness, but she wasn't putting the theory to the test.

Aline shifted Esther in front of her.

"See it. Taste it. Think of safety and hope and a ley line with
power we can follow."

With Magic at her back, Aline reached for him and slipped a
hand around Magic's wrist, a flood of desire hitting her. Longing to be alone with him, curled up together, safe and sound
with nothing but time and freedom spread out before them. For
things to be different and for their journey to be typical.

With one last thought to Three and the splintered madness
that had gone after them, Aline pressed a hand through Esther,
tethering the ghost to her, and shoved them forward, into the
hole that opened up to a haze.

Esther drove them into it . . . leaving the madness and Three
behind to face whatever chaos came next.

Sixteen

THREE WAS NEVER THE BRIGHTEST OF WITCHES. They didn't need to be. When Three was a child, they could anticipate what anyone would do at least a half an hour before they did it.

"Darling, you can't tell Made that she's going to lose her virginity to Ketut, and he's going to then sleep with Made's best friend an hour later," their mother would say.

"Well, someone should warn her he's a right horrible human," Three would argue.

"Puta told me you said she would fall off a cliff while I was speaking to the elders and then, within the quarter hour she did," their father would say. "This is very bad."

"If they listened to reason, it could be very good," Three would disagree.

But no one liked what Three had to say, and Three was not

like the others. Being different isn't bad, it's extraordinary, which is confusing for the ordinary and left Three lonely and often annoyed.

There were games in the village and stories and fires filled with laughter. Three might have been a proficient chess player, had they ever cared to learn. Instead, one night when Three was barely into their prime, a pretty-eyed woman with dainty wrists that wove sparkles in the air and a silver tongue that dripped promises from it arrived.

"You're not like the others," she told Three, her smile saying she liked that about Three very much.

"I fail at being typical," Three said, the sadness escaping as they built a fire for one.

"You know what's interesting?" she said. "Is how we never know when the world is about to change. When we can change it. You have great power, and with it you can protect the world."

Three thought on this, for three days and nights while the female witch went out into the surrounding villages and returned to them as the sun set. Three could be a hero—saving not just their village but everyone—Three could show them all.

"If I help," Three asked, "what do you need of me? To predict the future?" That they knew they could do, though it was never as fun as they wished it might be.

"No," the woman named Supreme told him. "I have something to enhance what you can do. It will make you stronger, more in tune with your power. You will see beyond what you can now, and you will be able to predict disasters and travesties on an epic scale."

"Losing a life is an event on an epic scale," they said.

"Seeing it coming months in advance would increase the scale."

Three nodded, thinking how they might win the village over finally. Keep them safe, keep their parents protected, and maybe even find their place in this world.

A fortnight later Three sat in a perimeter of crystals created by the witch. Lines of power ran beneath them. They vibrated up into their head, making it hard to think at all.

She sprinkled an old magic, bone magic, onto herself and them, and dripped her own blood onto the crown of their head.

Magic, the color of a golden mist, rose and entered into them. Three screamed in pain, writhed as the power took over, reshaped and molded them.

The sun rose behind the moon, knocking it out of its orbit; the stars fell and the skies lit with fire.

Three exploded and broke apart into a million pieces before they were pulled back together into something that never should have been.

History would say a volcanic eruption decimated the village of Three's homeland, but the only volcano nearby was underwater and inactive.

Three had been the power of the destruction of their mother, father, family, and village. The pretty-eyed witch with the silver tongue tricked Three, infusing them with enough magic to wipe out their town and the people in it, leaving Three stuck. Bound to the barren land to sit . . . and wait and wait and wait.

Because she needed the magic bound, but she never needed them. Once the magical transfer was complete, she was gone, and they were bound to a desolate land, living on the ashes of all they had ever loved or hoped to love.

But Three was made strong.

They used their new powers to heal the land. Infusing it with rich soil and crops, drawing the tides and the healing rays of the sun. In time, so very much time, it prospered. Three set about creating a sanctuary, drawing in new life—their monkey familiars and other creatures lured by the soothing power on the island. What had once been a land of destruction became one of ascendency.

Not all things changed, though. Three still liked power, only now they hated the Supreme Witch. Over the years, Three crafted a new mission. They collected power, pulling it from themself when they could, in the form of their own magic. A madness born of power the color of a golden sunset.

It was painful to drain themself. Bloody, too. But Three did it every half century, sacrificing the evildoers they lured onto their lands to cement the ritual with blood, much as the Supreme Witch had done so many centuries before. Siphoning the power into a well in a cave below their home was Three's secret the Supreme Witch did not know. It was the start of a new game, one only Three was privy to, because the witch did not visit Three; she had all but forgotten them.

Until now.

Three knew this, because Three was still the ultimate chess player who had never played the game. Instead, Three created a new game and wrote the rules. It was time to finally play.

Three sat, waiting, surrounded by madness in shades of cream and silver . . . and gold. The gold was Three's, grown and collected, and they wondered what she would think of it being free.

Of Three being able to control it.

The new twist in the game.

The wind blew cold, and the earth shook, and a witch with

pretty eyes and dainty wrists and a devious tongue stepped into their cave.

"Hello, [redacted]," she said, standing at the open mouth entrance, her hands loose at her sides. Three's name had been erased from the book of names, and try as she might, Florence could never call it back. Three made the choice the day Florence filled them with magic to prevent her from having further power over them ever again.

Her eyes tracked the golden mist swirling around Three, and the silver and cream she commanded sniffing at its edges. "I see you've been busy."

"I see you've been busier," Three said, standing tall, their face devoid of emotion. "And I go by Three now, since it's what you made me."

"Always so dramatic," she said, tapping her fingers against her thigh.

"How would you know?" Three asked. "This is the first time you've shown your face since you left me here and blew up everything I loved."

"You blew it up," Florence said, her eyes on the swirls of color circling them, and the gold strand that danced around Three. "With your power, I would have thought you would have seen it coming."

"I wasn't looking," Three said, and flashed a cold smile. "That was the last time I made that mistake." The gold shifted closer to Three. "You were clever to send the madness ahead, but only because you didn't think anyone knew what it was. I know, and I know you thought you could take back Four, finish her off completely. That Esther would be felled by the madness and lose herself in it. You were wrong. *You* are losing your touch."

"You think so?" Florence asked, lifting a hand and calling the madness back to her. The silver-and-cream strands swam around her like undulating eels before they rose above her, sliding into her hair and weaving around the darker strands until they were no longer visible and all that remained was the madness.

"I don't need to think." Three pulled a dagger from behind from where they'd hidden it in their boot, and stood, flourishing it. "I told you. I always look now."

Florence's hands came up as though to ward off the blade, and Three brought it down onto themselves, slashing their arms—killing blows that cut deep into their veins as blood poured from them and a golden light shifted out.

"I've spelled the cave," they said, as they stumbled forward. "You'll never get my magic now, and I have broken myself, so none of me will belong to you."

Then they tumbled into the open pit and landed with a thud.

Florence stood where she was, her fingers continuing to tap. Five minutes. Ten. Then the golden strand slipped up and out and wove around the room. She held up her hand.

"From me, back into me, I call to thee."

The madness swam toward her and climbed into her hair, adding a new strand of color, of gold.

Florence walked to the pit and stared down into it.

"When you took your own life, you broke yourself from your magic, [redacted]. Which means your spells no longer hold. You are broken, same as you always were. Why do you think I chose you and the others? You're weak. Fragments of souls with no purpose and no power outside of what I deemed to give you. Your magic is mine, and the broken bits are, too. You're just the shell now."

She turned and walked from the cave, her hips swishing from side to side as she flicked her wrists, sending sparks that looked like stars down into the cave. She sang softly to herself as she left. "None can stop me. I will reclaim what was meant to be mine and then, perhaps, everything will burn."

ACROSS THE SEA, IN THE MIDDLE OF AMERICA, THE EARTH GAVE A MIGHTY RUMBLE AND SPLIT APART. From Memphis to St. Louis a fault line that was one of the foremost ley lines in the United States opened and gave a mighty shout. Hitting 7.4 on the Richter scale, it decimated buildings, homes, restaurants, and lives.

A new virus rose from the earth, bringing with it a poisoning sickness. Unlike the one Three had set up to steal power, this one stole breath. Healthy lungs grew plagued with asthma and COPD; unhealthy lungs simply gave up.

The sea along California grew rough and spit out jellyfish larger than the average ranch house and dead baby sharks—missing their eyes.

Overhead the North Star disappeared entirely, constellations gave up—Orion changing places with Cassiopeia as Perseus fell from the sky.

Cell towers lost and crossed signals, like candles being blown out on a birthday cake. Whole grids went offline.

Whistleblown's bookstore shuddered; Jen S.'s home rotted from the inside out. Puddles became ponds that grew into lakes under the local middle and high school and swallowed them overnight.

The Supreme Witch's power grew, and the world shrank further into darkness.

As the world was upended, Aline, Magic, and Esther stepped through a crack in the world from Three's sanctuary. . . . and into a monastery.

THE GRAY STONE FLOORS BENEATH THEIR FEET WERE HARD AND COLD, AND INSET WITH INTRINSIC CARVINGS. Fractals of varying shapes and sizes spread out down the hall. The cream walls to the right were made of gorgeous stone blocks laid in and then set back to create space for offerings. To their left were balustrades that held up the roof and offered views of an expansive garden. One full of vines. Grapevines teeming with crop.

"Did we walk into a monastery vineyard?" Aline asked, looking at all the arches in the hallway and the vines below.

"Damn it," Esther said. "I was trying to think of where Three said to go, but I had a bad spell with Two, and so I brought us here. To the lonely mountain and the keeper of it."

"You chose a monastery over Stonehenge?" Magic said.

"You know about Two?" Esther asked.

Magic's eyebrow twitched. "No; Three's clues were fairly obvious on that one, though."

"Ah. Well. Two is a horrible partner, and she burns everything she cooks. While ghosts can't eat, we can smell, and I swear she only burned things when we were in an argument."

"Partner?" Aline asked. "When you were already changed into a ghost? How did you . . ."

"There are ways," Esther said, a dreamy look coming into her eyes.

"Okay," Aline said, turning to stare down the corridor. "So where did we end up instead?"

"A leyline in a once great monestary, known as the Hall of Six," Esther said. "Where the good Faerie waits."

"There are *fairies*?" Aline asked, her brow knitting together.

"There should be," Esther said, "considering Two. But no, I mean Faerilyn, one of the remaining Magics. She is the keeper of this lonely mountain."

As though she'd heard her name called, there was a whooshing from behind them. Aline turned slowly and found herself face-to-face with a gliding creature who might have been human at one point, but no longer resembled any person she'd ever met. Dark flowing hair, olive skin, and eyes the color of blue sea glass, Faerilyn the sixth Magic practically floated toward them, wearing an open expression of horror.

"What are you *doing* here?" she asked, her voice low and hoarse, her eyes roaming over each of them as though she hadn't seen another body in a thousand years. Aline realized that was likely true. Both Three and Faerilyn were tucked away in places no one dared go or knew existed—if the dust gathering in the monastery was any indication. Unlike Magic, who had lived in a town with privilege and power, these witches turned beings were practically locked away.

"We crossed over," Aline said. "I'm—"

"A hedge witch," Faerilyn finished, her eyes drifting to Magic. "And you're One."

Magic didn't answer; he simply took a step closer to Aline, so she was positioned slightly behind him.

"I'm Esther," Esther said. "But you can call me by my number if it makes you feel better."

"You're a Magic?" Faerilyn asked, sniffing the air. "You smell . . ."

"Comforting?" Aline asked.

"Like freshly baked biscuits," Faerilyn said. She shifted her robe, which was more like a burlap bag than a dressing gown. It did nothing to take away from her beauty. She wore it like she had forgotten it existed. But all that was left in the room was her. And she was something to behold.

Her dark inquisitive gaze flitted between the three of them. Eventually she sighed, and on bare feet, turned and started back down the hall. "If the world is ending, and surely you three wouldn't have gotten past my guards if it weren't, then you might as well come join me for tea before war comes for us all."

Faerilyn led them down the long corridor, then down a wide spiral stone staircase, into a main room that was as wide as a football field. The room was filled with herbs and tattered rugs and large dusty pillows. In the center was a square wooden table and single chair. On the table was a large book, half the size of the table.

As they drew closer, Aline let out a surprised puff of breath. "That's *Mischief, A Beginner's Guide.*"

Faerilyn looked at her, lifting a brow. "I'm sorry?"

"The book—I have a copy, too."

She reached into her bag and pulled it out, passing it to Faerilyn, who opened it and flipped through the pages. "This is not quite my story."

Faerilyn handed back the book to Aline, who slid it in her bag. Then she turned the large and heavy papyrus pages of the book. "Mine is the story of what has been. What the Supreme Witch told me, and what I divined."

"You're a diviner?" Esther asked.

"I was."

"You lost your power?"

Faerilyn shook her head. "It changed, and in my dreams, I see the truth of what was and what could be."

"You sleep?" Magic asked.

"Of course."

"You sleep," Aline said to him. "That's how we . . ." She broke off, blushing, thinking of their nights together.

"I only sleep for you," he said, and ran his fingers along the side of her arm, sparks chasing his touch. She shivered and swallowed around a pop of need.

Esther and Faerilyn stared at them. Then they exchanged a look.

"Oh," Faerilyn said.

"Yep," Esther nodded.

"How many of us are dead?" Faerilyn asked.

"Only me," Esther said, waving her hands as though about to put on a show, "as far as I know."

"Ten minutes before you arrived, the herbs in those flower beds shriveled and died," Faerilyn said, pointing to the row of empty flower beds. "There was a cosmic shift. It buckled the floors beneath me, the very vibrations of magic and power being pulled and splintered. These shifts only happen when a ley line is disrupted, when magic is freed from its forced form."

"Three," Aline said, looking up at Magic. "What if Florence—"

"We can't know anything for certain," Magic said, brushing his other hand down her cheek. She leaned into his touch.

"Like two cats," Esther said, nodding toward them as she spoke to Faerilyn.

"More like two halves," Faerilyn said, looking back down at the book.

"And that is a book of our history?" Esther asked, turning her attention to the pages Faerilyn was poring over.

"It's *The Book of Witches,*" Faerilyn said. "The first who came, the three who were banished, the Fates who let it happen, the axes of power, us. And . . ." She looked over to Aline. "Her."

"Me?"

"Yes, the one to restore the balance."

Magic wrapped an arm around her.

Aline looked over to Faerilyn. "The book I have, *Mischief,* includes the ghost who spoke in riddles, the traveler who was out of time, and the man made of smoke and lies because the truth had been locked away from him. But it's about the town and the one it was made for. About—"

"Yes, about Matchstick and the home of Magic the First," Faerilyn interrupted, with a small smile. "But your book is a story written for a specific purpose. By the Fates. Made with a mission."

"A mission?"

"For you."

Aline swallowed hard, thinking of Chlo and Liset and Atti. "What mission?"

Faerilyn's eyes took on a faraway look, as though she were seeing into a different time. "The Fates failed us in the beginning. When it grew too late to change things, we were stuck. But *they* had changed, so they decided to make a change."

"What was in the book?" Esther said, while Aline shook her head. "It was just a story, a soothing one. That's what they did. The sisters looked after me, cared for me."

"They came to you. They came to the little town where you were overlooked and forgotten—where you begged to be seen, and they saw you for what you could become. A hedge witch with pure magic."

"Oh gods, of course that's how they did it," Esther said, her mouth dropping. "Why didn't I realize it sooner? It's as clear as the ring of a bell."

"What are you talking about?" Aline said, while Magic's brows drew together.

"The book you carry," Faerilyn said. "What happened when you read it, the first time?"

"I . . ." Aline thought about it. "I found safety, comfort, and my place when I was lost."

"You found your place," Faerilyn said, studying her. "Yes, that's true. There was a reason for that, though."

"What are you getting at?" Magic asked, while Esther's gaze pinged back and forth between Magic and Aline.

"Did you never wonder why the Supreme Witch provided for you?" Faerilyn asked him. "Why she gave you a town to distract you? Did you never suspect that she was waiting?"

"Waiting for what?" Magic asked, his voice a low growl.

"For her," Faerilyn said, waving a hand toward Aline. "For the one who carries your magic, who is a part of you."

Aline sat in the chair at the table, her knees going weak. "What?"

"The book was once imbued with pure magic," Faerilyn said. "The Fates had it all along."

"A story is more than a story," Aline whispered, the hair standing on her neck as chills ran down her spine.

Faerilyn nodded. "Only the Fates could cull it, and it could only come from one source and be given to only the purest of hearts."

"You're saying I took Magic's magic? From a book?"

Magic let out an irritated rumble, rubbing a hand down Aline's neck, soothing the confusion and fear that soared through her.

"I'm saying the Fates found a way to *take* from the Supreme Witch. They found a vessel of their own."

Esther let out a shocked laugh. "They couldn't transfer all of his magic, or it would have killed *him*."

"Right," Faerilyn said, smiling softly. "But they could give enough to Aline so she would be powerful beyond measure and able to help them when the time comes." She looked dead into Aline's eyes. "You are Magic, Aline Weir, and you are a witch. You are more than you were, and you are a part of this. It will be the two of you who end this. It has to be."

Seventeen

As Aline stared down at the book beside Faerilyn, she remembered the day she put the porkpie hat on in the bookstore. How she went through the wall to the little room. The tingle in the crown of her head as she'd placed it on, how she'd read the book and taken it home. "It started with the hat."

"No." A voice came from the doorway. "I told you it was more than a story."

Aline's shoulders sagged in relief at the sound of the voice. At her friend. She turned and ran for her, stopping short.

Dragon came in carrying a person, her lacy dress and curls bouncing with the effort.

"Dragon, you're okay," Aline said, while Esther said, "Oh gods, Three?"

"Oh no," Aline said, rushing forward to stand in front of the small frame of Dragon and the large one of Three.

"Good thing hocus-pocus means I can be as strong as Anne and Gilbert combined," Dragon said, referencing *Anne of Green Gables*. "This one is extremely dramatic."

"They're not dead?" Magic asked, walking up behind Aline.

"Clearly, ducky, they are," Dragon said, glaring at him. "That's not the problem."

"The Supreme Witch," Three said, lifting their head. "That witch stole my madness."

"She killed you?"

"Of course not." Three raised to their full height of six feet. "I killed myself. Thought it would stop her from being able to take from me if I was the one who did the breaking."

"What do you mean, take from you?" Aline asked.

"He means the madness," Faerilyn said. "When you rip a soul from its essence, and we are bound with the magic once it bonds to us, you break it apart when you kill it."

"But madness?" Aline asked.

"What else is being mad but being broken?" Faerilyn said.

"Like the Hatter," Dragon said, still glowering at Magic. "Mad as mad can be because broken and sad as sad to see . . . the way things were."

"Shh," Aline said. "Why are you speaking in riddles?"

"Who are you speaking to?" Magic asked.

"Dragon."

"There she said it again," Esther said.

"Who do you think carried Three in?"

"They carried themself," Three announced.

"No." Aline shook her head. "*Dragon* was holding them."

They all turned to stare at her.

"There's no one here but Three," Esther said.

"What?" She looked to Dragon, safe and sound, and here.

Dragon gave her a small smile and shrugged. "Not everyone is you or the sisters. Not everyone knows what's before their nose."

"I think I'm about to lose it," Aline said, pressing a hand to the back of her head.

"It's a lot to process, that's for sure," Esther said, poking a pot of lavender that sat on the edge of one of the large herb garden boxes and watching it fall.

Faerilyn sighed as Magic waved a hand and wind shifted through the room, catching the lavender and sitting it gently on the ground. "You are such a child," he told Esther.

"No, that would be Dragon," Aline said, before she shook her head and turned to her. She didn't care if they couldn't see her. Her friend was safe. Aline could finally exhale. "What happened? Florence said you took a scroll and then were gone. She told me you were kidnapped."

"That one is tricky," Dragon said, "and full of lies and madness. I was never there. I was otherwhere. She used me to lure you to him, to this. To it all. I failed you. I am so sorry."

"You were never in Matchstick?"

"Not then. I came to the forest to try to find you, and the sisters were in peril. So I stayed quiet. Kept an eye out. Looked after you, as I do. Followed you through the portal, then the other. You forgot to close the last one, not very smart."

"I did close the portal, as soon as I opened it." Aline said, rubbing her temples, her voice rising as she tried to process everything Dragon said.

"You can't close it," Faerilyn said, turning to her. "Magic is no longer following the rules. The axes can't hold it, or us, so the portals will stay open."

"Florence will come," Magic said.

"No, she will not," Faerilyn said.

"What have you seen?" Esther asked.

"It's all written in *The Book of Witches*."

"You can't simply tell us?" Magic said, irritation crossing the planes of his gorgeous face. It made him even more devastating, and Aline drew closer, her hand sliding up his arm.

"No, I cannot."

Dragon shook her head at Aline. "That book isn't all true. But it is mostly a truth."

Aline looked to them all. "You all really can't see her?"

"See who?" Magic asked.

"*Dragon,*" Aline said, exasperated.

"No," Esther said. "No dragons, lizards, or dinosaurs here."

"You can see Three, though?"

"Hello," Three said, finally lifting their head. "I'm standing right here."

"Yes," Magic said. "Three is here in noncorporeal form. Still as frustrating as they ever were. Your dragon, she is here?"

"Yes."

Three snorted. "You're frustrating. I'm dead."

"I don't understand it," Aline said, trying to decipher how they could see the ghost of a Magic, but not the ghost of a girl. "You see Three, but not Dragon, and she helped get them here."

Magic pressed a kiss to her head. "Maybe you're the only one meant to see her."

Esther moved closer to the book. "How can anyone read this?"

Aline looked over at the pages. "What do you mean?"

"I mean it's nothing but gibberish."

"No, it's not."

"Yeah, it is."

Magic looked at it. "She's right, I can't read it, either."

"Nor I," said Three.

Dragon shook her head again. "Nothing good comes from the history of sadness and madness."

"But . . ." Aline looked at Faerilyn, confounded.

"I told you. You were chosen. You read story, and this is story. The language of the Fates. I dream it, write it, but it is meant only for you."

Dragon snorted. "Lot of good they do anyone when they are in that damn tree."

Aline gave Dragon a gentle smile.

"I don't think I want to read any more story," Aline said, rubbing her face against Magic's shirt, inhaling his scent of pine.

"And yet you will," Faerilyn said, before she crossed to a large dusty pillow and lowered herself like a queen onto a throne atop it.

Aline looked up at Magic.

"You don't have to do anything you don't want to do," he said.

"If I don't, we won't get answers. What if this tells us how to stop all of it?"

"What if it tells us how to make it worse?"

He slipped his hand in hers. "I'm here. For whatever you choose."

Aline nodded. She closed her eyes and ran a hand over the book. Soft, singsonging whispers rose up. She didn't know the words, but she knew the voices. Chlo, Liset, and Atti.

Aline opened her eyes and sat down in the chair at the table. She squeezed Magic's hand, and as soon as she looked at the book, the light in the room dimmed except for a small overhead glow. The others faded from her vision, even Magic.

It was only Aline and the book, and a story as old as Time.

THE SUN, THE MOON, AND THE DUSK

The vibration of magic is made from love. Love can be bent, but it is difficult to break. The Supreme Witch discovered this in Sun and Moon, two witches who lived in a small town on the axis in the Americas. Sun and Moon had slipped into our world through the crack between worlds. They were young and powerful, and besotted with the one the Supreme Witch called Magic.

It was hard not to love Magic, for Magic was kind and curious and didn't ask for power. Power had been forced, and he had little care for using it, other than to be the safeguard and to look upon the Supreme Witch with the lust she had sewn into his eyes.

"You should tell him," Sun said to Moon, one night as they sat by the river, watching the witch talk to the sky. "He'll never believe it, and she, she would destroy us."

"She can't destroy us," Moon said, taking Sun's hand. "We're side by side, together for always."

"She is worrying," Sun said, looking up to the sky.

"Her power, what she can do. It's not been day or night here since she came."

"I know." Moon nodded. "But more witches have come into town, people with abilities who need help. We have community. We have what we could never find before."

Before, the two had been outcasts, lost and alone—outside of having each other. Here, in this new world, they had found friends who were family. Witches new in their ways. Born because magic was waking up in the new world—because they had woken it when they came. Sun and Moon liked being useful. They loved having other witches to eat, laugh, cry, and sing with.

They did not like how the Supreme Witch called herself a new name. How she led Magic down a path of confusion and manipulation. How she'd compliment him one day to laugh at him the next, or tell him they didn't want him to be a part of their circle, when the opposite was true.

That was why Magic was here, on the other side of the river, building his house. Because he didn't think he belonged anywhere. Or to anyone. Not even the Supreme Witch, though both Sun and Moon knew he was deluding himself.

It was hard, though, when you've not had love to know what is fact and what is fiction. Magic thought if he believed she loved him, it was a fact, but he believed a lie.

That night, while the town slept, Magic sat under the moon, his feet in the water. Sun and Moon came to him, they told him what they saw and their suspicions.

"Why would she lie?" he asked them. "She loves me. She gave me power. She took me from a place where I had no purpose and delivered me to paradise. She made this for me."

"Yet she won't let you leave," Sun said, her voice soft. "Everyone else can come and go, but you cannot."

"I don't want to leave."

"Why?" asked Moon.

"Because...," Magic said, but the reason eluded him.

"Try," Moon said, "to walk across the boundary and back. If you are capable, I promise we will say no more on the matter ever."

"You will apologize," Magic said, "to her for this injustice?"

"Of course," Sun said, resting a hand on Moon's arm. She was always reaching for him. Finding a piece of his skin to press or hold.

"Fine."

Magic stood and marched across the woods to the side road that led to the veil that separated Matchstick from the rest of the world. He picked up the pace, breaking into a jog. Sun held her breath, Moon sat up straighter... and Magic came to a stop. He scratched his bare chest, looked at the dusky sky, and turned around. He walked back to the others and sat down.

"What are you two doing here?" he asked.

Neither Sun nor Moon spoke. After a few moments, Magic rubbed his head, stretched, and got up. He went back to chopping wood, working on his home, and they went to the boundary at the edge of the wooded forest.

"He did not remember," Sun said. She walked to the veil and ran her hands over it before she turned back. "I remember."

"We are not spelled," Moon said. "We don't need to be, because we're not threats."

A rustling came from beyond the small yew trees they had planted not long before. The Supreme Witch stepped out from behind them. "You weren't threats. I fear, though, that much like Time, things have changed."

"You can't keep him prisoner like this," Sun said. "It's unfair and it is going to hurt him."

"If anything hurts him, it will be me," the Supreme Witch said. Then she called the wind and rain down into the town, she pulled up earth and fire, and sent all four toward the two. They jumped out of the way, but the Supreme Witch pulled the earth back to her and sent the fire where it belonged, before she made a bubble of wind to capture the two and used the rain to ride the bubble up and cast the two witches out of Matchstick proper, and into the sky.

"You call yourself Sun, and you call yourself Moon," she said. "Why not provide us with what your namesake designs?"

Moon went into the moon and became Night, and Sun went into the sun and became Day, and Magic stayed as he was, besotted with the witch who kept him prisoner. The Supreme Witch soon stopped visiting the forest that reminded her of Sun and Moon, and the Fates eventually found their way there—to claim that which was nearly forgotten.

Meanwhile, Sun and Moon lived in the sky, where they waited and watched, biding their time for when Time shifted again, and Fortuna's Wheel would spin.

They lived on, divided by Dusk and the Watcher, who was trapped there, too. The Watcher was the only person the Supreme Witch truly feared, and the only being more dangerous than herself.

Aline looked up from the book. Magic stood guard at her shoulder, and the others in the room were quiet, waiting for her to speak. She tilted her face toward Magic, and as his eyes met hers, she was all he could see, and the need to touch her overpowered him.

"We need to talk," she said, then stood, took his hand, quivering at the contact, and led him out of the room and down the hall. He exhaled at the feel of her; it was easier to breathe when she touched him, and he was growing dependent on the connection. On her.

"She's coming," he said, and Aline blinked at him, the gears in her mind whirring so loudly he could almost hear them.

"Sorry, what?"

"Florence," he said. "That's what you wanted to talk about? How we defeat her?"

"I didn't, actually. I was going to ask you about Day and Night?"

"The hamlets in Matchstick?"

"No, the witches who are locked in those hamlets. Sorry, I mean Sun and Moon?"

The room tilted and Magic's head swam, his knees buckled, and he stumbled forward. "Whoa," Aline said, wrapping an arm around him, and he placed his hands on her shoulders to steady himself.

"How do you know of Sun and Moon?" he asked, his voice a soft whisper. He hadn't spoken of his old friends in centuries. Not since they left him behind. He'd forgotten, almost. How was that possible?

"The story in there, the one Faerilyn showed me: it was theirs, and yours, and Florence's."

"They left, Aline. Long ago." He closed his eyes, tried to look back and recall what happened. "Matchstick grew too big for them, so they went to find a better place."

"No." Aline shook her head. "They didn't go anywhere."

Magic stared at her, cycling back through what she had said. "You called them Day and Night, as in the hamlets Day and Night."

"Yes."

"Are you saying Sun and Moon became the actual sun and moon?"

"Yes."

Magic's brow furrowed together. He paced down the hall, then back up, then down, and then he turned and punched a wall—bashing half the bricks from it.

"Holy ghosts," Aline said, jumping as the stones tumbled free and crumbled down into the vineyard below.

"I didn't see it. It shouldn't be possible. We need to leave," Magic said, brushing his hand on his shirt as though he hadn't decimated half a wall, and turning to her. "She's coming and she will kill every single one of us, and I'm not waiting for her to stick you in a star."

"I don't need you to protect me," Aline said, her feet poised as though she were waiting to run to him. To soothe him.

He let loose a frustrated laugh. "You told me the person who is after us is reworking the sky by trapping witches in it, and you think you don't need protection."

"I think *I* am protecting you."

Magic studied the irritation flaring in her beautiful cinnamon eyes. He didn't understand. "Why can't we protect each other?"

"Because the Fates *chose* me."

"You don't know the Fates," Magic said with a grimace. "They only ever choose themselves, Aline."

"And you're only being nice to me because of this . . ." She waved a frustrated hand between them. Refused to meet his eyes. ". . . bond or whatever. As soon as we sever it, you'll go."

"If we sever it, we die," he said, running a hand through his hair. How could she think that was all it was? That was all she was? Still. "Which is why we have to go."

"What?"

"We're vessels for magic," he said, speaking methodically and with precision, trying to get her to hear him. The need and urgency to get her far away from this place. "We can't be separated from the magic, or we die. You and I are two vessels for one magic, same principle. You remove the magic from one . . ."

"They die."

He nodded. He would do anything to keep her from dying.

"That's why she wanted me, to get the magic from me into you."

He swallowed. "And then she would have killed me. We are pawns in her game."

"It doesn't make sense. Why not kill us both and then take the magic?" Aline looked out into the open space Magic had carved with his fist. "Maybe she didn't want to kill you. Maybe she really loves you."

"No." He shook his head. "Whatever she was doing to me was the opposite of love."

"Or the only way she knew how to love." Aline rubbed her arms, trying to push the chill out. "Either way, we can't leave."

"Aline."

"I won't leave Dragon, or the others. We're stronger together. Three ghosts and three Magics. We can defend ourselves if she comes."

"*When* she comes, and we still need to get to the last two Magics."

"We will. We need a plan." She tilted her face to Magic's. "If Sun and Moon are the two hamlets of Day and Night, who is Dusk? Who is the Watcher?"

Magic's eyes widened, surprise marking his face. "The Watcher?"

"Yes, it's in the book."

He took a breath. "I think you need to read me this story, and we need to see what else Faerilyn has seen and recorded."

"But who is it?"

Magic slipped his hand into hers, giving her a gentle tug, and they walked toward the end of the hall and the room with their friends waiting.

"The only person she has ever feared. Her father."

≪≪≪

ALINE TOOK THE BOOK OUT TO THE GARDENS. It was quiet in the vineyard, even with withering vines the color of decaying flesh winding through the rows. Rosebushes with white and pink flowers grew beneath them, and the sky overhead was a dusky gray. The earth smelled too oaky, like it had been turned one time too many and the ground was dying. There was a distinct line between life and death in the garden, and perhaps that was why Aline liked it there. It was familiar.

She stared at Dragon, as the others walked down the rows to where Aline waited. Dragon did not seem the least bit disturbed to be unseen.

"I still don't get it. Why don't they see you?"

"Can't see what you forget. Won't see what is hid."

"I hate when you speak in riddles."

"Bit of mad isn't bad."

"I guess not." Aline shifted the weight of the book in her arms. "Is it because you're a regular ghost?"

"Don't know any other ghosts like me," Dragon said, and smiled. It was crooked but sweet, a lot like Dragon, and made Aline grin in response. She always wanted to be in on the joke with Dragon.

The others came down the final row and sat on the tree trunks that were laid in a circle in the center of the garden.

"It's wonderful and strange to be in a coven again," Esther said, taking a seat across from Aline.

"You remember your coven?" Three asked.

"I do," Esther said. "I prefer to be alone, or thought I did."

"I wonder if it's an introvert-versus-extrovert ability," Faerilyn said with a smile.

"How do you know about introverts and extroverts?" Aline asked.

"I divine the ways of the world," she said. "Not just the magical ways, but all the ways."

"Does that make you more or less lonely?" Aline asked.

"Did reading stories make you more or less lonesome as a child?" Faerilyn replied.

"Less," Aline said. "Stories were mostly my friends. Sometimes they were my only friends."

"I think we all have that in common," Three said. "None of us quite fit. Maybe that's why she chose us."

"Or maybe she chose you because you're extraordinary," Aline said.

"Either way," Magic said, "it's not the lottery most people would sign up for."

"She gave you a whole town," Esther pointed out.

"A town that's really a prison."

"All she gives are prisons," Dragon whispered, tugging at Aline's shirt from behind her.

Aline turned, searching her friend's face. Suddenly, Faerilyn stood. The trees around them, the ones that formed a perimeter around the monastery, shook, leaves falling as the trunks cracked and the ground rumbled.

"She's here," Faerilyn said. "The Supreme Witch has found us."

"Ash on an old man's sleeve," Dragon whispered to Aline, and then she was gone.

Aline turned in a circle looking for her, but her friend had slipped beyond to the in-between. It was not the first time she had seen a ghost use the words she had carried through years as a talisman to cross to the other side, but it was the first time Dragon had uttered them.

"Shit," Aline said. She could only hope Dragon was safe wherever she'd slipped to.

She did not have time to dwell on it. One moment Dragon

was beside her in the lush garden behind the monastery, and the next she had crossed back into the in-between. The Supreme Witch had found them, and before Aline could so much as shout, the air filled with the sound of tuning forks and the ground beneath them vibrated. Faerilyn stood frozen to the spot where she stood. Only her eyes moved as she looked between Magic and Aline.

"Into the circle," Faerilyn said, barely able to move her lips. "I hoped I was wrong, but it's the only way."

"What?" Aline said.

"These are yew logs," Faerilyn said, her tone urgent. "Use them. Cross back into the in-between and find the remaining Magics."

"We aren't leaving you," Aline said, her eyes tracking the edge of the vineyard as the roses that ran along the ground withered.

"She has too much power already," Magic said, as cracks broke the ground apart. "It's curdling the land."

"Go," Faerilyn said, her eyes wide. "I'll find you. I promise. I have foreseen it."

"Aline," Esther said, stepping into the circle. "I don't think we're ready to fight this battle."

"We can't leave her," Aline said, opening the book, struggling to hold it as she flipped through it, looking for a spell or clue for how to stop Florence.

"Aline," Magic said, one hand lifting in the air. "We have to go."

Aline turned and her foot was rooted to the ground. She looked at the stiff form of Magic's outstretched hand, and her other foot tried to shift down, locking her in position.

"Oh," she said, looking at Faerilyn. The tuning fork, it was somehow tuned to magic—*their* magic—and it was freezing them in place.

"We *have* to go."

Aline tossed the book into the circle and shoved Magic. He stumbled in, and once inside, his arm fell free from the spell. He reached out and grabbed Aline and yanked her into the protective circle after him. The muscles in her legs released and she stumbled inside the circle. At the last moment, she turned to grab Faerilyn and wrench her in with them to safety. The ground shook fiercely. A crack boomed across the air . . . and the vineyard exploded. Earth, branches, flowers, and weeds flew into the sky.

For a moment, Aline was back in the parking lot. Staring at Noah, being told she was not enough. A zig of hate fused through her as though a tether tugging her up. The ground burst free of its roots, the monastery behind them crumbled down—an implosion of stone and then a tumbling of it like a volcano pouring ground and stone instead of lava and ash.

Vines and thorns rained down on them. They piled up and wrapped their way around Faerilyn like a cocoon, tugging her in tighter and tighter. She was no longer moving, her eyes the only part visible. She blinked once at Aline, and then she was gone.

Aline couldn't see her through the debris, and then the world gave out beneath them. Aline pinwheeled her arms and kicked her legs, her breath stolen as she tumbled through the crack in the world, a high-pitched keening chasing after them. She reached blindly, trying to find Magic's hands, grasping a pinky once before it was wrenched away again.

Everything went black.

Eighteen

✳

DAY WAS CONCERNED. Matchstick was a quiet but charming town, and lately it was an immobile one. Witches went about their routines and daily life, going to the café, grabbing a coffee, cruising on their golf carts, but they weren't smiling. They weren't performing spells or rituals. Worst of all, they weren't leaving their hamlets. No one had left the sleepy magical town since the portal opened and closed and Florence went off chasing those who were clever enough to escape.

Day wished *she* could leave. Instead, Day was watching the overgrown yew where the three Fates slept. There was a ticking in the air. Click, click, *click*. The sound of the wheel turning. Fortuna must be pleased, wherever she was, to know such mischief was being managed by beginners and in a place such as this one. Her sisters, the three Fates, were responsible. They were always responsible. Day knew this now. Being trapped in this prison had shown Day many things, including how to help—if only Day could escape.

The Watcher was waiting, too. Day knew this, and it would have made Day shiver had there been bones in her body. She was fairly certain there had been, once upon a time, but now Time had no face, and Day was alone, longing for Night . . . never quite able to meet him.

Day wished Magic was still around. Magic was always calm. But Day was alone with her thoughts, watching witches who were lost without their false leader, while they were unaware their leader was lining them up like pieces on a board.

But still.

It wasn't so bad.

At least the Watcher was caged.

If that changed . . . there it was again, the strange sensation of an almost shiver, trying to wrap around Day at the thought.

⫷⫸

MAGIC LET OUT A SCREAM THAT SENT A MURDER OF CROWS FLYING OUT OF THE TREE BESIDE THEM. Aline stumbled away from him, her feet tingly as she tried to get her bearings. They were standing on flat green earth, the color so bright it was near blinding. Overhead the sky was a cheerful blue, not a cloud in it. A narrow road ran to their right, and up ahead, in the distance, waited a circle of large rectangular stones. A wonder of the world so familiar Aline had a strong sense she'd been there before, until she realized it was because she'd seen hundreds of photographs of the sight standing before her.

Stonehenge.

Magic's voice rose, the scream distracting.

They had landed on Salisbury Plain, in Wiltshire, England.

"The henge of stones," Aline whispered, turning to look for Three, their words ringing in her ears. She reached for Magic, and as soon as her fingers brushed the soft linen of his shirt, he stopped screaming.

"Three isn't here," Esther said, from her perch up in the tree. "Those crows left when they never leave, and they were our only good omen. Thanks, Magic."

"It's just us?" Aline asked, squeezing Magic's hand, exhaling when he pressed back.

"Yep," Esther said, hopping down.

Magic was breathing heavily beside her, as though he'd just run a marathon or five. The muscles under her hand bunched, constricting as he nearly hyperventilated. Aline rubbed small circles on his back, trying to soothe the rage boiling inside him.

"What was she doing?" Magic said, a minute later, finally drawing in a broken breath. "To *us,* Florence, how did she do that?"

Esther shook her head. "I can't be sure, but. . . . I believe she was killing you?"

"Is that . . ." Aline bit her lip, released it. "Is that how you died?"

Esther shrugged. "I don't know. I woke up dead. Free."

"Dead isn't free," Aline said, her voice gentle.

"It is when you've been imprisoned for most of your life." Esther stretched. "I've lived a long time as a Magic ghost. It's not that unlike being human, outside of not aging. Other ghosts, they live in the shadows, but we own the shadows once we're shades."

"It's not a life," Aline said. "It's an echo. You deserve to live."

"Says the woman who lived in stories."

"Back off," Magic says, his voice a growl. "You haunted that cemetery because you were chained there. Aline freed you. She's the reason we're all free."

"Yes." Esther nodded. "But who freed her?"

"The Fates," Aline said. "That's what Faerilyn said."

"They chained you to him. That's the opposite of free. There's a reason they chose you and gave you that book. It's not because you're special. We are all special."

"We're all stranded," Aline said, "and I don't want to be dead, so we need to make a plan."

Esther waved at the monument ahead of them. "We better get moving if you want to warn the second Magic and find out if they can be of any use in helping us stop that witch. Though I'm not putting any bets on it."

"We'll see."

"Don't forget *that*," Esther said, pointing to the middle of the road and Faerilyn's book. Aline crossed to it and scooped it up.

"Maybe we'll get lucky, and the witch of Stonehenge will know what to do with the stories, tell us how to fix all this, and we can go home," Aline said.

Esther slid her a sly smile. "I would imagine she can, though I really wouldn't expect her to be willing to help."

"I don't expect anyone to help," Aline said. "It won't stop me from trying."

Esther only grunted, and Magic took the book from Aline, before slipping his fingers between hers. Together, the three of them started up the road for the tourist trap that was almost as old as Time.

≪≪≪

DRAGON STOOD IN THE FOREST OF MAGIC'S HOME IN MATCHSTICK, OUTSIDE THE LARGE YEW TREE THAT HELD THE FATES. She paced in front of it and back again, around it and then climbed up it and down it. The bark was warm to the touch, the leaves of the tree pungent and sweet. The crisp air had her wanting to draw in a deep breath and curl into the arm of the thickest branch and proclaim, "Isn't it wonderful to live in a world full of Octobers?" But Dragon had seen many Octobers during her time being hidden from most of the world, and though her thoughts were occasionally murky, her heart was not.

She needed to help her friend Aline. While Aline thought of Dragon as her oldest friend, Dragon knew Aline was her only one. Dragon had watched Aline for some time before that night at the slumber party when Aline was a child. She had slid along the shadows in the school, eager to be among people Anne of Green Gable's age—even though Dragon did not age. She had watched Aline making her notes, trying to learn the ways of the others just as Dragon had. Aline was clever. She thought of specific compliments and paid close attention. Her memory was vivid; she did not really need the notebook. But Aline didn't know what Dragon knew—that the child had power.

Aline's mother had power, too, but didn't want it. Broken people have a harder time living, and when you ignore your gifts . . . well, magic has a way of unraveling when it's not claimed. So, Aline was left in the hands of two broken adults, one a witch who did not realize she was a witch and the other a mortal without morals. There was no one to tell Aline what she truly was. A witch. No one to explain how mortals were often uncomfortable around people with power.

Aline was a lonely witch, but a witch, nonetheless. Dragon saw her and understood. Dragon was lonely, too. Sheltered in the small town of Whistleblown, on an axis forgotten by even the Supreme Witch, remembered only by the Fates. But the Fates were not helping Dragon, because they were only helping themselves. That was the way of the Fates.

Until Aline.

Until Dragon went to the slumber party and interfered . . . and the Fates, too, saw Aline. As worthy. For what she was. Powerful. Capable. The way home.

Dragon was mad at herself for that, because she only wanted to protect her friend. Had known they were friends long before that night from watching her. That they were future friends. Then when it mattered, Dragon had messed it all up.

The Fates were clever and knew more than anyone. Spinning their yarn, letting Fortuna's Wheel guide them.

Actually, as Dragon rethought it, lazy is what they were.

She told them so through the bark that now protected them. "Lazy, lazy, lazy."

Dragon banged the back of her head against the tree, and the sky flickered overhead. Dusk, trying to change colors from a rosy hue to a deeper purple.

"Something wrong with that sky," Dragon said. "Lots of somethings wrong with Matchstick." She turned to face the tree, thought about smashing it to bits and forcing the Fates out. "You'd probably crawl into the earth, burrow to another tree if I did it. Lazy, but not eager to face what you've done. She's not stopping. Not going to stop until she has what she wants and is whole and everyone else is broken."

The sky flickered again, and the wind blew colder. Dragon shivered and climbed down from the tree. She wandered from the forest, the leaves crunching beneath her patent leather shoes. She rubbed at goose bumps sprouting along her arms, before she picked up her speed and skipped out of Dusk and into Day. Dragon thought the skies were confused. Or maybe it was the town. She watched a witch with purple hair and black glasses pull lavender from her garden. Every bunch she pulled regrew. The witch had tears running down her cheeks in frustration.

Dragon looked up at the sun and blinked.

"That is more than a sun, and now it's more than it was," she said. The sun shimmered. A ring around it pulsing power. Dragon skipped on, pausing to dig her fingers into the lavender and stop their regrowth. It was simple magic, pulling from the soil and sending the power up into the air. It would find its place along the vibration of the earth . . . or it should.

Dragon watched the air shimmer where she'd tugged the excess free and float up to the sun.

"Interesting," she sang, before passing a circle of witches who were charging crystals in a pond full of phosphorescent water. It glowed an aqua blue, and when they dipped their stones in, they came out shimmering, too.

Magic in the town was wonky, and the people were moving like they were coated in molasses, repeating their motions or— like the two sitting outside a café—hardly moving at all. Holding their cups of spiced tea and blinking with the precision of a slumbering owl, a pile of scones on their table.

Dragon hurried on, and when she got to Night, she sat down and looked up. There was a circle here, too, tinged in red. A harbinger of change.

"Hello," Dragon called up to the man in the moon. "I see your shadow." Because she was sure that's what it was. The story of Sun and Moon made real. So much did and didn't make sense, but then that was the problem with her mind being a bit scrambled, like eggs.

Dragon knew too much, but the knowledge didn't like to stay. It wanted to hide, like Dragon had been hidden, but Dragon wasn't going to let anyone, or anything, hide her anymore.

Aline needed help, and Dragon would help her. As she had learned from Anne of Green Gables's example, there was nothing she wouldn't do for her bosom friend.

She stood up and turned, walking up the street, feeling the eyes of the moon following her. She didn't mind, and she waved without turning her head as she skipped on—in the direction of the House of Knowledge.

ALINE, MAGIC, AND ESTHER STOOD OUTSIDE THE INTIMIDATING CIR-CLE THAT WAS STONEHENGE. Up close, the air appeared to waver, threads of magic shifting around them. The wind was perfumed with a familiar scent, and Aline tried and failed to place it.

"I know that smell, but I can't figure out how," she said, trying to rub the tickle from her nose.

"It's palo santo," Magic said. "Incense of the gods, or so it was reputed." He looked down at Aline, and for a moment Aline forgot everything else. Where they were, what their worries were, and why she couldn't just stay where she was, standing in front of Magic with his eyes locked on hers, the world disappearing beyond them.

"She likes to burn it to keep out negative energy and witches," Esther said.

"I don't see anyone," Aline said, dragging her gaze from Magic and squinting at the rocks.

"Because that's a magical mirage," Esther said, giving what Aline assumed was a fake yawn. Ghosts didn't get tired, did they?

"How do we enter?" Magic asked, shooting Esther a look that would intimidate a scarecrow. Esther only shrugged. "I've never gone in this way."

"There's another way?" Aline asked.

"Always."

"And we didn't take it?"

"Can't."

"Care to elaborate?" Magic said, his tone dropping to what Aline had started thinking of as sexy-menacing.

"It's enchanted," Esther said, waving toward Stonehenge. "Like Alcatraz. Only Magics can enter."

"And the other way?" Magic asked.

"I am not at liberty to say. You'll understand if we make it inside."

"If?" Aline said.

Magic handed Aline the book. "There's always a cost." Then he moved quickly around Aline, took a step forward, and broke into a run.

The scent in the air bloomed—what had been a hint of incense perfumed into a gust—and Magic disappeared.

"Hello, sexist," Aline said. "As if I needed him to go first."

She gave Esther one last look and strutted in after him, her heart hammering in her chest.

As she passed the first marker, a small stone on the ground, the air grew warm. The hard earth softened beneath her feet. Birds chirped, but they were nowhere to be seen.

A sharp wind tugged at her, and she lost her breath. Aline stumbled to the ground, clawing at it as she tried to inhale. Her bones ached, snapped, and she curled in on herself. The blood rushed to her head and boiled beneath her veins. She was dying. In a gruesome and cruel way. She couldn't swallow, couldn't scream, could not make a sound.

All she wanted was him.

Magic crawled to her. He laid his hands over her face and brought his mouth to hers. "Steady now," he said, his voice hoarse and cracking. He blew his sweetened breath across her mouth and brought his lips to hers. Aline drew in a breath.

His hands rushed down her side, over the bones that had cracked. He was whispering, but she didn't understand the words. Everything in her caught fire. Pain poured through her as her body fought against being mended. Magic kept his mouth to hers, and tears poured out of Aline's eyes. She didn't want him to keep going; she wanted him to stop. She wanted it all to stop.

"No, my love," he said, and pressed a palm to her heart. "You are mine and I am yours."

He pulled the ribbon from her ponytail and wrapped it around her limp wrist, bound it to his. "We are ours."

She nodded, the motion causing the world to spin and her stomach to twist so excruciatingly she let out a scream.

He pressed his lips to hers again, his own tears falling on her cheeks. His mouth kept moving, his hands roaming, and the pain, which had been a death promise, abated.

It pulled back, receding slowly and steadily, until Aline could draw a breath, until she could register her body as her own and not a barrier from which to escape.

She lay, curled into Magic, for a long time. The sun shifted in the sky, the air blew cold and hot, rain fell in angry sheets across them, and the moon rose and brought a warm wind with it, drying them off.

"Can you sit?" Magic asked when it seemed day and night had become one. His voice was a deep throaty crack, and it shivered its way down her spine.

"I . . ." Aline coughed the vowel out. She cleared her throat three times and nodded. He helped her up, and she found she no longer hurt. In fact, Aline was rested and revived. She helped Magic up, took a step back, and tested her strength. Raising her arms overhead, stretching her back, and rolling her neck. Magic smiled at her, and the way his cheek lifted curled her toes.

He took a few steps away, deeper into what appeared to be a desert before them. She watched as he took care where he stood, his eyes seeking, his strong jaw clenching. He looked back at her, a question in his eyes.

Magic stood before her, his hands in his pockets, his head tilted to the side. Aline swallowed. There was a warning in how he crooked his hand. Not beckoning her, but asking. She stepped forward and something crunched.

She looked down and found she was standing on a bone. A femur? She studied the earth and shuddered. Bones were littered everywhere. All sizes. All, she feared, human.

"We weren't lying on this," she said, horror caking her tone.

"No. We hadn't breached the perimeter."

"And now?"

"Now we have."

How? She needed to ask, but first . . . she was standing on decaying parts of the dead.

"Magic. What *is* this place?"

"Bone graveyard," he said, his hand finding hers. Their fingers intertwining. Her fear lessoned infinitesimally. "Strong protection. You can't pass unless your intent is pure and you do not mean to harm."

"Was what we went through a test, then?"

"Yes and no."

"What does that mean?"

"It was a test, but not for two."

"But we're both here."

"Yes."

Aline looked down at the ribbon still bound to her wrist. "Magic?"

"Old magic needed older magic. We are two into one."

Aline took a deep, slow breath.

"We already were," he said. "This was symbolic. The power we share, that's the truth."

"Yes, but I was out of my mind with pain."

"You regret it?"

He asked with a straight face. No emotion in his voice. It was his way, she'd learned, to give her space to speak the truth. And as for that?

"I don't know what it means?"

The corner of his mouth curved, a sharp bright flash of a grin. "It means I am yours."

"And I'm yours?"

"As long as you will it."

Butterflies danced themselves into a dervish in her stomach. "Then I do not regret it."

He nodded, licked his lips, and she found even her ankles went weak. Until her gaze drifted to the bones beneath her feet.

"Did she kill these people?"

"I . . . don't know," Magic said. "Rather not think about it, to be honest."

"It's all I can think about when staring at it."

He tugged her closer and Aline took a breath and a step, and another and another until they were side to side. The bones crunched and she shivered as she slid her hand into his back pocket. She tried not to think about who she was walking on, if they had lived a good life, a short life, or a sad one. The bones rolled beneath her shoes, and she swallowed back a pop of fear. Would she end up like this? Littered bones in a forgotten graveyard?

Magic bent down, brushing his lips across her head, and she exhaled. A sense of rightness settled over her, and she squeezed his palm. He squeezed back three times, and they faced the same stones as before. Only now, as they stood side by side, a light lit at the base of the closest stone.

SPEAK AND ENTER, LIE AND DIE. read the words carved along the closest boulder.

"Speak what?" Aline whispered.

"I assume our intent," Magic said.

"'We wish to save your life'?" Aline said. "Is that what it means?"

"I suppose that's better than 'we wish to not end up decayed and degraded in your front yard,'" Magic said, his tone wry.

"Ha-ha," Aline said, trying hard not to move so she didn't have to step on another bone. "Let's not risk even joking about that."

"I've vowed, I will protect you," he said.

"We've gone over this," Aline said, shifting to face him. "I'm the one protecting you and the rest of the Magics—"

The stones trembled before them. Aline staggered back and Magic tugged her close, wrapping both arms around her waist. He held her close as they observed the stones of Stonehenge shift and reshape. One by one, they toppled like dominoes, and then crawled toward each other.

"That's not normal," Magic said, amusement filtering his tone.

Aline peered through the gap in their shoulders. "No. Nothing about this is, and we're here alone. Where *is* Esther?"

"Not standing on a sea of bones," Magic said. "Or would it be floating?"

Then he made a startled noise that had Aline's head turning. The stones had shifted into the formation of a house. It was a squat but sweet cottage, and the shape stirred at Aline's memory.

"Magic, I've been here before."

As the stones settled, the air glistened with a bright light that filtered in. Aline lifted her hand not wrapped around Magic's solid back, and she squinted through the glaze of the world as it shifted from what had been to what was.

The bookstore inside of Matchstick, which bordered the outside of the House of Knowledge, stood proud and a little cocky. It was a shop that wore the clothes of another. A place not quite in time. The only place in town Aline had seen Florence not visit.

"Is that . . . ," Aline started to ask, unable to finish the sentence, because she couldn't quite accept that it had been under their noses the whole time.

"The Crone's bookstore?" Magic said, unable to suppress a slightly unhinged laugh. "Yes, it is."

The door opened and Esther walked out with the Crone—all four and a half feet of her—trailing behind. They stood on the porch, Esther leaning against the wall, and the Crone with her arms crossed, an irritated smirk on her tiny heart-shaped face.

"It figures," the Crone said, staring at Magic, "that we would come to this, but I still would have preferred a less-involved resolution. I so do not like to get my hands, nose, feet, or toes dirty."

Then she waved them in with the crook of a tiny finger and skulked back inside. Esther offered a bemused shake of her head. "She's not so bad, really. Or she is, but she's not always what she seems. Give her a chance, and a little time. I have a feeling we may need both."

Then Esther was walking through the wall, and Aline and Magic were left outside.

"What do you think?" he asked.

"I think, if I've learned anything, what will be will be."

He nodded, blew out what Aline took for a breath of acceptance. "What will be will surely be," he said, and followed her inside.

Nineteen

INSIDE, THE BOOKSTORE LOOKED THE SAME. The scent of incense was strong, the books on magic inviting, and the child with needles for teeth (who most certainly wasn't a child) stared at them, tapping her foot and leaning against a case that held books advertised as being FOR SELFISH HELP. Books on *How to Get Your Way* and *What to Use to Poison Your Cheating Lover*. It was a stark reminder that there was nothing normal about anything Aline was experiencing, and yet as she looked to Magic, everything steadied inside her.

"You know, I really did hope you wouldn't return again after reading about the Fates, after my exceptionally and exponentially gracious warnings," the small being told Aline.

"Yes, but you failed to mention something critical to all of this. You're *a Magic*?" Aline asked, studying the Crone, finding her as intimidating as ever . . . and yet she did not seem to be as off-center as the others. She was psychopathic, but she seemed confident in her abilities, and very much as though she was who she was always meant to be. As terrifying as that thought was.

"I am."

"But I thought you were here running a bookstore. In Matchstick."

"I'm between spaces," the Crone said. "I'm not *in* anywhere. It is still a store, of course, can't change the outer for the inner no matter how hard one tries."

"The Supreme Witch could come in anytime," Aline said, rubbing the back of her neck. "Couldn't she? You're in her town. Isn't this like baiting a piranha?"

"I'm a shark, and I'm *between* her town and Stonehenge. The rules for both entrances are the same. Flo doesn't want to tell me where her bones are, so she won't enter." The Crone flashed her teeth, and Aline recoiled.

"She's taken out Three and, I presume, Faerilyn," the Crone said, as Esther towered over her protectively. Aline looked up at Magic. He was mimicking Esther without realizing it, standing sentry over Aline. Aline might have laughed if the stakes weren't so high and the situation so dire.

"Yes," Aline said, her voice catching. "I saw her fall."

The Crone let out a sigh that was shockingly human. "There is a town in Egypt where every single one of the stars blinked out of the sky not more than thirty minutes ago. I'd say she's killed Six dead."

"Six?" Aline whispered.

"Faerilyn," Magic said, his voice low.

"Which leaves you, *this* Magic"—she waved at him like he was an STD—"and the last Magic," the Crone said.

"No one knows where the last Magic is," Esther said, leaning into the Crone. "That one's been hiding for a century or two."

"Really?" Aline asked. "How is that possible?"

"We're Magics," the Crone said. "Anything can happen, child, anything we want can be." The Crone displayed her shark-toothed grin. "If Flo has made her move, then she has to have an idea of how to get that one."

"You don't know if it's a he or a she or a they?" Aline asked.

"We are whatever we are meant to be," the Crone said.

"He's changed," Esther added, nodding to Magic. "Magic the First became your Magic. It happened years ago. One day he wasn't much more than a being. Then the skies split apart, and the world shook. Over time, he evolved. He's more of everything now. Taller, wider. You haven't noticed?"

Aline had. He was slender like a dancer the first time she saw him under the lamplight, but now he was built like a quarterback. Still trim but filled out.

"I am what you need," Magic said to Aline, his eyes meeting hers.

"Aww," the Crone said, her voice flat. "How sweet."

Aline looked at her, flashed her own teeth. "You know Florence wants you dead."

"Duh." The Crone leaned forward.

"You don't seem concerned."

The Crone rolled her eyes and dropped to the floor, tucking her knees beneath her. She looked up at Aline. For a moment, she looked so much like a child, one Aline knew. Almost like . . .

"Dragon," Aline said.

The Crone wiggled her brows. "Ah."

Aline and the Crone stared at each other, neither blinking. "Why?"

"Why not?" the Crone asked, batting her lashes.

"I . . . I didn't notice before," Aline said, a bubble of panic popping beneath her breastbone. "Your hair is so much shorter, and you have those teeth." She steeled her spine. "You *do* look like her. Why?"

"Because it hurts Flo." The Crone dropped her smile, left her pretenses beneath her feet on the floor. She stood and stepped toe to toe with Aline. "This image cuts her, and it gives her pain, and that brings me the sort of pleasure I can sink my teeth into and gorge on the blood for days."

Aline fought the urge to swallow and vomit at the way the Crone licked her chops, smacking when she was done.

"Why would you looking like Dragon hurt Florence?"

The Crone flashed those pointy teeth, little spikes in her mouth. She snapped them. "That's the wrong question."

"How do we kill Florence?" Magic said, inching closer to Aline.

"That's the right one," the Crone said. "And you can't."

"What do you mean, we *can't*?" Aline asked. "Isn't that our job? Stop her, stop this whole thing?"

"That book can't tell you the future," the Crone said, wrinkling her pert nose at the one Aline held. The one Faerilyn had written. "It simply had a need to return to where it belonged." She stood up and held her palms out to Aline. Aline passed the book over and as soon as it was in the Crone's hands, the book shrank. It shifted forms and became smaller, thicker, and perfectly proportioned to be placed on a shelf. "You won't find *how* she kills us in this, and that's what you need. To reverse the ritual and to stop the change you need knowledge."

"Stop which change?" Magic asked.

The bell chimed as the front door opened. Dragon walked in.

"Stop the Supreme Witch from changing," Dragon said, waving at Aline. "Hello, my bosom friend. Sorry about earlier." She nodded to the Crone. "Thief."

"It's not stealing if it's a glamour," the Crone said. "It's a compliment."

"You can see her?" Aline asked, as she turned and surveyed the group. They were all gaping at Dragon, except for the Crone, who was doing her best to glare and looking more miserable than successful. "Truly?"

"Of course, I can," said the Crone.

"We all can," Magic said. "Who is she?"

Aline looked from him to Esther, and both were staring at Dragon.

"I don't understand," Aline said. "Why can you see her *now*?"

"The bookstore is in a place out of time," the Crone said.

"It's in the shadows, so anyone can see me," Dragon added, with a smile that was too bright to be joy-filled. "There's no hiding here."

"That's Dragon?" Magic said, looking to Esther, then Aline, and back to Dragon.

"No staying, either," the Crone said. She turned to Aline. "You need to discover the ritual and there is only one way. Pick your bait, set your trap. You can't use yourself or your other self." She nodded to Magic. "She won't come for me looking like her."

"Why?" Aline said, staring at Dragon. "I don't understand."

"I'm not just *your* Dragon," Dragon told Aline. "I'm also hers."

"You're not a real dragon," the Crone said with a snort.

"She's a little girl," Magic said.

"She's a treasure," Aline argued.

Esther looked at Dragon. "Sure. But. Who are you really?"

"I'm Dragon, and I do not answer to you." Dragon turned to Aline. "I can help. I'm excellent bait."

"Bad idea, that," the Crone said, rubbing her tiny, pointed chin. "I *like* it."

"We need a Magic," Aline said. "Not a ghost."

"She's no ghost," Esther said, giving Dragon the side-eye.

"Of course she is," Aline said. "She's the first one I met."

A shout came from outside and the Crone sighed. "Three and Six have arrived. They can't come in. They aren't sure what's going on inside and have murder in their bones. You better get out there, Aline. Maybe you'll be lucky and Four will remember her death. Or maybe you'll be unlucky and you'll all die. In which case you won't need me. Either way, I'm staying here where I'm meant, so you're on your own."

"Didn't take you as a coward," Magic said.

"I'm not a coward, Flo's boy, I'm clever," the Crone said.

Magic charged for her, and the Crone lifted a finger. A single pointer rising up.

Magic floated to the ceiling, stuck and stretched. The Crone grinned, and Magic screamed.

"*Stop*," Aline shouted.

The Crone shook her head. "It will be better this way, child."

Aline couldn't stop it. That burning rage inside her, the fuse lit and burst at the sight of Magic writhing on the ceiling. She turned to the Crone and let it out, a single flame of intent, and the Crone staggered into the books, sending row after row of stories to the ground.

"Goddess, you're a live wire," she said, as smoke billowed up around the edges of where Aline stood.

Dragon drifted closer to Aline. "It's going to be okay," she said, placing a tiny hand on hers. "It's easy to be wicked without knowing it, isn't it?" she asked, whispering in her ear. "Just remember. All the Beyond was hers with its possibilities lurking rosily in the oncoming years—each year a rose of promise to be woven into an immortal chaplet."

Then she reached in Aline's bag and pulled out her book, *Mischief*.

"You're not in this," Dragon said to the Crone.

"No?"

"No."

"Shame, as I really am the most interesting thing here."

"But you aren't here. You said it yourself. You live between. You don't really exist. You don't matter. You watch and you refuse to get involved."

The Crone raised her brows. "I do like to watch."

Dragon slid the book onto the shelf. "Fine. You can have it. We don't need it anymore." She turned to Aline, found her still shaking with rage. "There are real people you care about now. Come back to us, dearest Aline."

Aline blinked, quavered, and trembled again. "I don't like her," she said, between chattering teeth.

"No one does," Dragon said, rolling her eyes. "Such a Jen S."

Aline let loose a laugh that shook the walls, and her rage slithered into nothing.

"You're trying to hurt her," Magic said. "It's too real for you, that's it, isn't it?"

"How real are vessels?" the Crone asked with a sneer. "Or ghosts? They're like smoke. You can't hold them or catch them. You chase them, but you'll never be satisfied. You were all meant to be alone, like me."

Aline shot the Crone a frown, and then she reached for Magic's hand, and together they left the shop, Dragon following them and Esther pausing at the door.

"Is that what you truly believe? You're meant to be alone?"

The Crone sniffed, turning back to the books.

She did not see Esther's eyes fill with unshed tears. "You're really not going to come?"

But the Crone was already slinking back amongst the shelves, disappearing around the corner, and it was Esther who was left alone to follow her friends into the fray.

FAERILYN AND THREE STOOD OUTSIDE THE BOOKSTORE, UNDER THE MOONLIGHT OF NIGHT. Faerilyn was indeed dead. She looked the same as she always had . . . except her shadow was gone. Aline looked from her to Three, to Esther as she stood on the porch. All three were missing their shades. Aline should have realized it before.

Aline bit back a sob and moved to Faerilyn. She hugged her, and it was like hugging an icy stone. "I'm so sorry."

"I knew it was coming," Faerilyn said, patting her briskly on the back and releasing her. "As I knew I would see you again."

"Do you remember how she did it?" Magic asked.

"I saw the trees falling, branches and leaves and vines, and then I tasted roses. They decayed on my tongue, and I no longer could speak. There was a flash, and the next thing I knew, Three was standing over me, helping me up."

"I didn't see it," Three said, crossing their arms over their chest, giving their head a shake. "I was halfway to you all, through the portal, when I felt the vibration of the earth splinter. I snuck back into the monastery and found her spirit waiting."

"Before I died, I knew how she did it," Faerilyn said. "I dreamed it, and I knew . . . but now it's gone." She ran a hand through her long dark hair. "So much of what I was is missing."

"Maybe—" Aline said, but the rest of the sentence did not come.

The ground beneath them vibrated, the air filled with a high whine of a tuning fork, and the light of the moon blinked out.

"She's coming," Aline said, her limbs growing heavy. She turned to run and found her feet frozen to the spot.

"Oh no," Esther said. She, Faerilyn, and Three stood around Aline and Magic, forming a circle trying to protect the two as they both shifted into a frozen state. Neither moving. Their hands bound together, their eyes roaming from each other's to the darkness before them.

The Supreme Witch, better known to the denizens of Matchstick as Florence, came striding in. She walked along the tops of the hedgerow that bordered the House of Knowledge's garden, holding a gold divining rod and a tuning fork. She moved with precision and without care. Her hair shimmered; it was the main part of her visible through the darkness. What had been cream and silver was now cream, silver, gold, and violet.

Dragon stepped forward from where she was waiting at the edge of the porch, Aline opened her mouth to scream, and the bookstore door swung open.

"Hello, Flo," the Crone said, from where she slid out onto the porch. From the corner of her eye, Aline saw Dragon sigh, duck her chin, and then she was gone.

Florence stopped and stared. "Get that face off," she said, biting the words out.

"Make me," the Crone said, blowing her a kiss.

Florence opened her mouth and let out a scream that echoed through the air, ripping into the space around them. Like a cyclone of sound, it circled their heads.

The Crone didn't blink.

Florence lifted her hands and ran them through her long locks, tugging the color free. It uncoiled like a snake, undulating against her palms. She threw it forward, and it raced in the air—straight for the Crone.

The Crone met Aline's gaze; she didn't look away. She had plenty of time to react. Instead, she stepped out onto the steps of the porch.

"It's more than a story," she said, raising her arms out as though receiving an embrace.

Instead, she welcomed death.

Esther let out a shrill call, which morphed into a keening scream as the madness unspooled into four threads, wrapping itself around the Crone. There was a strong blast of wind, knocking Aline down. Florence raced forward, stepping up to the edge of the stairs. She sent the wind behind her, blocking the others and the ghosts.

She stayed on the ground, staring up at the Crone, and pulled a small matchstick from inside her jacket.

The ritual. It is more than a story; this was what the Crone meant. This was how she did it, and the best way for Aline to see it and understand it.

Florence turned the match sideways, and the end glinted against the light of the madness. Sharper than one of the Crone's teeth, Florence cut into one of her own palms, then the other, and then dragged it across her third eye. She tossed the matchstick into the air and spoke three words.

"*By my will.*"

The matchstick dove at the Crone, slicing into her hands and forehead. Blood trickled out and a light followed . . . and grew.

The softest shade of red followed the blood, blending with a brighter tone of crimson. The Crone splintered apart like a thousand puzzle pieces breaking off into the air. Her cries filled Aline's mouth, and from the corner of her eyes she saw Magic and the others with their mouths opened, mimicking the pain overtaking them all as it poured from the dead Magic.

Light exploded, the colors swirling overhead, and suddenly Aline was unstuck. She grabbed for Magic and yanked him after her. Then they were racing in the darkness toward the garden. Jumping over the cracks skittering through the earth ahead of them. Rain poured down, sogging their steps, but they pushed on.

Esther and the others called from behind them, their voices blending together in a single shriek of rage and pain. Aline couldn't look back. She dove through the rosebush, thorns scraping against her as she let go of Magic. She called for him to follow and crawled out of the other side of the bush. She stood and stared into the eyes of Noah.

Aline screamed, shoved through the ghost of her childhood, and ran. It was impossible. He couldn't be there. The sisters had said they sent him to the other side. It was her imagination, fear, and shock conjuring the boy who had once broken her heart, the boy she'd killed so many years ago.

Panic was the pulse of her beating heart. Aline sprinted. Her blood rushed loudly in her ears; soon it was the only sound she heard. Her breath whooshed from her lungs, burning as she kept moving forward. Noah raced alongside her, the same blue shirt he'd worn that last day flashing as they became a blur of legs pumping.

She ran through Dusk and into Day and into the forest that held Magic's home. She dove into the river. Swam across the clear water, not stopping until she pulled herself to the other side and Magic's home was in sight. She looked for Noah, but he—or the hallucination of him—was gone.

She crawled toward Magic's home and the front door opened.

Time stopped, Aline's thoughts dropped off, and fear engulfed her.

Magic walked out from inside his cottage.

His shadow missing, his eyes full of despair.

She didn't need him to say a word. She could see him for what he was, and what he wasn't. Magic no longer. A ghost now stood staring back at her. She had escaped, but he had not.

Aline stopped crawling. She collapsed into a ball there on the shore of Magic's former haven and sobbed and screamed into the earth.

Twenty

✳

THERE IS A MOMENT BETWEEN LIFE AND DEATH, BETWEEN REALITY AND DREAM. Aline wanted to linger there. To become her own version of Schrödinger's cat: stuck in the box, when one could forget to open the door and cross from a single impasse to the other. Where Magic was still alive.

"It's tomorrow," she said, her lips pressed into the dirt. "You said you wouldn't kill me yet. We've had quite a few tomorrows, so how about now?"

The ghost of Magic stood at her side, waiting.

"I can't do this without you," she sobbed.

She gave a silent yell into the earth. Tried to pour out the pain and sorrow, frustration and fear. The truth, the very uncomfortable and horrible truth, is that the cracks caused by heartache aren't the type to fade.

"I could never hurt you, Aline Weir," Magic said, sounding far more tired than she'd ever heard before.

"I let go of your hand," Aline said, remembering. "In the bushes. I should have held on to you."

"No," Magic said, "I let you go. I had to distract her. I know Florence. I knew what she wanted. It was me or you. The clock is ticking, and she's grown desperate."

"She'll come now," Aline said, pressing her head into her arm. "It's over."

"No," Magic said. He nodded toward the giant yew tree across the river. "The Fates built a bridge she cannot cross. They protected it long ago, and now their roots are deep into the ground here. They inhabit it. She can't come into the forest."

"So I'm safe and you're dead."

"It had to be this way."

"The Crone knew what she was doing," she said. "She was our bait."

"Yes, and now you know how the Supreme Witch kills. You know the ritual."

"And I lost you. It wasn't worth it. Don't you see that?"

He was so stoic. His face empty, his arms loose at his side. The passion, the need, nowhere did it emanate from him.

"I don't want to kill anyone," Aline said, moaning into her arm as she slid it under her face. Salty tears dripped onto it and she rolled over, looking more closely at Magic.

"I know," he said. "Perhaps when you find them, you can tell them you won't kill them today, but maybe you will change your mind tomorrow."

"That's not funny."

He sat down. "No, I suppose not."

Aline stared at him. He was there but not. Like all ghosts, he was a piece of who he'd been. But he was not her Magic. He wasn't whom she had fallen in love with.

It slammed into her, the truth. Aline was in love with him, and he was no more.

Aline was all alone yet again.

Reality was fading, her grasp on it loosening. Hysteria creeping in. "All my friends are ghosts," she said, through her tears.

"I don't know that I would call us friends." He said the words with a smile, but it did not meet his vacant eyes.

She stared at him, wishing she knew what he was thinking. A cold whisper trickled along her skin, the wind kissing down her arms. "I can't feel you anymore."

"We are no longer tethered," he replied.

Magic studied her, his gaze raking over her body where she lay on her side, curled into herself. There was a hint of intensity to his gaze.

"Does it matter?" she asked, her voice catching. She wanted to ask, *Do you love me, too?*

He stood and walked over to where she lay. He squatted beside her. "I never belonged anywhere until I belonged to you."

Aline swallowed. He ran three fingers along her cheek, like ice dripping down the planes of cheekbone.

Then he looked away. He rose and crossed to the edge of the river. His gaze on the yew tree in the distance that harbored the three Fates. Then he nodded, once, turned, and continued his journey down the water's edge.

He did not look back.

Tears flooded Aline's gaze until she could no longer see him. He hadn't said it, but if he was walking away, he didn't belong to her anymore. He could not love her after death.

Maybe he'd cross on now that she wasn't his, since he was so easily able to walk away.

Aline sat on the shore by the river, staring after him until she couldn't see him any longer. Her hand automatically reached for the book she kept in her bag, but it was gone. There was no comfort to be had. Three, Faerilyn, Esther, and the Crone did not show up as she hoped. Aline sat by herself as the hours ticked by, tears running down her cheeks.

She was back in the room in Jen S.'s house, alone once more, rejected again.

What was the point of any of it? Living, dying, trying?

Aline crawled closer to the water. She let her fingers graze against the surface, trying to judge how deep it was. Wondering if it hurt to drown, to choke to death on water, if it was as simple as letting go, or if letting go lasted an eternity.

When Aline had been a child, she'd been afraid to swim. It wasn't until she had read a story about a girl who turned into a mermaid that she overcame her fear. She wished she could turn herself into a mermaid. She would swim away.

"Tomorrow is a new day with no mistakes in it yet."

Aline didn't look up. She simply sighed. "Hi, Dragon."

"You are sad."

"I am."

"Because of me."

"No. Because of me."

"No." Dragon sat and pulled her knees up so her slender

arms could wrap around her legs. "It's me. I am the cause of this, why you're here."

Aline looked over her shoulder, wiping tears with the back of her hand. She sobbed out a hiccup. "You know, you told me not to read the book. You tried to stop me."

"They chose you because of who you are, brave and powerful, and I chose you because we're alike. Lonely and sad, and a little strange."

"I'm not strange."

"You're a witch who talks to ghosts."

"Okay, I might be a bit odd." Aline emitted a watery laugh she didn't feel. "But I don't regret you. You have always made things better."

Dragon sighed. "That's both true and it isn't."

"I wish you wouldn't speak in riddles right now."

Dragon reached over and shoved Aline forward. She tipped into the water, sputtering a gasp as she went in and under. She came up to the surface with a burst, splashing water as she lurched forward and climbed out onto the bank.

"You shoved me!"

"I thought showing you would be easier than the telling. My words get twisted in my thoughts. Madness does that to a girl."

Aline blinked. Dragon had *pushed* her. No other ghost had ever done that, and while Aline assumed spirits had the power to manifest energy and move things—

"Madness? You have madness?"

"I've never been a spooky spook," Dragon said, her smile small. She reached up and toyed with one of her curls, pulling it down and releasing it. "I was hidden by the Fates, but not dead. Florence doesn't want to kill me, or she might, but can't."

Aline's mind raced as she tried to sort what Dragon was telling her. "You're a Magic?"

"The original Magic," Dragon said.

Aline gaped at her. "Like in the book. *Mischief.* I assumed it was Magic."

"I should have told you from the beginning, but I didn't know what I didn't know. I knew the book had untethered magic from Magic, knew you wanted to read it. I was afraid it might hurt you, not use you. Then I couldn't find my way back."

Aline took in a shaky breath. "Back from where?"

"I was mad mad, so I crossed back into the in-between, and it's hard to follow my laid lines. The vibrations aren't the same there as here. I tried to get back, but then when I did, you were sadder and you were Magic and you needed me. So I stayed as long as I could."

"Why did the Fates hide you?"

"The Supreme Witch. She's been looking for me for a long time."

"You said she doesn't want to kill you, though?"

"Nope."

"But you're a Magic."

"Yep."

"I don't understand."

"She doesn't want to, but she will have to. If she can."

Aline waited, watching Dragon tug at the white lace of her dress.

"The Fates hid you, but you're here now."

Dragon nodded. "They can't do much from inside that tree and I am tired of hiding."

"If she finds you, she'll kill us both," Aline said.

"True. If she could. You are stronger than you know."

"Are you the final Magic, then?" Aline asked, rubbing the space between her brow.

"No, I am the original, but I am not the Magic you seek. The last vessel is still tucked away."

"Do you know how to find them?"

"No, but I know who will." Dragon looked up. "That's why we have to free him." She pointed to the sky. "Only Night knows what the Supreme Witch has hidden."

⤜⤛

NIGHT GETS LONELY, BUT NIGHT WASN'T LONELY NOW. No, now Night was concerned. The ley lines were shifting, and Matchstick was faltering. Every twelve hours, there was a moment when the sky would lighten, when the cycles of life would shift and in a typical part of the world the sun would rise or set, and night would enter or leave. Every twelve hours, Night would swear he could taste Day rushing past, cycling once more since one never set and one never rose. It was the moment Night lived for—if his existence could be considered living.

Night found, as he watched the hedge witch filled with Magic sneak back into his domain with a creature Night had assumed was a myth, that he might have another moment to add to his incredibly short list. Dusk grumbled, his skylines shifting another shade of ocher, and Night ignored him. Matchstick was faltering, yes, but perhaps there *was* salvation after all.

The Magic in the girl was bright. She was made from Magic, and the world Night lived in was made to bend to Magic's will.

Which meant the witch who could be their blessing or curse was about to step into the arena.

Night hoped she was ready, and he hoped Day would be, too.

⟨⟨⟨

ALINE STOOD BENEATH THE NIGHT SKY, STARING UP AT IT. She and Dragon had snuck across the hamlets, Aline holding her breath, Dragon stopping every so often to lean down and whisper to the earth. The streets were empty, the moonlight cascading across the tall pines that ran between houses that were shut up tight. The oversized front porches sat empty of conversation. No steaming mugs of tea or empty glasses of wine littered the side tables. No blankets or books were left on the daybed swings. It was the stillness of it all that left Aline shivering in the warm October air.

"Tomorrow is the full moon," Aline said.

"If tomorrow comes," Dragon replied. "Tonight, though, I will help you free Night, and when I do, he will have our answer."

"For where the last Magic is."

"Yes."

"Then you'll help me find them?"

Dragon did not answer, holding up a hand instead. She cocked her head, listening. "The vibration is louder here." She knelt and pressed her ear to the earth. Aline crouched down, following her lead.

"What are we looking for?"

"A rip in the betweens," Dragon said. "A space for you to open the door."

"How exactly can I open the door to Moon? That's who is in there, right? Faerilyn was correct?"

"Yes. You can pass in between, so you can open the door to the prison. It's not here, and not there."

"That means it's nowhere."

"No, it's a where. It's a between where."

Aline bit back a scream of frustration. Her nerves were shot, her palms were sweating, and she was standing in a hamlet where only hours before Florence had killed Magic and the Crone and almost killed her. She thought she might as well have a target painted on her forehead, and yet Dragon was confident they were safe for the moment, and this was the only way forward.

She was trusting her best friend who was a ghost child who was not a ghost or a child, and about to free an imprisoned being who controlled Night but was called Moon.

Aline let out a hysterical laugh, and Dragon cut her eyes to her. "Now is not the time to fall apart, bosom friend."

"Why *Anne of Green Gables*?" Aline asked, looking up at the moon. "If you're the original Magic and not a ghost of the 1900s, why that story and why didn't you know there were more of them?"

"I don't stay out of the in-between for long," Dragon said. "I come and go, but hidden means the realms aren't safe for me. I popped in and found Anne's story, which is more than a story, but all books are, and then I popped in a hundred years later and found you."

"How? Why?"

"I was lonely," Dragon said. "I followed the laid lines and one day, I found a town called Whistleblown and a girl in a school who had power but didn't know it, who was in the midst of people but felt alone, and I saw myself."

"So you ambushed me at the sleepover?"

"The Fates cloaked me well. I didn't think about how revealing myself to only you would look to the other girls, or how it would reveal you to the Fates." Dragon shrugged and rubbed her left eye. "I wanted a friend. No, I wanted *you* as my friend."

Aline thought Dragon had never looked more human, and she was right. Aline had been alone and lonely, and Dragon had changed her life in more ways than one. She wouldn't regret meeting her or all that came from it. She couldn't. She thought of Magic and swallowed a sob as it stuck in the back of her throat. She reached over and hugged Dragon, found her warm and real, and the truth of it punched a hole in Aline's heart.

"My power means I can open this door to Moon?"

"It does." Dragon nodded to her bag. "You have his marble, after all."

Aline looked down at her bag. "*His* marble?"

"You are the finder of lost things, and Moon is most certainly lost even though he is imprisoned. He's separated from where he belongs. The first step to getting him there is releasing him."

"He's a ghost, then?"

"No, but he's not mortal, either. He's magical, and I think you do yourself a disservice to limit who you help." She gave her a pointed look. "Your powers mean you can see the otherworldly. People like me, ghosts like those you've helped, and the Magics."

"Dragon?"

"Yes?"

"Noah? Is he . . ."

"Sometimes we tie things to us," Dragon said.

"The sisters said they sent him on."

"They did. He didn't stay gone."

Aline took a deep breath. "How do I help him?"

"You save the worlds. Then you show him to his next one. For now, you do what you always do. You've got a key, and I've shown you the space where the door waits. Open it."

Aline reached into her bag and pulled the marble out. It was warm to the touch and vibrated in her palm. "Oh."

Dragon smiled. "Go on, bosom friend."

Aline took a step to where Dragon stood, indicating the space she believed the door was. As Aline moved closer, the vibration in her palm grew.

The marble whispered, "*Yes, yes, yes.*"

Aline saw the faint outline of a door; like an aura around a person, it shimmered in gold. She held the marble out, and the door solidified. Aline reached for the handle and turned. Opened the door, and a man, tall and disheveled, tumbled out.

Twenty-one

✳

THE MAN IN THE MOON, MOON HIMSELF, WAS SHAKING. He was free, no longer bound to the cage created by the Supreme Witch. The witch before him was small and pale, with skin the color of clotted cream, freckles, and auburn hair. She held up his marble and Moon's fingers closed around it.

"You found it," Moon said.

"I did."

"You opened the door."

She nodded. Then she held out her hand. "I'm Aline."

Moon let out a laugh that was more sob than chuckle. He shook her hand, and said, "I'm Moon, but for the past thousand years I've been Night."

"Moon and Sun," Aline said.

He nodded, looking to the horizon. "Day."

"She imprisoned you both."

"And another," he said, turning his face toward Dusk. "She is fond of her prisons, but I would think you've figured that out."

"The Magics, the towns, yes, I would say she is."

Aline looked around; he thought she was most likely seeking the one who left as Moon arrived.

"She can't stay for long," he said. "Your guardian. She will draw the Supreme Witch's attention if she does."

Aline swallowed. "Right. I'm on my own." She wiped at her brow. "Dragon said you'd know where the second Magic is?"

"I know where all the points are along the ley lines. They are stars in the sky."

"And this one?"

Moon smiled. "The nowhere man waits on the rock of Uluru."

"Uluru?"

"Australia?"

"Ah."

Moon smiled.

"How do I get there?" She waved her arms toward the houses. "Those trees are pine, not yew. Do I go back to the river and forest beyond it?"

The wind whipped behind them; lightning crossed the sky. Moon tilted his face up. "Those coming will help you, I believe. I cannot follow you. I must seek Day. She is all there ever was for me." He looked down at her, his eyes warming. "Thank you, Aline Weir. May Magic keep you safe."

Moon turned, and his legs picked up pace, for he was going to find his Sun, and nothing could stop him now.

ALINE WANTED TO RUN AFTER MOON, BUT THE WIND HELD HER
BACK. It curled around her, forcing her to retreat one step, then
two. With Night out of the sky, the atmosphere was caught between Matchstick and the world beyond. Storm clouds shifted
overhead, and Aline dug her heels into the earth.

Aline spun in a circle, opened her mouth to call for Dragon,
and inhaled a familiar scent. The wind smelled of spices, and she
tasted cinnamon on her tongue. She turned and let out a relieved
sob at the sight before her.

Magic walked toward her, through the rain that fell softly
at first, light smatters cascading from the skies, before it turned
angry and pelted down, drenching her. Magic remained unaf-
fected, not a single drop touching him . . . or falling onto the
ghosts who walked behind him. Faerilyn, Three, and Esther.

"The Crone needed a bit of sorting," Magic said, giving her a
half smile, "and I knew you needed us all, so I rounded them up."

"I thought you left," Aline said, tears mixing with the rain
that streaked down her face.

Magic tilted his chin, his eyes penetrating as they stared into
hers. "I will never leave you."

"But you're free," she said. "Of our bond, and you walked
away without looking back and—"

Magic pressed a hand to the side of her face. It was cold and
yet, somehow, it still caressed like him. "I am yours. Not because of magic, but because of you. It's more than a tie between
us, Aline."

She nodded, placing her hand on his cheek, bringing her
forehead to his. "I am yours. In life or death."

"Bound. Always."

A throat cleared. "Hello," Three said. "We are all here with you."

Aline wanted to fall apart in Magic's arms. She wanted to kiss life back into him, rip off his clothes, and devour him. But his heart wasn't beating, even if it was hers, and they were short on time.

"Thank you," Aline said to them.

"It's not too late," Esther said. "We can't save ourselves, but we can save you, and you can stop her."

"I can try, but I don't know if I can succeed. The second Magic is in Australia," Aline said.

"Uluru," Faerilyn said, eyes lighting. "Of course. It's the rock of the one who sits and waits. There must be a way there from here."

"How?"

"The one place where you can find anything," Three said. "The House of Knowledge."

"It's made of yew," Magic said. "We can open the portal there."

"What if it doesn't work?" Aline asked. "You're a ghost, and I don't think spirits unlock the in-between."

"I'm still Magic," he said, slipping his hand into hers. "I'm now of the in-between, so who better to open it?"

"And if Florence shows?"

"We fight. You know how she does it, how she kills now. You can reverse the spell, bind her."

Aline shook her head. "It's too risky."

"No," Magic said. "You can do this. We believe in you."

Aline didn't agree, but she wasn't ready to fail. She couldn't.

"We can open the portal from the outside," Magic said. Aline nodded, squeezed his frigid hand, and hurried in the direction of the House of Knowledge. She found it as silent as the town. It was as if a spell had been cast across Matchstick: nothing stirred outside of the storm that raged overhead.

She walked up the steps and stood in the doorway, Magic to her right. Aline looked over her shoulder and found the others there, waiting at her back. She held up her left hand, and Magic mirrored her with his right.

The wind cackled, the ground shook, the trees cried—and the door swung open to a portal. Aline didn't hesitate. She crossed through, walking into a void before the light returned, and she was standing on an unfamiliar land, staring across a desert interspersed with tufts of tall grass, at a giant red rock.

"It looks like the sleeping back of a red lion," Aline said.

"Never met a lion I liked," Magic replied.

"I would find a red lion more intimidating than a blue one," Three said, stepping closer.

"You think red minds that it gets a bad rap?" Esther asked, her eyes shifting to Aline's hair.

"I think blue and red aren't worried about it when there are teeth chewing their way through," Faerilyn said. "What does color matter when the bite is worse than the bark?"

"I thought you all lost your madness," Aline said. "Is this really relevant right now?"

"Is it distracting you?" Magic asked.

"Yes."

"Then it's worth the contemplation," Esther said.

The rock in front of them groaned, and Aline shuddered. "What was that?"

"I'd say they know we're here," Three said, rubbing their hands together. "This should be fun. I bet this one is the most unhinged of us all, living in the desert on a boulder. Maybe he has a red lion waiting at the entrance."

Aline barely suppressed an eye roll at the glee in their tone. "Terrific. I've got to save a possibly bloodthirsty Magic and you're excited by the prospect."

"It's a bit less concerning when you're already dead, love."

Aline threw her shoulders back and marched ahead, muttering to herself about the unlikely nature of ghosts and being their keeper. She reached the edge of the rock, not finding any lions or bones or gatekeepers.

"It seems odd that nothing is barring the way," she said, studying the rock.

"The lack of stairs is a deterrent." The voice came from beneath the boulder, where there was a slight overhang and a single hand-carved wooden chair.

The young man sitting in the chair didn't look a day older than twenty. He had long hair the color of sand and intense brown eyes. He was slender and of medium height, but his voice and expression were startling. Deep in timbre and shockingly bright. He didn't glare at Aline but gave her the slow blink of a child waking from a restful sleep.

"Hi," Aline said.

"Hello," he replied. "You're not who I thought you'd be." He looked beyond her. "If you're here, then Moon sent you. Which means he's dead or couldn't leave Sun, and the Supreme Witch is killing us, and he thought by giving my location he'd be saving me."

"Uh, yes, to all of that."

This Magic sighed. "He's wrong, of course, but the Fates aren't a blanket. You can't pull a thread and unspool their work."

Aline's brows pinched together. "I don't understand."

"She'll have been following you," he said. "This was the only ley line she couldn't see."

"But she sent you here," Aline said. "All the Magics to their prisons."

He shook his head. "No, she used me, but she didn't set the ley line here. She didn't set any of them. She left me along St. Michael's Sword, and I found my way here, where Magic was meant to be."

"Which means I've . . ."

"Shown her the way, yes." He nodded and stretched. For someone who knew the reaper was coming, he seemed little concerned.

"Why aren't you terrified?" Aline asked. She pointed to the group around her. "They were like you, and now they're ghosts. You know what that means?"

"It means the wheel is spinning, so there's hope yet," he said, flashing a smile offset by two perfect dimples. "Moon assumes you have a chance at winning, so tell me, what do you have that makes this worth it?"

"If you're living in a desert under a rock," Esther said, "I think anything might make it worth it."

"You don't even have monkeys, mate," Three said.

"Do you have a name?" Aline asked.

"No one ever gave me one," he replied.

Aline looked at Magic, who lifted a brow. "Right. Can't have two Magics."

"Only one of me, *love*," Magic said, shooting Three a warning look.

"I'll call you . . ." Aline looked to the others, and Three mimed growling and pawing the air. "Leone."

Leone grinned, and never had a name seemed more appropriate. "I'm your lion, am I?"

"He's not blue or red," Faerilyn said, humming a little under her breath. "It still suits, I'd say."

Leone winked at her, and Faerilyn's cheeks went rosy.

"Oh, for all our sakes," Aline said. "We know how to stop her, the Supreme Witch. There's a ritual she uses to kill Magics. We need to reverse it."

Leone walked to join them, let out a low whistle, and a fog rolled in. As it did, it revealed a staircase made of red rock that went from the base of the mammoth stone to the top. "What are we waiting for? Come up and teach me how to level her before she comes for us both."

THEY RAN THROUGH THE RITUAL THREE TIMES, ADDING A LAYER OF ELEMENTAL MAGIC. Aline set the circle with a perimeter of salt and crystals. Leone lit the black candles made of volcanic ash, and Aline sprinkled in water from the river in Matchstick. The four dead Magics took the four corners, pulling the wind to them to draw in air.

In the center of the circle, Aline and Leone sat, going over the words of the spell and the places to cut—when the time came.

"What if she comes for you first?" he asked, leaning back

on his hands. "We're wagering she's after me, but what if we're wrong?"

"If she kills me, then you keep going," Aline said, swallowing around the fear that knotted in her stomach. "The goal is what matters, killing her, binding her, stopping her—the rest must be details. We've already lost too much. We can't fail." She looked up to Magic, who stood in the fading light of the sun, his eyes on her.

"You should both try and sleep," Magic said, his words soft, though he was speaking mainly to Aline. "We'll wake you when the time comes."

Aline was exhausted. At the suggestion, she found her eyes could barely stay open. She nodded and fell asleep curled on her side, staring up at Magic, the stars behind him blinking out— one by one.

When she awoke it was to the crackle of a fire. She opened her eyes to see Magic still standing sentry, the others at their corners. Leone was tending the flame and had a plate of food waiting for her.

"It's not much," he said. "Bit of bread and honey and goat's cheese. I'm good at provisions, but I don't have visitors, so while the honey is fresh, the others aren't. There's dried meat and fruit as well."

Aline's stomach growled and she ate the food without tasting it. Leone laughed and passed a jug of water to her. "I'm sure it's delicious," she said, drinking deep.

"It's not," he said, "but you make me thankful I had it."

They shared a smile, Magic growled, and the earth shook beneath them.

"She's here," Esther said, her eyes watching the horizon.

"The last supper is complete," Leone said. He gave Aline a slight bow. "Whatever comes, we won't go hungry."

"No," Aline said, the food sitting heavy in her stomach as her nerves ramped up. "I guess not."

She started to ask him what he had done, to pass time for so many centuries, when a loud current ripped through the sky, followed by a vibration that rattled the boulder so ferociously, Aline and Leone both fell to their hands and knees.

"Aline," Magic said, his eyes on Aline.

"I'm okay," she said, reading the question there.

She pulled herself to her feet as the sound of the tuning fork sang through the air. Aline waited, fearing the paralysis would follow, but it didn't. Their circle held.

"Phase one complete," she muttered to herself.

She nodded to Magic, and Aline reached over and blew a sliver of their circle away. A tiny crack, a rip, even. Just enough to allow the four ghosts to call their madness home.

The spirits of Magic shifted their attention and elements and drove them toward the other end of the boulder, where Florence waited at the top of the stairs. The four elements swirled around her, tugging at the strands tucked in her hair. Waking their madness. Much like what had happened at Three's hut, the madness recognized where it came from. It unraveled from Florence, one thread at a time, and the freed madness swirled out, turning for the four corners of power trapped inside the circle.

Florence followed, her eyes blazing as she took off running for the spirits. Her hand raised, and Aline nodded to Leone, who slammed his fist into the boulder—and much like Magic punching the walls at the monastery, the power dove into the rock. It split down the middle, and the four ghosts shifted into the air, provoking their madness and drawing it with them—to the opposite side of the split.

"It's working," Aline said. "We're overpowering her!"

"*Now,*" Leone said, and Aline reached out and grabbed Florence's ankle. She dragged her into the circle, closing it, and then she and Leone jumped on her and bound her hands and gagged her mouth.

"Quickly," Aline said, and he pulled the rock they had chipped and shaped. So it resembled a match, with a knife-sharp point.

"*By my will,*" he said.

He turned the matchstick sideways and cut into his forehead where his third eye was, and then each palm, and then he jabbed each palm of Florence, before dragging it across her third eye. She bucked under their restraint but couldn't rise with her wrists captured.

The sky darkened; Florence's eyes went wide. The wind shifted from the ghosts' grasp and blew through the circle, lightning danced across the sky, and a shimmer of clear light pooled in Florence's palms.

"You're doing it," Aline whispered, her eyes on the pieces of Florence breaking free. "You're really doing it!"

Leone smiled at her, quick flashes of his dimples, before he turned back to Florence. He leaned in, and Aline watched in horror as the ritual that had seemed to be going so right went utterly wrong. Florence snarled and bucked Aline off her. She yanked her hands back and lifted them up, dragged lightning from the sky, and threw it at Leone, striking him over and over. He fell to the rock, and Florence turned to Aline.

"It is not the time for you yet, hedge," she said, before she blasted her from the circle.

Aline skidded across the rock, tumbling over and over before she landed on her stomach. She lifted her head in time to witness Florence pull the pin from inside her sleeve, cut into her skin, and bend over and strike into his. She chanted as she slashed and pulled the magic from Leone. A deep-blue shimmering light poured out, and it climbed up Florence's body, slithering over her chest and neck and settling into her hair.

"Aline," Magic called, trying to hold the madness that was now revolting and seeking its way back to Florence. "Get out of here *now*."

Florence turned and hopped over the edge of the circle. The wind blew her hair forward but did little to move her from her path. She sauntered to Aline, her hair a vibrant, angry rainbow of color and madness.

She ran a hand through the strands and brought her fingers to her lips, licking the tips of them. "He tasted of sourdough and figs. I wonder how you'll taste when I finally devour you."

Aline dragged herself to her feet. "You'll never have me."

"Never is a long time," Florence said, flashing a smile. "You should have worked with me from the beginning. It would have been so much simpler for us both. Alas, now we'll do this the hard way."

Florence knelt and punched into the rock where Leone had cracked it. There was a loud groan as the boulder split apart, and Aline let loose a scream and toppled down into the darkness just as Florence's hand came around hers and she whispered the word "Matchstick" in her ear.

Aline pushed through for the portal, and it dropped open, catching them both as they fell to the earth.

Twenty-two

MATCHSTICK WAS CRUMBLING. The streets were caked in cracks formed along the ley lines. They zigged and zagged through the town like stress fractures down a crushed bone. Aline stood in the center of it, Florence wearing a smile on her cold and beautiful face. Florence's left hand wrapped around Aline's throat.

Trees were down in the yards surrounding them; a few had toppled through porches. Golf carts sat abandoned on sidewalks, and there was a loud buzz in the air, like too many live wires exploding at once.

Aline's eyes tracked the changes and Florence gave a gentle squeeze to her neck. Aline choked, and Florence released her. Aline's feet dragged. She was so tired; she wanted to give up. She remembered Magic's eyes, how steady they were when they held hers and how much faith they contained as they looked at her. He'd made her stronger, given her hope by believing in her. She'd finally fallen in love and she may have lost him to death, but she wouldn't let his death be in vain.

Florence whispered the words "bind, tether, tame," and from the cracks in the road vines erupted, snaking around Aline's hands and binding them to her sides. Florence picked up one end of the vine and tugged Aline forward. Aline had no choice but to stumble after.

"I bet you thought you were clever. That you were getting somewhere."

Aline swallowed panic and tried to work her hands free, but the tethers wouldn't give.

"It's no use," Florence said, giving her shoulders a little shimmy. "Magic is disrupted, and that means you." Then she looked to the corruption of the fallen trees and damaged houses. "It was always you. If you hadn't destroyed the boy, well, the cracks wouldn't have splintered and none of this would be possible."

Aline blinked and thought she saw Noah at the edge of the town. A flash of blue and gone.

Florence's voice quieted. "I have to get the people of Matchstick out of here before it breaks entirely." She cleared her throat, lifted her chin. "Before your Fates are swallowed by the earth and we're all doomed."

"You did this, not me," Aline said, terror clouding her vision. She tried to calm her breathing but every exhale was ragged with rage and revulsion. "You forced the magic into them and when you took it, it disrupted the power and it is destroying *everything.*"

"I put the magic in them because it was too much to hold

in the earth, and I couldn't take it all in or it would kill me. I needed to build a tolerance, and I needed to siphon off the excess somewhere safe until I could find safe passage for the people here, and myself. I'm not a monster, Aline. I am . . . a leader."

"From where I'm being dragged, you are a tyrant, and everyone would be better off without you."

Florence spun on her heel. "I brought you here, to help you. You did start this. Without you, it would never have happened. You have great power. I was trying to work with you."

"By lying? Tricking me? And when you had the magic out of me? I'd, what, be a normal and happy person?"

"There was a sixty to eighty percent chance you would be comatose, but I was mostly sure you wouldn't be dead."

"You're awful."

"I'm a trailblazer. This is what we do. You're a follower." She turned and started walking, yanking Aline after her. "That is what you do."

"You *killed* Magic."

"Collateral damage. He made a poor choice and so I made the only one I could."

"And now what?"

"Now I'm going to have you do what you were always meant to do," Florence said, running a hand through her hair, the colors of madness distracting Aline with how they swished and swirled together. "You're going to open the portal for me to the in-between and I'm going to leave this forsaken place and destroy those who've stood in my way."

"Yeah, I'm not going to do that."

"It's sweet how you think you have a choice."

"Where would you even go?"

"There are places where Fortuna's Wheel does not spin. Worlds where life can begin anew without the interference of the controlling gods. I'll tear a rip into one of them if I must, once you get us over."

They crossed into Day, and the light splintered. Aline tracked a ray of sun as it lit upon Florence, illuminating the invisible chains Aline wore woven around her arms.

"As I said," Aline repeated, studying the chains, "I won't be getting you anywhere."

Florence sighed, and turned, and there was a loud pop. Dragon appeared, striding out of thin air, and walking through it with her head high as she marched toward them. "She really won't, ducky," Dragon said, a smile breaking over her face. Aline's breath whooshed out in relief, and then her stomach flipped at the idea of Dragon being killed.

Dragon moved so fast, Aline couldn't react. She reached to the left and yanked a brick from the wall. It flew at Florence, who let go of Aline's tether when her hands flew up. Dragon's opposite hand came up and she shielded Aline, giving her time to run toward her friend.

Florence flew back as the bricks tumbled onto her; Dragon sent siding, concrete, and clay after her. All clamoring down and burying Florence. Dragon turned to Aline and yanked her hands free.

"We have to chop-chop," Dragon said, nodding to where the sunlight cascaded over the hoard of bricks and mortar covering Florence, illuminating those strange chains. "She won't stay down for long."

"How do you chop invisible chains?" Aline asked, out of breath.

Dragon glanced at them. "I would think your Magics might help. Where are they?"

"Florence pulled me through a portal. They didn't follow."

"Stuck, then," Dragon said. "Which means we spell it open."

"How?"

Dragon held Aline's hands between hers. She stared deep into her eyes. "You are a hedge witch with enormous power. You are also a Magic. See it opening, like you open a portal—you ask it and will it."

Aline took a deep breath. "What if I can't?"

"What if you can?"

"I guess we find out."

Dragon grinned, and for a moment it was a thousand other days, Aline and Dragon, and an adventure. Then the ground rumbled and Aline swallowed hard.

"Say it with me," Dragon said. "*Cut the ties that bind, that do not serve. Send the prison open, free from her.*"

Aline squeezed Dragon's hands, and they chanted together. As they did, Aline imagined each knot breaking, slipping free. As their words became a request, then a demand, the chains unclasped one by one.

The rubble of debris shifted, Florence let out a wail, and the wreckage exploded into the air, raining down on Dragon and Aline.

Aline and Dragon were knocked down, their hands breaking free. Florence stood, dusting off and eyeing the two. She smiled and then charged toward them, arms outstretched, eyes blazing.

She opened her mouth, the beginnings of a curse slipping past her lips. "Banish thee—"

Overhead, clouds erupted. Shades of magenta, golden yellow,

crimson red, and charcoal gray bled across the sky. Thunder rolled and then the heavens split into two.

⪡⪡⪡

WHEN THE DUST CLEARED, AN OLDER MAN LANDED ON THE GROUND, CROUCHED BEFORE THEM. He slowly stood, staring at Aline. He was around her height, with shaggy gray hair, a thick beard, and tattered linen pants and a shirt. His feet were bare, and his skin was as pale as freshly ground flour. He had clear blue eyes, watery in color, and his teeth were bared at them, yellow and sharper than the Crone's.

Aline took a step back, and Dragon's palm shot out. Dragon stilled her, holding tight to Aline's wrist with her small hand.

The sky above them was broken, splintered in two shades of muddy brown. Beyond them, Day had darkened to something closer to Night. The wind blew angrily through the trees, rattling the branches of the pines, stirring the scattered fragments on the ground. Aline breathed in, and it smelled strongly of ashes and pine needles.

"You," he said, his eyes falling on Dragon, skimming over her, then coming back to her face. "Look different, but your aura is the same."

"Hello, Watcher," Dragon said.

He inclined his head. "Where is she?"

Florence was frozen to the spot, and she took a step back at his growled question. He pivoted, and she stopped. "Daughter." She opened her mouth, and he shook his head. "I don't think you need to speak, do you?" He brought his hands together in the prayer position, a loud *thwack* echoing through the land, and Florence dropped to her knees. "That's better." He walked over and picked up a handful of dirt scattered from the strong winds that had blown it across the cracked street.

"You were a fool to try and steal the magic from the original Magic, the creature born out of time," he told her, sprinkling the dirt around her in a circle. "You were as imprudent as ever to lock your father away in Dusk, thinking you could ever punish or contain me. I was simply biding my time."

"I couldn't understand it," Dragon said, her eyes tracking his movements. "Why she did it. Why imprison her father, whom she loved so dear."

He continued laying the circle, adding another layer of earth as he muttered the incantation of a binding spell.

"You're the being out of time," Aline said, her eyes falling on Dragon.

"I'm almost out of time," Dragon said, "but not quite."

"I thought you were the ghost who spoke in riddles."

"I am more than one thing," Dragon said. "Haven't you learned that by now? We all are." She turned her attention back to the Watcher, keeping her hand gentle but firm as she held Aline. "I realized, though, that Florence was trying to free herself. From him." She spoke louder now, so she was talking to the Watcher. "She locked you away and thought if she had enough power, she would be able to escape you forever."

He paused in his muttering but didn't look over at Dragon.

Finally, he said, "Why would you think any of us can escape the other? We came together, and this is where we belong."

"No," Dragon said. "You followed me. I did not realize it then, and that simple act bound me to you both."

The Watcher turned, and as he did, the elements followed. The last rays of the sun, the wind's cold exhale, the dirt and scattered bits of earth, and the water from a nearby well rose and aimed in the direction toward Aline and Dragon.

Dragon yanked Aline behind her, released her friend, and then fisted her hands, one on top of the other. The elements flew at her but bounced off the invisible shield she held.

"You do not understand Magic," Dragon told him. "You've always underestimated those with true power, seeking instead to own it, teaching your daughter that the only way she is worthy is to be owned by it . . . and you. Withholding the one thing that could have changed the world."

"He caused all of this," Aline said, power crackling in her palms.

Dragon looked over her shoulder to Aline and nodded. "The dragon she wears, it was meant to remind her that there are things more precious than gold. I fear it failed to do its job in the way I had hoped. The key in your pocket waits. Unlock the bridge between the ghosts and the living. It is the only way to bring over your Magic."

"I don't understand," Aline said, reaching for her, the magic needing a place to go.

"I created the ley lines and the axes, and I can use my magic with your help to aid them."

"Dragon," Aline said, swallowing, "I don't want anything to happen to you."

"Me, either," Dragon said, flashing her sweet smile, before she took two steps away from Aline, her gaze sweeping back to the Watcher. Her voice turned cold. "Get to the forest. Find the tree with the key-shaped hole. Go, now!"

Aline barely had time to comprehend what Dragon was saying before the Watcher released the elements at them. Then he reached over, picking up a copper pipe that had come loose, holding it overhead like a pole. He charged for Dragon on a warrior's cry. Dragon flew into the air and somersaulted over him.

"*Now,* Aline," she yelled, before reaching back, grabbing the Watcher, and flinging him into the ground. It sank around him, fragments exploding into the air. Dragon reached into the earth and pulled a rock loose, smashed it into her hands, and then threw her palms up into the air. The road rose to meet her, and she sent it careening down into the Watcher.

Aline took off running. She sprinted through the town, into the cemetery, and crossed into the forest. Her heart was ramming in her chest, her lungs screamed in protest, but she kept pushing forward until she came to the river, and there she shuddered to a stop.

Magic's home, the cottage the Fates had made him, had crumbled to ruins. All that remained was a single door framed by stone.

"It's made of tourmaline," a familiar voice said. Aline turned to see Noah.

"Oh gods, you are real."

"Not quite," he said, "but they are."

Aline looked over her shoulder to see a woman with copper skin and dark curly hair standing next to Moon.

"You must be Sun," Aline said, her gaze pinging from Noah to the woman to Moon.

Sun nodded. "You must be the witch who freed me."

"That was as much Dragon as it was me."

"A dragon is a great protector."

"This one is certainly trying to be that," Aline said, panting a bit as she wiped her brow and studied the stone door. "Tour-maline, as in the crystal?"

"Yes," Moon said. He had one arm wrapped around Sun, the other cradled to his chest. "It's meant to be a conductor. Electrical, recharging, it's one of the strongest of crystals."

"I'm guessing the door is made from yew," she said, her scalp tingling with awareness.

"You're opening the portal, aren't you?" Noah asked.

"Yes."

"To the in-between?"

"I need the other Magics," Aline said, looking at him. "I need my Magic."

"Ah," Sun said, and exchanged a look with Moon. "That's why you feel familiar. You're a bit of him."

Aline nodded.

"And he," Moon said, nodding at Noah, "is a bit of you."

Sun sighed in what sounded like relief. "Good. We didn't want to leave him, either of them, but . . . this is no longer our fight or our world."

"Where will you go?" Aline asked.

"Back through the crack in this one," Moon said.

"Where is that?"

"Beyond. It is where they came from, the original three, and it is where we will travel through," Sun said, and then she crossed to Aline and gave her a hug so great it squeezed her ribs in a pain-ful way. And yet, she felt better for it, when Sun let go. "Good luck, little Magic. May your dragon prove worth her name."

Holding hands, the two exited the forest, slipping beyond the veil of Matchstick and into the outer world.

Aline turned her gaze back to Noah. "I am sorry, you know."

"I don't think now is the time for amends."

She nodded, turned her attention to the door, and summoned as much strength as possible. She closed her eyes, thinking of what Dragon had said, trying not to fear for her friend. She had opened the wrong door, freeing the Watcher. But she knew now what to do. She was meant to open the portals, to help the ghosts. To help Noah.

She was alone, but she didn't need to stay lonely for long.

Aline saw the in-between, how it was a dark place with no walls, and a forest of trees that you never reached. She saw her friends on the rock of Uluru, and Aline reached out with her hands and her heart, and she opened the door.

When she opened her eyes, the door was sparking with light and electricity. It reminded Aline of a television set from when she was a child, how if there was no cable, it only showed wavy and dotted lines of energy. Then the door shifted into all light, blinding Aline so she had to duck and cover her eyes with her arm.

The light dimmed and she stood, dropping her arm to see her friends standing before her, Magic in front, Three and Esther behind him, Faerilyn and Leone behind them. Aline let out a watery laugh, and Magic ran for her. He caught her and spun her around before setting her down and running his hands over her face and hair.

"I've never tried to break through a boulder the size of a town before today," he whispered, pulling her in close again.

Aline shivered at the connection, not minding that his skin was like ice, and she was already trembling from the adrenaline and use of power. The others closed in, and Aline took in the looks of relief and focus on their faces.

"We are all so glad to see you," Esther said.

"Though only one of us tried to pummel through the earth's core," Three added.

"Not even a magical ghost has that ability," Faerilyn said.

Leone simply winked, and Aline bit back a sob. "I'm so sorry, Leone."

"It's done, and it was almost worth it to have companions again and be off that godsforsaken rock."

"What now?" Magic said. "Where is Florence?"

"And who is that?" Faerilyn asked, her gaze drifting to Noah.

"This is Noah," Aline said. "He's a ghost, and I'm the reason why."

He waved.

"Dragon and I freed the Watcher," Aline said, running her hand down Magic's arm, not wanting to let go of him. "She was battling him after he turned on Florence."

"You freed the Watcher?" Magic said, his brows rising.

"And Day and Night," she said. "Well, Sun and Moon. They left in search of the crack in the world. They said they're returning through it to find a better one."

"Too bad they didn't take Florence with them," Three said.

Magic's eyes met Aline's. "Oh," she said.

"Yes," Magic said, tapping his bottom lip, his eyes twinkling. "It *is* too bad."

"Do you know where the rip is?" Aline asked him.

"I don't know that I need to." He looked back at the door.

"Aline," Noah said. "You know there are more spirits waiting, don't you?"

"Waiting?"

"For you," he said.

"In the in-between," Leone added. "We heard them whispering your name as we moved through the forest there."

"It's like a mirror, isn't it?" Aline said, looking around. "The forest, the worlds. A shadow inside of it."

"It is," Magic said.

"What if we use that?"

"How?"

"I don't know," Aline said, trying to see it, the answer almost there.

Magic rubbed his face, then dropped his hand. He looked up, pulling Aline behind him. "They're coming."

"Who?"

"The three who came first," he said. "Your dragon, the Supreme Witch, and the Watcher."

No sooner had the words left his lips than the water in front of them churned. It bubbled and sprang up, like a geyser shooting from the center in front of them. Florence came over the path, her hands raised. She lifted them higher, and the water followed suit. It crested and swirled, forming multiple ropes that she wove into a spiral and sent crashing toward Aline.

Magic gathered her in his arms and spirited her across the pond, through the spaces between the ribbons of water, landing behind Florence on the opposite side of the river.

"Stop," he commanded to her, and she laughed.

"You have no power here," Florence said.

"You don't deserve the power you have," Magic replied.

Light flickered overhead, breaking through the broken barrier Day left behind. Wind swirled around Florence, and she was shoved forward, her arms dropping and the water cascading down.

She let out a scream, and the four ghosts across from her pulled the wind again, drawing her closer to them.

"That's it," Aline said. "She doesn't deserve the power we have. What if we strip her of it?"

"How?" Magic said.

"It's not hers. It's yours."

"We're ghosts."

"And?"

"We can't hold it."

"You don't need to," Aline said. "We can pull it from her and send it back where it belongs, into the earth and the axes."

Florence turned and reached into the water. She lifted a single drop and sent a flood forth. It washed Aline off the shore, tossing her into the sky. She fell, her arms windmilling as she tried to find safety. The wind whipped past her, trying to catch her, and it slowed her enough that she was able to reach out and grab for the branch of the closest yew. She smacked into it, her arms straining as she held on.

"It isn't what gave me power," Florence called. "It only amplified it."

"You're killing everything you created," Magic said, walking toward her. "You are destroying Matchstick, and the witches in it will fall, too. You drain the world of the power that fed them. Don't you realize you're creating a city of walking corpses?"

He waved a hand toward the door across the river, and an opening into the hamlet that had been Night's appeared. Five witches stood outside the café, their shoulders collapsed forward, their faces drawn. Life, magic leaching from them.

He looked up to Aline, who swung herself down onto the next branch, crawling to its edge where it met the trunk and pressing her hand to its side. The scent of chocolate and vanilla, lavender and citrus drifted by.

The Fates. She was sitting in their tree.

"You don't know what love is," Aline told Florence. "You were never taught what love is. Instead you learned it's controlling those you wish to have power over. But love is the opposite, love is trusting in those you care about and giving them the power to live their lives. You can't write history for us, and you should never have stolen the magic meant to mold the witches of this world. By putting it in us, you have done us all a disservice."

"I gave you more than you deserved," Florence argued, her face flushing red.

Aline thought of the love the Fates had given her as she lowered herself another branch, and then one more. The permission to live, to be free, and to be seen.

She knew what she needed to do.

"I think it's time we returned the favor," Aline said, and jumped from the tree. She landed on the other side of the river, by the door. She pressed her palm to the crystal, and the energy crackled through her arm, shooting up to her skull. She lifted her other hand, crooking a single finger. The madness rose. It cascaded up from Florence's hair, shooting up and off the crown of her skull.

Aline yanked and tugged it forward, sending it rushing to her side. She bound it at her right hip, and then used it as a lasso to whip Florence into the air, wrapping around her waist.

"The in-between," she called to Magic. "It's the perfect place."

He nodded and turned his attention to the door she could not see. Aline was bound to him, and he to her, in a way that was separate from magic. She let him be her eyes, trusting him completely, and then she pushed the door open.

Aline screamed as she yanked on the madness that clung to her and sent Florence, the once Supreme Witch, careening in through the open portal.

The air crackled and snapped, and then silence descended across the forest.

Aline let out a laugh of disbelief before she looked over and met Magic's eyes. She opened her mouth to call to him, and the madness rushed into her.

Twenty-three

✳

WHEN ALINE WAS A CHILD, SHE WAS RARELY UNDERSTOOD. No one saw her, and when they finally did, they disliked what they found. Too strange, too different, too much. What had Noah told her? He didn't know what he wanted, but it wasn't her.

Aline Weir was many things, but none of them fit in with the mortal world. None of them served her, until she met Dragon. The little girl who liked her and stood up for her was the key that unlocked who Aline was and could become. Magic and the Fates did the rest.

As Aline inhaled the madness from five witches turned into power, she thought of how sad she was to let her friend Dragon down. Time slowed. The colors of the world bled into many and then dispersed, leaving only darkness. In the darkness, Aline tapped into the world beyond Matchstick.

She saw babies crying, abandoned in the street, cities falling into ruin, the sky overrun with clouds and fog. Families fought. Lovers walked away from one another without a word. Trees splintered, one side dying and the other thriving. Magic was revolting, the ley lines breaking apart. Power failed, cemeteries flooded, hospitals sank into the earth. It was chaos uninterrupted.

Aline tried to draw in a breath, and there was nothing to inhale but fog and pain. She screamed and it came out like a foghorn, cutting into the night.

"Hang on, bosom friend," a voice whispered in her ear.

Aline tried to hold the sound, but it was tinny, an echo of something she once knew. Perhaps once loved.

She let go and floated into nothingness. Silence cascaded around her, the cocoon of an embrace, one she'd never known when she'd had a mother and father in her home.

The scent of lavender, of citrus and chocolate drifted in.

Aline gasped as air flooded into her chest and her eyes flew open. Dragon stood over her, one hand to her heart, the other over Aline's rib cage. She pulled strand after strand of magic from her, the gold and silver mingling with the cream and teal, each ribbon lifted out of Aline until she could exhale, and Dragon's bright-blue eyes had turned black.

"That was reckless," Dragon said, offering a hand. Aline accepted, and Dragon lifted her up into the air, gently dropping her back down. "Oopsies, didn't realize the sparks that would come with that fire."

Magic was at Aline's side in the next breath, his eyes on Dragon. "Thank you," he said to her. He was vibrating with power, Aline realized, her eyes turning back to the door and the open portal.

"Don't go," she said.

He gave a single nod.

"She's right," Dragon said. "You all don't need to leave."

The Watcher walked out of the forest, and Dragon lifted a finger. "He does."

He stared at the group of them and smiled a grin a snake would envy. Then he lifted a fist and punched a hole into the yew tree beside him. The one housing the Fates. He tugged a strand of bark and the entire tree crumbled.

The forest around it fell, trees tumbling like dominoes onto where the Fates slept. Aline cried out and tried to run for them, but Dragon held her back.

"You have the power to send him where he belongs," Dragon said.

Aline looked at Magic, then up to the broken sky. "The rip."

"Where the others can do with him as they see fit," Dragon said. "Where he can be lost to time or claimed by it."

Aline nodded. She glanced at the tree once more, then took a breath and held out her hand. Dragon sent the madness from her palm to Aline and from Aline into Magic. One by one, the ghosts stepped up to clasp hands and form a circle. Power rolled from each of them, the pieces of them coming together and apart, as they sent their intention into the earth.

The balance shifted, restored, and they poured the power they had cultivated into Aline, who turned and blasted into the door that had once led into Magic's house. The crystals broke in a thousand pieces and each one floated up and shot into the sky where it pierced beyond the veil into the natural world.

It was as though a giant vacuum turned on. The wind yanked on the uprooted trees and debris from the town of Matchstick.

Anything not nailed down or held down by the madness was pulled through.

The Watcher screamed, and he was lifted up and out of the town and world.

"Close it, you wonderful fools." The words floated past them as the Crone sailed by. Aline tried to reach for her, and the Crone cackled, waving her fingers. She turned, and her form changed into a woman with bright-red curls, then she broke into breast-stroke as she swam up and out of the rip.

"She's bonkers, that one," Magic said, his voice growing thin.

"She really is," Esther said, longing in her voice.

"We have one chance." Dragon leaned forward and whispered into Aline's ear. "We can send the magic back into the axes and restore the world. Or I can send it to the other Magics and restore them."

Aline's gaze sharpened as she looked to her friends. Joy, hope, love. All three flooded into her. They could live. Together. She would have her forever family, and everything would be as it never had before.

Then the images from before, of the world beyond and its destruction and decay flooded back through her mind. The devastation. The destruction and loss of life.

Aline looked at her dearest friend, who had saved her and loved her before anyone else would. Dragon would not choose the selfish route. Aline knew it without asking because she had chosen to be selfless from the beginning. She might have thought she caused the events of the past to unfold, but Dragon had only ever acted with love and care.

"We have to save them," Aline said, swallowing hard. "The

world needs magic, and we need to send it back into the axes and give them a chance."

Dragon's eyes filled with tears, and Aline realized with a start her own cheeks were wet.

They nodded to one another and let go of the ghosts of magic. Aline raised a hand to close the rip, and Dragon dropped to her knees to slam her palm into the earth. The madness, the broken bits of the witches that were really strength and power, flooded into the ley lines.

The town of Matchstick's obliteration shifted into reverse. Trees rooted back into the ground, water refilled the river. The falsely created skies imploded and those bits shifted into the air before rising up into the ether, forming new stars.

Aline let out a watery laugh as her hand stayed clasped in Magic's palm.

Dragon turned toward her and reached up, hugging Aline as tightly as she could. Only then did Aline realize, once the last dose of madness was gone from her friend, that Dragon's shadow was gone, too.

"*No,*" Aline said, letting go of Magic and looking down at the sweet face of the girl with blond ringlets and bright-blue eyes. Her hair was perfectly coiffed, her dress untattered. Her shoes were shiny and patterned in black leather.

"It is right," Dragon said. "It is what I wanted."

Aline leaned down as Dragon's cold arms came around her waist. When she reached the child, Dragon whispered in her ears, the words softer than a caress. "True friends are always together in spirit." As Aline shook her head, tears clogging her throat, Dragon smiled. Noah stepped toward Dragon, taking her hand. Dragon nodded to him, turned to Aline, and quoted the whole of the stanza from the T.S. Eliot poem Aline had adopted as an almost-prayer for the dead, before squeezing Aline three times.

> "Ash on an old man's sleeve,
> Is all the ash the burnt roses leave.
> Dust in the air suspended
> Marks the place where a story ended,
> Dust in breathed was a house—
> The wall, the wainscot and the mouse.
> The death of hope and despair,
> This is the death of air."

Then Dragon was gone, Noah was gone, and Aline was left grasping at the air.

⟨⟨⟨

MAGIC DIDN'T TRUST THE OTHER MAGICS. He thought them as useless as the Fates, but as he watched Dragon drain herself to heal the world she had helped create, he decided true magic couldn't be all bad.

Aline's heart was broken. He could see the pieces of it shattering as she sank to the ground. He knew Dragon had done what was needed, and she wasn't really gone, and had returned to the in-between, but it cut him to see the person he loved the most in the world hurting.

"I'm so sorry," he told her, feeling useless.

"She's gone," Aline said. "I didn't realize she would go, too. I thought I would at least get to keep one of you."

She sobbed into his arms, and he wished more than anything he could feel her again. Instead, all he tasted was ash; all he touched was ice. He looked beyond him to the door that waited, the one that led to the in-between where Dragon and the other spirits, those lost and hopeless, waited.

"It's not fair for us all to leave you alone," Magic said, brushing a tear from her cheek.

Aline sobbed harder, and the others moved in, crouching down to wrap their arms around Magic and Aline.

It might have been hours or maybe it was only endless moments, but eventually the air blew warm. Birds chirped in the far-off yew tree, and the river babbled on as the water rode a current downstream.

"Really, dearie," a voice said, "you'd think true love would have a better rap, but here it is, a disastrous recipe."

"Oh yes, absolutely. Why fall in love when you can fall in a jar of caramel or a vat of chocolate pie?"

"Pie, that is absolutely the thing to love, but here we are, stuck with Magic."

Aline looked up to see the three Fates standing before her. Chlo, Liset, and Atti. Behind them, a door formed out of the limbs of the largest yew. A limb that had been bent from the storm but not broken. It created a rectangular arch.

"Chlo, Liset, Atti?" Aline said, her voice hoarse from crying. "How are you here?"

"How could we be anywhere else?" Chlo said, her finger busy as she knitted a heart-shaped cozy.

"Really, child," Liset said, working on a tiny pair of pants, "don't you know us at all?"

"We should have left the shop to Leanne," Atti said, as she cross-stitched a pair of eyes that looked remarkably like Magic's. "She wouldn't have left it to come here and save the world."

"True, true," said Chlo, "but that's part of the problem."

"It's not saved," Aline said. "Beyond these borders, who knows what's become of it. I saw it destroying itself, and now I've given up . . ."

"Yes?" Chlo said, pursing her lips. "What did you give up?"

"Love," Aline said, swallowing hard. "I gave up love."

"Pishposh," said the other two Fates at the same time, before they raised their knitting needles to clink them together.

"Who do you think you're talking to?" Chlo asked. Then she nodded to her sisters, and they blew across the heart Chlo held. The threads unraveled. Chlo tossed the strand into the air and pulled a wheel from her jacket. She gave it a spin and dragged the thread back so it looped and looped around the wheel, over and over.

Aline's mind fuzzed, her ears rang, her limbs buzzed.

"Be happy, dearest," the Fates whispered. "We love you, and you've taught us more than we could ever say."

Aline tried to respond but her mouth was as fuzzy as her head. She reached out and toppled over and down, into the softest bed she'd ever fallen into. Then she fell deeper and deeper into sleep, where dreams were kind and the world was filled with promise once more.

※

ALINE WOKE TO THE SMELL OF BACON FRYING IN A PAN. She jerked up and looked around the room. It was pristine, inviting, and exactly as it had looked those many weeks ago at the cottage when she first arrived in Matchstick.

Had it all been a dream?

She sat up, and a weight around her neck had her lifting her hand. She pulled the necklace out far enough to see it. A dragon.

Aline threw off the covers and ran downstairs. In her kitchen, wearing a bright-green apron, stood Magic. He was frying bacon and humming along to the radio.

"Magic?"

He turned and winked.

Aline launched herself at him, and he laughed, kissing her full on the lips. She pulled back, staring at the changes in him. The flush pinkness to his olive skin. The way his golden eyes were suddenly more honey and brown, and how they lit in delight.

How *warm* his skin was.

"You're alive."

"The Fates made what they called an executive decision, and they wove our threads back into being. Only this time . . ."

"You're alive-alive, like human alive?"

Magic flipped the spatula, waved a hand, and blew a breath up to it. It hovered in the air. "Not *only* human."

Aline's body sagged in relief, and she pulled him to her. She could use an elemental witch's help while guiding the ghosts home, and she had a feeling with Magic, there was no limit to the help they could provide.

"The bacon," he protested, with a smirk at the edge of his lips.

"Can burn," she said.

"The others might not think so kindly on that."

"Others?" Aline looked over her shoulder, seeking them.

"They're giving us the morning off."

"Everyone?"

"Except the Crone and Dragon," he said. "I'm sorry, love."

Aline let out a disappointed sigh.

"They didn't want to return," he said. "Their stories aren't done, but they aren't for this world."

"A story is more than a story," Aline said.

He nodded.

She reached behind him and turned off the burner. "I think you promised me a poem," she said, her eyes on his lips.

"I did," he said.

"I suppose this means you aren't going to kill me today."

"There's always tomorrow." He tilted his head to hers, bringing their foreheads together. He stared deep into her eyes, seeing her, and loving her. "Love walked in the door, not knowing way from way, where it met a truth, it had overlooked, and decided it wanted to stay."

He brought his lips to Aline's, and she lifted her chin, opening her mouth to meet his. Their lips brushed once, twice, and then his tongue met hers. Aline melted into his arms, and soon they were so busy losing their clothes and their selves in each other, they never noticed the bacon as it burned, or their power as it exploded out, carving a new axis and opening a tiny door. They never heard the Fates cheer, or their needles clack and Fortuna's Wheel spin on.

They didn't need to because they finally had each other.

Acknowledgments

So many incredible people championed and supported me in the writing of *What Became of Magic,* and without them, this book would be but a twinkle in the ley lines.

I am forever grateful to my editors, Monique Patterson and Vicki Lame, for their support, vision, and brilliance. I am also over-the-moon thankful to the following rock stars at Macmillan and St. Martin's Griffin: associate editor Mara Delgado Sánchez; assistant editor Vanessa Aguirre; jacket designer Olga Grlic; mechanical designer Soleil Paz; designer Gabriel Guma; managing editor Chrisinda Lynch; my marketing team, Rivka Holler and Brant Janeway, and my publicity team, Sara La Cotti; production editor Layla Yuro; production manager Jeremy Haiting; copy editor MaryAnn Johanson; audio producer Steve Wagner; and audio marketer EmmaPaige West. It's such a team effort to create a novel, and I have the out-and-out best team!

My dream agent, Samantha Fabien, you are one in a million. Thank you for helping me to grow into the best writer I can be and believing in me. I adore you.

I have an incredible community of fierce and fantastic women who encouraged and aided me in the creation of this novel. From The Porchies to my Shield Maidens, I am the luckiest lady to have such a loving sisterhood of story.

Megan Niedzwiecki and Kayleen McTurner, thank you for letting me cry, rage, and roll through a litany of grief and emotions. You are the witches who keep me sane, and I love you dearly.

Ben and Evan, thank you for listening to me work out the conceit of this book, and telling me that it was not ridiculous, and I should in fact go for it.

My full moon sisterhood in Serenbe, you are legion, and you are magnificent. Thank you for making the world (especially mine) brighter.

JT and Myra, thank you for always holding space for me and carrying my heart in your hearts. Nell and Amy, thank you for having more vision than even I could, and making all launch dreams a reality.

Katy, Sara, Juls, Mel, and Dali, thank you for the decades of always having my back, front, and sides. I love you all to the moon and back.

Amy Mass and Marcus Crutcher, thank you for being brilliant speed readers and helping me pull the knotted threads of this story out and weaving it back together. You are unicorns and you are both forever the cat's meow in my book.

Daddy, I love you. Josh, you are the best big brother. Brin, you are pure magic. Jocilyn, you can do anything.

Lynne, thank you, thank you, thank you. I love you.

Marcus Crutcher, you are my everything. Thank you for keeping me going, feeding me cheese and encouragement, and getting lost in the forest with our two beautiful children whenever I need a break.

Isla Doll and Rivers, this, and every story I create, is for you. Always.

I wrote *What Became of Magic* in a sort of fevered dream, in about six weeks' time. I lost my mother during the writing of this book, and it was through the story of Aline and Magic that I was able to grieve, and make sense of the deepest level of loss I have experienced thus far. I hope this book of magic has reached my Meme and my Granny in the in-between, and that they know they are forever and always loved.

I hope you know, dear reader, that you are forever and always loved. If you should be lost, may you find your way home again with a little magic on your side.

Finally, to the girls who created the I Hate Paige Club when I was in elementary school . . . thanks for letting me get the last laugh.

PAIGE CRUTCHER is the author of *The Orphan Witch* and *The Lost Witch*. She is a former journalist, and her work appears in multiple anthologies and on-line publications. She is an artist and yogi, and when not writing, she prefers to spend her time trekking through the forest with her children, hunting for portals to new worlds.